"A perfect read for STORMY SUMMER NIGHTS."
—*The Boston Globe*

"If you liked *Beautiful Creatures* (the book or the movie), *Between the Devil and the Deep Blue Sea* is right up your alley. It has a similar GOTHIC ROMANCE you'll be rooting for the whole book through!"
—Seventeen.com

"Magnificent prose, fascinating histories of residents in the seaside town, and a boy with a DISTURBING ability rarely seen in today's young adult books. Share the first of this trilogy with fans of Laini Taylor's *Daughter of Smoke and Bone*."
—Shelf Awareness

"We totally want this book to be our new BOYFRIEND."
—MTV.com

"A CHILLING supernatural exploration of free will and reality's fluidity."
—*Publishers Weekly*

"Will slip under your skin and capture the darkest corners of your imagination. This is a HYPNOTIC, terrifying debut that won't soon escape my mind."
—Nova Ren Suma, author of *Imaginary Girls*

And that's when I saw him.

I felt River fidget beside me. He was also watching Jack's pa. His eyes had narrowed into tight slits, and his face looked . . . eager. So eager, his jaw was clenched tight with it.

The eagerness scared me. Sitting there in the booth next to River, fear began to claw and claw at me like water claws at a drowning man, until my throat constricted and I half choked. Something was going to happen. Sunshine and Luke were busy flirting, and not paying attention. River's hand gripped mine underneath the table, but his skin felt cold and my fingers went limp inside his. I watched Jack's father, swaying in the square. I watched as he put a hand into his pocket. I watched as he pulled out something silver, something that sparkled in the fading sun.

I watched as he lifted it to his neck.

I watched as he slashed it across his throat.

Books by
APRIL GENEVIEVE TUCHOLKE

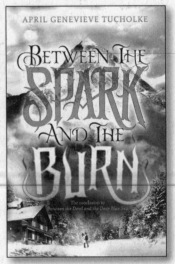

APRIL GENEVIEVE TUCHOLKE

BETWEEN THE
DEVIL
AND THE
DEEP
BLUE SEA

speak

An Imprint of Penguin Group (USA)

SPEAK
Published by the Penguin Group
Penguin Group (USA) LLC
375 Hudson Street
New York, New York 10014

USA * Canada * UK * Ireland * Australia
New Zealand * India * South Africa * China

penguin.com
A Penguin Random House Company

First published in the United States of America by Dial Books,
an imprint of Penguin Group (USA), 2013
Published by Speak, an imprint of Penguin Group (USA) LLC, 2014

THE LIBRARY OF CONGRESS HAS CATALOGED THE DIAL EDITION AS FOLLOWS:
Tucholke, April Genevieve.
Between the devil and the deep blue sea / April Genevieve Tucholke. p. cm.
Summary: Violet is in love with River, a mysterious seventeen-year-old stranger renting the
guesthouse behind the rotting seaside mansion where Violet lives, but when eerie, grim events
begin to happen, Violet recalls her grandmother's frequent warnings about the devil and
wonders if River is evil.
ISBN 978-0-8037-3889-8 (hardcover)
I. Title.
PZ7.T7979Bet 2013 [Fic]—dc23 2012035586

Speak ISBN 978-0-14-242321-9

Printed in the United States of America

1 3 5 7 9 10 8 6 4 2

TO ALL THE READER KIDS

I should hate you,
But I guess I love you,
You've got me in between the devil and the deep blue sea.

—Cab Calloway

CHAPTER 1

"You stop fearing the Devil when you're holding his hand."

Freddie said this to me, when I was little.

Everyone called my grandmother by her nickname, even my parents, because, as she put it, *Freddie, short for Fredrikke* was her name. Not Mother, or Grandmother. Just Freddie.

Then she asked me if I loved my brother.

"Luke is a damn bully," I said.

I remember I was staring at the pink marble of the grand old staircase as we walked up together. There were black veins running through it, and they looked like the blue varicose veins on Freddie's white legs. I remember thinking that the staircase must be getting old, like her.

"Don't say *damn*, Violet."

"*You* say damn." And she did, too. All the time. "Luke pushed me down this damn staircase once," I said, still looking at the marble steps. The fall didn't kill me, if that's what he'd wanted, but I knocked out two teeth and got a gash in my forehead that bled like hell. "I don't love my brother," I said. "And I don't care what the Devil thinks about it. It's the truth."

Freddie gave me a sharp look then, her Dutch eyes a bright, bright blue despite her age. She had given me those blue eyes, and her blond hair as well.

Freddie put her wrinkled hands on mine. "There's truths and then there's truths, Violet. And some damn truths shouldn't be spoken out loud, or the Devil will hear, and then he'll come for you. Amen."

When Freddie was young, she used to wear fur and attend parties and drink cocktails and sponsor artists. She'd told me wild stories, full of booze and broads and boys and trouble.

But something happened. Something Freddie never talked about. Something bad. Lots of people have bad stories, and if they wail and sob and tell their story to anyone who'll listen, it's crap. Or half crap, at least. The stuff that *really* hurts people, the stuff that almost breaks them . . . that they won't talk about. Ever.

I caught Freddie writing sometimes, late at night, fast and hard—so hard, I heard the paper tearing underneath her pen . . . but whether it was a diary or letters to friends, I didn't know.

Maybe it was her daughter drowning so young that made my grandmother turn righteous and religious. Maybe it was something else. Whatever had happened, Freddie went looking to fill the hole that was left. And what she found was God. God, and the Devil. Because one didn't exist without the other.

Freddie talked about the Devil all the time, almost as if he was her best friend, or an old lover. But for all her Devil talk, I never saw Freddie pray.

I prayed, though.

To Freddie. After she died. I'd done it so often over the past five years that it had become unconscious, like blowing on soup when it's too hot. I prayed to Freddie about my parents being gone. And about the money running out. And being so lonely sometimes that the damn sea wind howling through my window felt closer to me than the brother I had upstairs.

And I prayed to Freddie about the Devil. I asked her to keep my hand out of his. I asked her to keep me safe from evil.

But, for all my praying, the Devil still found me.

CHAPTER 2

I LIVED WITH MY twin brother, Luke. And that's it. We were only seventeen, and it was illegal to be living alone, but no one did anything about it.

Our parents were artists. John and Joelie Iris White. Painters. They loved us, but they loved art more. They'd gone to Europe last fall, looking for muses in cafés and castles . . . and blowing through the last bit of the family wealth. I hoped they would come home soon, if for no other reason than I wanted there to be enough money left for me to go to a good university. Someplace pretty, with green lawns, and white columns, and cavernous libraries, and professors with elbow patches.

But I wasn't counting on it.

My great-grandparents had been East Coast industrialists, and they made loads of cash when they were really damn young. They invested in railroads and manufacturing—things that everyone was excited about back then. And they handed down all the money to a grandpa I never got to meet.

Freddie and my grandfather had been about the richest people in Echo in their day, as much as being the "est" of anything in Echo mattered. Freddie told me the Glenships had been wealthier, but rich was rich, in my mind. Grandpa built a big house right on the edge of a cliff above the crashing waves. He married my wild grandmother, and brought her to live with him and have his babies on the edge of the Atlantic.

Our home was dignified and elegant and great and beautiful.

And also wind-bitten and salt-stained and overgrown and neglected—like an aging ballerina who looked young and supple from far away, but up close had gray at her temples and lines by her eyes and a scar on one cheek.

Freddie called our house Citizen Kane, after the old film with its perfectly framed shots and Orson Welles strutting around and talking in a deep voice. But I thought it was a depressing movie, mostly. Hopeless. Besides, the house was built in 1929, and *Citizen Kane* didn't come out until 1941, which meant that Freddie took years to think of a name. Maybe she saw the movie and it meant something to her. I don't know. No one really knew why Freddie did anything, most of the time. Not even me.

Freddie and my grandfather lived in the Citizen until they died. And after our parents went to Europe, I moved into Freddie's old bedroom on the second floor. I left everything the way it was. I didn't even take her dresses out of the walk-in closet.

I loved my bedroom . . . the vanity with the warped mirror, the squat chairs without armrests, the elaborate, oriental dressing screen. I loved curving my body into the velvet sofa, books piled at my feet, the dusty, floor-length curtains pushed back from the windows so I could see the sky. At night the purple-fringed lampshades turned the light a hue somewhere between lilac and dusky plum.

Luke's bedroom was on the third floor. And I think we both liked having the space between us.

That summer, Luke and I finally ran out of the money our parents had given us when they'd left for Europe all those months ago. Citizen Kane needed a new roof because the ocean wind beat the hell out it, and Luke and I needed food. So I had the brilliant idea to rent out the guesthouse. Yes, the Citizen had a guesthouse, left over from the days when Freddie sponsored starving artists. They would move in for a few months, paint her, and then move on to the next town, the next wealthy person, the next gin bottle.

I put up posters in Echo, advertising a guesthouse for rent, and thought nothing would come of it.

But something did.

It was an early June day with a balmy breeze that felt like summer slapping spring. The salt from the sea was thick in the air. I sat on the fat front steps, facing the road that ran along the great big blue. Two stone columns framed the large front door, and the steps spilled down between them. From where I sat, our tangled, forgotten lawn sprawled out to the unpaved road. Beyond it was a sheer drop, ending in pounding waves.

So I was sitting there, taking turns reading Nathaniel Hawthorne's short stories and watching the sky blurring into the far-off waves, when a new-old car turned up my road, went past Sunshine's house, and pulled into my circular driveway. I say old, because it was from the 1950s, all big and pretty and looking like really bad gas mileage, but it was fixed up as if it was fresh-off-the-block new, and shiny as a kid's face on Christmas.

The car came to a stop. A boy got out. He was about the same age as me, but still, I couldn't really call him a *man*. So yeah, a *boy*. A boy got out of the car, and looked straight at me as if I had called out his name.

But I hadn't. He didn't know me. And I didn't know him. He was not tall—less than six feet, maybe—and he was strong, and lean. He had thick, dark brown hair, which was wavy and parted at the side . . . until the sea wind lifted it and blew it across his forehead and tangled it all up. I liked his face on sight. And his tan, been-in-the-summer-sun-every-day skin. And his brown eyes.

He looked at me, and I looked back.

"Are you Violet?" he asked, and didn't wait for my answer. "Yeah, I think you are. I'm River. River West." He swept his hand through the air in front of him. "And this must be Citizen Kane."

He was looking at my house, so I tilted my head and looked at my house too. In my memory, it was gleaming white stone columns and robin's egg blue trim around the big square windows, and manicured shrubbery and tastefully nude statues in the center of the front fountain. But the fountain I saw now was mossy and dirty, with one nose, one breast, and three fingers broken and missing from its poor, undressed girls. The bright blue paint had turned gray and was chipping off the frames. The shrubbery was a feral, eight-foot-tall jungle.

I wasn't embarrassed by the Citizen, because it was still a damn amazing house, but now I wondered if I should have trimmed the bushes down, maybe. Or scrubbed up the naked fountain girls. Or re-painted the window frames.

"It's kind of a big place for one blond-haired, book-reading girl," the boy in front of me said, after a long minute of house-looking from the both of us. "Are you alone? Or are your parents around here somewhere?"

I shut my book and got to my feet. "My parents are in Europe." I paused. "Where are *your* parents?"

He smiled. "Touché."

Our town was small enough that I never developed a healthy fear of strangers. To me, they were exciting things, gift-wrapped and full of possibilities, the sweet smell of somewhere else wafting from them like perfume. And so River West, stranger, didn't stir in me any sort of fear . . . only a rush of excitement, like how I felt right before a really big storm hit, when the air crackled with expectation.

I smiled back. "I live here with my twin brother, Luke. He keeps to the third floor, mostly. When I'm lucky." I glanced up, but the third-floor windows were blocked by the portico roof. I looked back at the boy. "So how did you know my name?"

"I saw it on the posters in town, stupid," River said, and smiled. "*Guesthouse for rent. See Violet at Citizen Kane.* I asked around and some locals directed me here."

He didn't say "stupid" like how Luke said it, blinking at me with narrow eyes and a condescending smile. River said it like it was an . . . endearment. Which threw me, sort of. I slipped the sandal off my right foot and tapped my toes on the stone step, making my yellow skirt swing against my knees. "So . . . you want to rent the guest-house?"

"Yep." River put an elbow out and leaned onto his shiny car. He wore black linen pants—the kind I thought only stubble-jawed Spanish men wore in European movies set by the sea—and a white button-down shirt. It might have looked strange on someone else. But it suited him all right.

"Okay. I need the first month's rent in cash."

He nodded and reached into his back pocket. He pulled out a leather wallet and opened it. There was a thick stack of green inside it. So thick that, after he counted out the money he needed, he could barely close the wallet again. River West walked up to me, grabbed my hand, and pressed five hundred dollars into my palm.

"Don't you even want to see the place first?" I asked, not taking my eyes off the green paper. I let my fingers close down on it, tight.

"No."

I grinned. River grinned back at me, and I noticed that his nose was straight and his mouth was crooked. I liked it. I watched him swagger, yes swagger, with panther hips, over to the trunk of his car, where he pulled out a couple of old-fashioned suitcases, the kind with buckles and straps instead of zippers. I slipped my sandal back onto my right foot and started down the narrow, overgrown path through the bushes, past all the ivy-covered windows, past the plain wooden garage, to the back of Citizen Kane.

I looked behind me, just once. He was following.

I led him beyond the crumbling tennis court and the old greenhouse. They looked worse every time I saw them. Things had gone to hell since Freddie died, and it wasn't just about our lack of cash. Freddie had kept things up without money somehow. She'd been tireless, fixing things all on her own, teaching herself rudimentary plumbing and carpentry, dusting, sweeping, cleaning, day in day out. But not us. We did nothing. Nothing but paint. Canvases, that is, not walls or fences or window frames.

Dad said that kind of painting was for Tom Sawyer and other unwashed orphans. I hadn't been sure if he was kidding. Probably not.

The tennis court had bright green grass breaking through the cement floor, and the nets were crumpled on the ground and covered with leaves. Who had last played tennis there? I couldn't remember. The greenhouse's glass roof had caved in too—broken shards were still on the ground, and exotic plants in shades of blue and green and white grew up the building's beams and stretched out into the sky. I used to go there to read sometimes. I had many secret reading spots around the Citizen. They'd been painting spots, back before I'd quit painting.

We slowed as we neared the guesthouse. It was a two-bedroom red brick building covered in ivy, like everything else. It had decent plumbing and twitchy electricity, and it stood at a right angle to the Citizen. If the ocean was a mouth, then the Citizen would be the wide white nose; the guesthouse, the right eye; the ratty old maze, the left eye; and the tennis courts and the greenhouse two moles high on the right cheekbone.

We both went inside and looked around. It was dusty, but it was also cozy and sort of sweet. It had a wide-open kitchen, and chipped teacups in yellow cupboards, and church bazaar patchwork blankets on art deco furniture, and no phone.

Luke and I had run out of money to pay the phone bill months ago, so we didn't have a working phone at the Citizen, either. Which is why I hadn't put a phone number on the poster.

I couldn't remember the last person who had stayed in the guesthouse. Some bohemian friends of my parents, long ago. There were dried-out tubes of oil paint lying on windowsills and paintbrushes still in the sink, where they'd been rinsed and then forgotten about. My parents had a studio on the other side of the maze, called the shed, and had always done their art things in there. It was full of half-finished canvases, and it smelled of turpentine—a smell I found both comforting and irritating.

I grabbed the paintbrushes as I walked by, planning to throw them out, but the bristles that hit my palm were damp. So they didn't belong to old friends of my parents. They'd been used recently.

I noticed River watching me. He didn't say anything. I set the brushes back down where I'd found them and walked into the main bedroom, moving back so River could throw his suitcases on the bed. I had always liked this room, with the red walls faded almost to pink, and the yellow-and-white-striped curtains. River glanced around and took everything in with his fast brown eyes. He went to the dresser, opened the top drawer, looked in it, and closed it again. He moved to the other side of the room, pushed back the curtains, and opened the two windows to the sea.

A burst of bright, salty ocean air flooded in, and I breathed deep. So did River, his chest flaring out so I could see his ribs press against his shirt.

The guesthouse was farther away from the ocean than

the Citizen, but you could still see a thick line of blue-blue-blue through the window. I noticed some big ship, far off on the horizon, and wondered where it was going to, or coming from. Usually, I wanted to be on those ships, sailing away to some place cold and exotic. But that itchy, gypsy feeling wasn't in me right then.

River went over to the bed, reached up, and took down the black wooden cross that hung above the pillows. He brought it to the dresser, opened the top drawer, set the cross inside, and bumped it closed with his hip.

"My grandfather built Citizen Kane," I said, "but my grandma Freddie built this cottage. She got religious later on in life." My eyes were fixed on the dark red shape left on the wall, where the cross had shielded the paint from the fading effects of sunshine. "She probably hung that cross up there decades ago and it's been there ever since. Are you an atheist? Is that why you took it down? I'm curious. Hence the question."

I flinched. *Hence?* My habit of reading more than I socialized made me use odd, awkward words without thinking.

River didn't seem to notice. And by that, I mean he seemed to be noticing everything about me, and everything about the room, so that I couldn't tell if he noticed my use of *hence* more than anything else.

"No, I'm not an atheist. I'm just somebody who doesn't like to sleep with a cross over his head." He looked at me again. "So, what are you . . . seventeen?"

"Yeah," I said. "Good guess. Because my brother says I still look about twelve."

"We're the same age, then." A pause. "My parents went down to South America a few weeks ago. They're archeologists. They sent me here in the meantime. I have an uncle who lives in Echo. But I didn't want to stay with him. So I found your poster and here I am. Sort of strange that both our parents took off and left us, don't you think?"

I nodded. I wanted to ask him who his uncle was. I wanted to ask him where he came from, and how long he was going to stay in my guesthouse. But he stood there and looked at me in such a way and I just couldn't bring myself to do it.

"So where's this brother of yours?" River brought his fingers up to his hair and gave it a good shake. I stared at him, and his tousled hair, until he stared back at me. And then I stopped.

"He's in town. You'll have to meet him later. And I wouldn't get too excited. He's not as nice as me." Luke had walked into Echo after breakfast, intending to track down this girl he knew, and try to grope her in broad daylight at the café where she worked.

I pointed out the window. "If you want to walk into town to get groceries, there's a path that starts back by the apple trees, behind the maze. It hooks up with the old railroad trail and leads right onto the main street. I mean, you can drive if you want to, because you have a car, but the path is really nice if you like walking. It goes by this old train tunnel . . ."

I started to back out of the bedroom. I was beginning to feel stupid, talking on and on like some dumb girl who opens her mouth and lets all her thoughts fall out of it. And feeling stupid made my cheeks blush. And I had no doubt that this observant boy next to me would observe my cheeks turning red, and probably guess why.

"Oh, and there's no lock on the front door," I continued as I sunk into the welcoming semi-darkness of the hall-way and put my hands to my face. "You can get one at the hardware store if you want, but no one will steal anything from here." I paused. "At least, no one ever has."

I turned and left without waiting for his reply. I walked out of the guesthouse, past the collapsed greenhouse, past the tennis courts, around the Citizen, down the driveway, down the narrow gravel road to the only other house on my street: Sunshine's.

I had to tell someone that a panther-hipped boy had come to live in my backyard.

CHAPTER 3

S UNSHINE BLACK HAD soft brown hair to her waist, and dimples in her elbows and knees.

She was sitting outside, on her cabin's porch swing, one leg bent and dangling over the edge, drinking a glass of iced tea and staring off into space. We were the same age, and while we weren't really friends, we were each other's only neighbors. And I guess that amounted to the same thing.

She looked at me as I walked up the wooden, uneven steps (Sunshine's dad had built the cabin himself), and then moved her legs so I could sit down beside her.

"Hey, Violet. What's up?"

"Lots, actually."

A crow cawed in the trees above us, and I breathed in

the sharp smell of the pine trees, which you could smell better at Sunshine's. Her little house was farther back from the ocean, set right into the forest. Tomato vines grew up the side of the porch and gave off their own faint earthy scent too. I took another deep breath.

"Oh, yeah? Where's Luke? What's he doing today?"

"Luke is pestering Maddy. He knows how much I hate that he's kissing her. She's too stupid to say no to him. It's manipulative. He's being manipulative. I once said that she seemed sweet and innocent like a girl in a fairy tale, and so he had to go corrupt her. But enough about Luke. I've got news."

Sunshine raised one eyebrow, half interested.

"I had a taker on the guesthouse," I said. "He's already moved in."

Sunshine's eyes widened a little. She had sleepy brown eyes, which made her look seductive, and very Marilyn Monroe, and probably made boys imagine what she would look like after being kissed. My eyes were big, and, according to Luke, staring and know-it-all. Which I think means I have a penetrating gaze. Which might be the same thing, but sounds a hell of a lot better.

"Is he old? Is he a pervert? Is he a serial killer? Is he going to rape you in the middle of night? I told you not to get a renter, you know. I can't see why you don't just get a job if you need money."

I weaseled the glass of iced tea from her hand and took a drink. "I can't get a job. If you come from old money, you have to run through it all and then drink yourself to death in the gutter. Getting a job isn't allowed. Anyway, the guy isn't old. Or a serial killer. He's young. Our age. His parents left him, like mine. And he's come to live in Echo. He was supposed to stay with his uncle, but he didn't want to. So now he's in my backyard."

Sunshine wrapped her arm around one creamy knee. "Well, our summer just got more interesting. What's he look like?"

"He's . . . he's all right. He looks expensive. In a vintage way. He has a good smile. It's kind of crooked."

Sunshine grinned. "What's his name?"

"River West."

"Really? That sounds made up."

"You should talk, Sunshine Black." I tilted the glass to drink the last of her tea. "Maybe he did make it up. I never asked to see any identification."

Sunshine shook her head. "That was dumb. Violet, you're so naïve. Look, we'll need to get a hold of his driver's license then and check. Leave that to me. Does Luke still have any of that chokecherry wine he made last fall?"

I shrugged. "Yeah, I guess. I think there's two bottles somewhere in the cellar."

"Good. Then we'll all get drunk, and I will let the stranger in your backyard kiss me, anywhere he likes. Meanwhile, I'll steal his wallet."

"Or I could just ask him if I can see his ID." I didn't like the thought of Sunshine kissing River. Or doing anything else with him. At all. An entire summer of the two of them sweating and moaning in my guesthouse filled me with a cold kind of horror. Besides, River was mine. And by mine, I mean I saw him first. And by saw him first, I mean he didn't seem like the kind of boy who would get drunk on homemade wine and try to kiss Sunshine.

Sunshine laughed. "Where's the fun in that? Violet, you're scowling."

"No I'm not," I said, though I knew for certain I was.

I heard feet on gravel and looked up.

Luke. He was walking up Sunshine's dark, tree-lined driveway, jeans hanging low on his narrow hips and a too-tight T-shirt hugging the stupid muscles in his stupid chest in a way that, I'm sure, poor Maddy loved. And Sunshine too.

Luke had our mother's hazel eyes. But he mainly looked like our dad, with his auburn hair, and his wide forehead, and his square face.

The crow cawed again overhead, and a strong sea

wind came in and burst through the trees, making the green pine needles shake themselves all over the place. That sound always gave me goose bumps, the good kind. It was the sound an orphan governess hears in a book, before a madwoman sets the bed curtains on fire.

"Hey, Sunshine. Hey, sister."

Luke smirked at Sunshine, tossed his hair back, and tried to look cocky and reckless. I thought it came off stupid, but Sunshine didn't. She lowered her eyelids, then reached back and pulled her long hair over one shoulder so it would swing across her ribs in the way she thought was sexy.

"Hey yourself, Luke. How's Maddy?" Sunshine squeezed closer to me so that Luke could sit down on the other side of her.

"Maddy smells like coffee. But that's good, because I like coffee. Violet, why don't you go on home and make me some."

"Shut up, Luke. You should be the one making *me* coffee. I just got us enough money to buy some food. And get the phone back." I paused, for effect. "Someone answered my poster, and we've got a renter for the guesthouse."

"You're kidding. That dumb idea actually worked?" Luke raised a hand and then let it fall back down to settle on Sunshine's thigh.

Sunshine smiled.

I reached over and knocked it off.

If Sunshine had been a boy, she and my brother would have been best friends. But Luke would never be friends with a girl, even if they were into the same things—like locking me in closets with brutish boys from school, or setting the books I was reading on fire.

Sunshine and Luke had been teaming up since she moved here. Before that, she'd lived in Texas, Oregon, Montana . . . wherever her librarian parents were needed, apparently. Five years ago, right after Freddie died, my parents got so broke, they had to sell off six wooded acres of our estate. Sunshine's dad had grown up here, and so he bought the land, built a little cabin on it, moved back to Echo with his family, and started running the little library in town with his wife.

Sunshine squished closer to Luke and he put his hand back on her thigh, higher up than it was before.

"Stop it. Both of you. I'm sitting *right* here."

Luke laughed. "Who cares? I want to hear about this stranger in our cottage. Girl? Guy? Did you get paid already? Where's the money?"

"Yes, he paid. And no, you're not going anywhere near it. I'm getting groceries this afternoon."

"His name is River West," Sunshine slipped in. "And

Violet's decided she's going to be mad as a hatter in love with him."

"That's not remotely true," I said, looking at her with my penetrating, know-it-all gaze. "That couldn't be less true."

But Sunshine was dead right, and we both knew it.

CHAPTER 4

THE THREE OF us walked back to Citizen Kane, squeezing through the jungle path that led around the house, trying not to let the branches scrape up our arms and legs.

Sunshine had decided that we should all go grocery shopping together, and we should invite River to come with us. So I went up to the door of the guesthouse and knocked. I heard River call, "Come in," and so I did. I found him in the kitchen with his hands deep in soapy water.

"Thought I would clean up a bit. The dishes were dusty." He looked at my brother. "Are you Luke?" River pulled his hands out of the water, reached into a drawer, and grabbed a white towel embroidered with a smiling lamb.

I watched him dry his hands and it occurred to me that the towel he was using was probably a thousand years old like the rest of the guesthouse, and the fingers that stitched the red grin on that sheep were nothing but bones in the ground.

The dead are all around us, Freddie used to say. *So don't you go being afraid of the dead, Violet. And if you aren't afraid of the dead, then you aren't afraid of dying. And if you aren't afraid of dying, then the only damn thing you have to be afraid of is the Devil. And that's the way it should be.*

I missed my parents. I missed the sight of my mom's fingers, covered with splotches of paint, and her dreamy green-brown eyes that weren't like my eyes at all, because mine were, as I said, blue and staring. I missed the way her teeth showed too much when she laughed, and how her nose seemed just a bit too big if you looked at her from the side.

And I missed my dad. I missed standing in the dark doorway of the servants' entrance and watching him carrying a canvas around the backyard as he tried to find the best light. I missed the way he sighed whenever he looked at the crumbling greenhouse, then shook his head and went back to his painting. He was a lot older than my mother, and his brown-red hair was thinning. I missed the way it looked copper in the direct sun. I missed the way he would drink sherry after supper in the library, and then snore so hard, I could hear him all the way upstairs. I missed the wrinkles by his eyes, and his wide forehead.

But it was nothing to the ache I felt inside my insides for my gosh-darn always-around-because-my-parents-weren't Freddie. Always around until she died, that is. I missed her white-blond hair, bobbed and wavy and unchanged since the '30s. I missed the woolly berets she wore even when it was warm out, and the way her clothes sometimes smelled like lemons and sometimes like expensive French perfume. I missed the soft skin of her face, peachy-white and clear, with no wrinkles. Some women were like that—their faces stayed young, and their eyes bright, no matter how old they got. I wanted to look like Freddie when I hit the upper decades.

Luke fidgeted. I pushed the sad, missing-Freddie thoughts out of my head and caught River's eye. "Yeah, this is my brother, and our neighbor Sunshine. She lives in that cabin down the road."

River shook Luke's hand. I noticed that Luke was several inches taller than River, which surprised me, since I remembered River being really tall.

Or did I? No, when I first saw him, I thought he was very not-tall. Average. River had grown a foot in my mind, just in the last hour.

Sunshine eyed River, and then looked over her shoulder at me and ran her tongue over her lips. I ignored her and watched Luke. My brother treated all girls pretty much the same, but he did one of two things when he met a guy. He either talked down to him, using a special, condescendingly hateful Luke tone. Or he worshipped him, with all the pent-up fervor a fatherless boy could muster.

"River. Glad you found Violet's poster." Luke paused and scratched his elbow, all forced nonchalance and faux easygoing. "It'll be pretty cool having you around. Nice to have another guy. I usually have to spend my summers with these two." He thrust his chin at Sunshine and me. "I need someone who can drink whiskey without whining. And I could use a spotter when I lift weights. I got a set in one of the rooms on the third floor of the Citizen. You lift?"

Worship it was, then.

River smiled at Luke but didn't answer.

"We're going to the grocery store. Want to come?" Sunshine sidled her way in front of Luke, and flipped her hair, and seemed to take up the whole kitchen all of a sudden.

"Yeah," River said. "I just plugged in the fridge. I need some food. Hence, I'll come with you to the grocery store." River looked at me and winked.

I stared at him, and then kind of laughed, and he flashed

his crooked smiled at me. My cheeks started going red again, so I ducked out and went back to the Citizen to grab a few canvas bags. Then the four of us walked down to the apple trees. White apple blossoms were blowing around in the sea breeze, and a few fell on River's shoulders as we passed under the trees. He left them on, didn't brush them off, and I liked that. Our feet hit the dirt path, and we started toward Echo.

Luke kept asking River questions about where he came from and what he liked to do, but River somehow managed to avoid giving my brother any direct answers in a way that seemed casual but was actually pretty brilliant, if you were really paying attention. Which I was.

Sunshine walked along beside me, all long hair and round butt and round thighs, curving and sliding against each other, happy as a clam that she had two pretty boys to flirt with. I smelled dirt, and leaves, and forest things, and felt in a pretty good mood too.

When we'd gone about a half mile, we came across the old railroad tunnel, lurking back in the green trees. No trains ran through there, and hadn't for years. The tracks were all gone, but the tunnel still stood, pitch-black and winding for a mile or so into the hill. Where, I guessed, it ended in a cave-in. I'd gone maybe twenty or thirty steps inside, but never coughed up enough courage to go in all the way and find out what was in there, in the dark, at the very end.

It had always surprised me that no joy-killing adults had ever tried to board up the entrance. Maybe the tunnel was too far from town for any group of stupid teens to have gotten lost in it and died. Or broken a leg. Or smoked pot. Or knocked up some poor straight-A student and set the town afire with moral certainty and anti-tunnel evangelizing.

Or maybe the lack of tunnel interest was because of Blue Hoffman. And the rumors. We all came to a stop in front of the tunnel and stood there, staring, like four people facing down an old foe.

"You know," Luke said, "no one even knows how far back that thing goes. I say we men skip the grocery store and go check it out. What do you think, River? Should we send the girls to get us food while we go exploring?"

Sunshine groaned. "Right. I'm a girl, so I'm too scared to go in the tunnel. Screw you, Luke."

"They say a lunatic lives in there," I said, turning to River. I put my hands on my hips and swayed them a little so Freddie's yellow skirt would move against my legs in an engaging sort of way. Then I realized it was something Sunshine would do, and stopped.

"Go on," River said, and he was smiling and his brown eyes were amused and cool, but also kind of dancing and eager.

"The story's been going around since we were kids, maybe longer," I said. "There was a man named Blue Hoffman, who went to war and killed people. It made him crazy. He came home, and then kids starting disappearing. The cops finally went looking for Blue, but by that time he'd disappeared too. They never found the missing kids. They say Blue lives deep in the tunnel and keeps the missing kids as slaves, and they never see the sun, and they run around like bats in the dark, and they've gone practically blind, and they live on raw rat meat, and they're all mad as the Devil."

Luke shook his head. "I can't believe you remember all that, Violet. I stopped believing that story in kindergarten."

I shrugged, and refused to feel stupid. "It's Echo's own personal urban legend. It's not about whether or not you believe it. You just have to keep the story going."

Despite what Luke said about not believing, I knew the tunnel scared him. It was so dark inside that a flashlight barely dented the blackness. And the thought of some poor missing kid with clammy white skin and half-blind milky eyes following you as you stumbled around, waiting for the right moment to drag a moist finger down your face before sinking two sharp bat-like teeth into your neck . . . well, it was enough to keep everyone, even my brother, out.

Sunshine, Luke, and I had spent five summers together, counting this one, and we'd walked past the tunnel hundreds of times on our way into town, but not once had any of us gone in more than a few dozen feet. Not even that time last year when Sunshine dared me to go to the end, and then threatened to make out with Luke in front of me if I didn't. They had kissed, a long, loud kiss, and *still* I didn't go in, though I was squirming.

The thing is, they both knew I was as un-touched and un-kissed as a nun, and they both figured that I probably preferred not to be. Besides, their kissing made things two against one all of a sudden, instead of all for one and one for all.

But anyway, now River was watching and Luke was looking to impress and the tunnel was sitting right there.

River shot an arm out and wrapped it around Sunshine. "How about me and Sunshine go check it out, while you two twins stay here and hold down the fort. What do you say, Sunshine? Should we try to find this rat-eating lunatic?"

Sunshine grinned, and Luke looked pissed. I wasn't

happy, either. River led Sunshine to the mouth of the tunnel. They took one step in, and another, and then disappeared into the damn murk.

Luke stomped around, his light skin turning pink in the heat, and his red-brown hair looking redder in the sun, like our dad's. Finally he just lay down on the ground and looked up at the sky.

I plopped down on the ground too, on a little bit of grass off the path, near the tunnel. I slipped off my flip-flops and wondered what the hell River meant by taking Sunshine into the tunnel. Alone.

Luke turned and blinked pissed-off hazel eyes at me. At my clothes. "I see you're wearing Freddie's skirt. Why do you do that? It's weird, sister. It's so damn weird. That thing looks a hundred years old. It makes you look crazy."

I smoothed out the yellow skirt, my thumbs running over the soft pleats, and didn't answer him. I had started wearing Freddie's clothes earlier that year, just some of her old skirts and dresses from when she was young. I'd finally grown up enough to fit into them properly. It wasn't *that* odd.

Besides, it was summer again, and summer was the season when the missing-Freddie feeling was the sharpest, and the deepest. And if I wanted to wear her old dresses, then I would.

Why is my brother like this, Freddie? Why can't he just be nice to me once in a while?

Maybe he is. Freddie's husky voice flooded my brain. *Maybe you're just too damn busy disliking him to see it.*

I looked at Luke. "You know, there are some of Grandpa's suits hanging in one of the closets on the second floor. You could try on his vests, or maybe wear one of his ties, or his hats. It's kind of . . . nice, wearing old, lived-in clothes. Who cares if it makes you look crazy? Everyone already thinks we're crazy because Mom and Dad are missing and our house is so big and we have wealthy, illustrious ancestors."

Luke looked at me for a second. Then he shook his head. "No wonder you don't have any friends, Vi. Do you really think for one second I'm going to walk around town with you, wearing the clothes of our dead 'illustrious ancestors'?"

I sighed.

A few more minutes passed. I began to wonder if River was kissing Sunshine in the sunless tunnel, and if she was trying to steal his wallet.

I felt kind of sad.

Then I heard the scream.

I snapped my head toward the tunnel entrance. Sunshine stood there, at the edge of the sunlight's reach, face tilted back. She was screaming. She screamed and screamed while

I jumped to my feet and ran. I reached her as she hit the ground, skirt up to her waist and sheer black underwear shining against her white thighs. I was right there next to her. I should have knelt beside her, moved her skirt back down, and tried to wake her up. But I didn't. I was afraid that if I touched her, I would faint too, and my own skirt would fly up as I slid to the ground.

River came out into the light. He and Luke dropped to their knees beside Sunshine, and whispered things to her, and tried to wake her up. But I did nothing, absolutely nothing. Finally, River slipped his hands underneath her and lifted her to his chest. He carried Sunshine away from the tunnel, back to the patch of grass. I followed, my arms hanging at my sides. River set Sunshine down and she opened her eyes.

"I saw him, Violet," she said, looking straight at me, brown sleepy eyes haunted and scared as hell. "I saw Blue."

CHAPTER 5

WE DIDN'T GO to the grocery store.

Sunshine said she wanted to go home, so I took her. The boys went back to the guesthouse. Luke thought we should call the cops, but I told him to leave things be until I could talk to Sunshine. Luke never took orders from me. But he shut his mouth this time and did as I said.

Sunshine lay down on the couch, drank some iced tea, and wouldn't talk to me, not for a long time. I watched a streak of sunlight move across the floor, and waited.

Sunshine's house was small, especially compared to mine. The Citizen was a rambling labyrinth of turns and twists and stairways and spare bedrooms and floor-length windows and rotted-out balconies and forgotten closets and cellars inside cellars. But Sunshine's cabin was cozy and comprehensible and cluttered, with every corner lived in and covered with books. I loved it.

Two glasses of tea later, and Sunshine finally looked at me. "He's in there, Violet."

"Blue?"

"Yeah." She paused. "It's funny, River and I didn't even walk that far into the tunnel before we saw him. River had a lighter, one of those old refillable gold ones—do you know what I'm talking about?"

I nodded. The ones that look like they fell out of Jack Kerouac's pocket. We had a few of them lying around the Citizen.

Sunshine swiped the condensation off her glass with one hand and then held it to her forehead. She was pale. "River held up the old lighter, so we could see, but it was still dark. Really, really dark. All I could hear was our feet echoing on the stone. The air kept getting colder and danker, and I thought River was going to stop and kiss me. I was giggling and swinging my hair, and he had his hand on my arm. Finally, he stopped walking, and tugged on my elbow to turn me around. I licked my lips, because I thought I knew what was coming."

Sunshine shivered. She was sitting in the direct sunlight, and it was warm, almost hot, but she shivered.

"I think I'm going to be sick," she said.

I slipped my hand into my tea and grabbed an ice cube. I knelt beside her and put it to her forehead. "Here, Sunshine. You're all right. Tell me what you saw, when River turned you around."

Sunshine blinked. The melted ice ran down her temples and made a wet stain on the couch. "I turned, and I saw a man, crouched near to the ground. I saw him, clear as day. His eyes were huge and milky blue. He smiled at me with these little sharp teeth, and they looked fuzzy, somehow, as if he had been eating fur." Sunshine's voice came faster and faster. She sat up, and gripped her knees under her chin. "I was screaming by this time. I was already scream-ing, when I saw it. Violet, there was a small boy, or maybe a girl, lying by Blue's feet. It had horrid white skin. And long, pointed ears. And the same fuzzy teeth. And every time I think of that thing, that white furry-teethed kid-thing, I—"

Sunshine put a hand to her mouth. She jumped to her feet and ran to the bathroom.

I called the library and told her parents to come home.

≈≈≈

Cassandra and Sam were nothing like their daughter. They were skinny. Skinny like gangly teenage boys, not skinny like older people who exercised a lot or starved themselves. Cassie put her hair back in a bun, like a ballet teacher. She wore thick round glasses like Aldous Huxley, and liked wearing gray things with white scarves. She had faint lines around her mouth, and raised blue veins criss-crossing her hands. Sunshine's father, Sam, had a scruffy beard and mostly wore corduroy. His eyes were sleepy like Sunshine's.

They closed the library early and came right home. I told them what happened; Sunshine was still in the bathroom. I checked up on her once, but she was lying with her cheek on the cold white tiles of the floor, her hair spread out around her like a soft brown shawl. She told me that if she moved, she would throw up again, so I left her there.

After I told them about the tunnel, and Blue, and Sunshine, Cassie started to make tea and Sam stared off into space for a moment, looking puzzled and a little bit lost. It was a look he wore well.

"You do know, Violet, that the story isn't true," he said at last. "Blue was just a sad, confused man, and the children he was supposed to have kidnapped walked back into town a week later. Turns out they read *Tom Sawyer* in school and got inspired." Sam's fingers fiddled with the bridge of his nose. He didn't wear glasses, but I got the impression that he wished he did. "They ran off into the woods," he continued, "and lived off berries and peanut butter sandwiches. Eight days later they showed up, hungry and dirty and surprised at the fuss. Blue disappeared all right, but into a mental institution up north. This happened thirty-odd years ago, when I was a teenager. I can't believe that story is still going around."

I nodded. And then shook my head. "But Sunshine's not lying. She *saw* something. She was screaming and screaming. It was . . . it was terrifying."

"Did this other boy see anything?" Cassie turned and handed me a cucumber sandwich. It was wafer thin, with the crusts cut off. She grew up in England and thought cucumber sandwiches and tea solved problems. Which they sort of did, sometimes.

Cassie took a sandwich for herself and began to nibble at it, her skinny elbow jutting out in the air.

"Yes," Sam added. His thin face looked even thinner when his eyebrows were raised. "This new boy who is staying in your cottage. Did he see a man in the tunnel?"

I opened my mouth, then closed it. I had forgotten to ask. In all the excitement of Sunshine's fainting, I had flat out forgotten to ask River if *he* saw Blue. I looked at the small triangular cucumber sandwich between my fingers. The nightmare of the tunnel was wearing off, quickly, as nightmares do, and Sunshine's story was sounding more and more outrageous.

"I don't know," I said. "I'll go ask him."

The bathroom door opened. Sunshine stepped into the kitchen, pale and sweaty, her hair tangled. Her brown eyes didn't have their usual sleepy, semi-bored look. Instead they were frustrated. Violent. Two emotions I'd never met before in Sunshine. She was not the kind of girl who got . . . passionate. Not in that way.

Sam went over to his daughter and gave her a hug. "I always said that you were harboring a brilliant imagination, Sunshine. It had a funny way of rearing its head, but I knew it would come out sooner or later." Sam gave a low sort of chuckle. "Violet talked about the Blue legend, and then you went in the tunnel, and that's who you saw. But Sunshine, that story isn't true. You know it isn't true, don't you?"

Sunshine said nothing.

"It's okay, Sunny." Cassie wrapped a long, thin arm around her daughter's waist, hugged her tight, and smiled. Unlike her body, Cassandra's lips were full and pouted, like a cute little kid's. Like Sunshine's. "We all see things sometimes. When I was your age, I was so in love with *Wuthering Heights* that I convinced myself Heathcliff really existed. I still lived in Cambridge then. I took a bus up to Yorkshire and set out to find him. I walked for twenty miles across the moors, following what I thought was Heathcliff's shadow, stretching across the heather, calling me to him. I ended up in a pub, hours later, tired, cold, and embarrassed."

Sunshine caught my eye over her mother's shoulder. She was still angry. Really angry. And it unsettled me.

"I'm going to go talk to River," I said.

CHAPTER 6

I KNOCKED ON the guesthouse door. Luke answered. He scowled when he saw me, but stepped back so I could come in. The scent of coffee hit me, and it smelled like caramel and chocolate and black soil and time to wake up in the morning. A large moka pot was steaming on the stove. My parents had Italian artist friends, and a moka pot was what they used for espresso. It looked like a stout woman in a silver dress with her hand on her hip, and I was mildly surprised that River knew how to use it.

"I borrowed some coffee from the Citizen," River said.

I pictured River going through my kitchen cupboards, uninvited, looking for coffee . . . and found I didn't mind.

Liked it even. "How did you know what the moka pot was?" I asked. "Have you been to Italy?"

River smiled. "I spent a few years in Naples as a kid, living in a tiny flat on a busy street with an aunt."

"Italy? Really?" I'd always wanted to visit Italy. "Say something in Italian."

"Io non parlo italiano." He winked at me. "It means I don't speak Italian."

"Yeah, I kind of guessed. But you're lying. If you lived there for a few years, you'd have to speak it pretty well. Say something else."

He didn't. "So how's Sunshine? She all right?"

"Not really." I wanted to ask River more about Italy. But he was staring at me, half smiling, his eyes twinkling, almost as if he *wanted* me to ask him another question, so he could dance around it again.

I fidgeted for a second under his gaze. "River, did you see a man, in the tunnel? Sunshine said she saw Blue, and a little kid. Did you see them too?"

River took three espresso cups from the cupboard, dusted the insides with the lamb towel, and filled them with creamy brown espresso. He handed one to Luke, and me, and then sipped at his own.

"No," he said at last. "I didn't see anything. We were in the tunnel, walking in the dark, and then Sunshine started screaming. She ran out and I followed her." He paused. "So she thinks she saw Blue, huh? She must have one hell of an imagination."

"But that's just it." I took a sip of my coffee. It was smooth, and hot, and very good. "Sunshine doesn't have an imagination. Well, not that great of one, anyway. She doesn't believe in ghosts, or monsters, or fairies. She doesn't even read. She believes in realistic horrors, like global warming and serial killers, but not urban legends and men with furry teeth."

"Furry teeth?" Luke asked. "What the hell?"

"That's what she said. The man she saw had furry teeth, like from eating furry animals. Sunshine couldn't make that kind of detail up. So I know she saw someone in that tunnel. And we need to go back in and check it out ourselves. If there *is* some crazy guy in there, we need to find him, and tell somebody."

River turned and poured himself another espresso. But before he turned, I caught a smile. It was fast, so fast I almost thought I didn't see it—like maybe I blinked, and saw it in my mind. I held out my cup for more coffee.

"Oh, Violet." Luke ran his hand over his chin, which still didn't sprout much of a beard. I guess he thought it made him seem wise. It didn't. "River already said he didn't see anything. It would be a waste of time to go back to the tunnel. Sunshine's just being a girl. She heard your story about Blue and got hysterical."

"You didn't think that two hours ago. Two hours ago you wanted to call the police."

Luke ignored me. He put down his cup, reached his hands toward the ceiling, and stretched. The thick tendons in his arms looked swollen and stiff and stupid. Whereas River, standing next to him, was all straight, lean lines. Luke's shirt was two sizes too tight and his jeans two sizes too big, while River's clothes hung perfectly on both halves of his body, as if they'd been made just for him. Which maybe they had.

"Man, my muscles are sore," Luke said, stroking his pecs with both hands, as if to prove my point. "I did some really hard lifting this morning."

"You know what, Luke?" I said. "Your muscles are boring. And don't think I didn't notice you changing the subject. If you want to distract me, I suggest you talk about something other than weight-lifting."

Luke grinned, happy he'd managed to annoy me. "Maddy doesn't think my muscles are boring. Maddy doesn't think my muscles are boring *at all*. Speaking of Maddy, her shift is over in half an hour, and if me and my muscles aren't there waiting for her, like a big-eyed puppy, I won't be getting to second base. River, it's been great.

Glad to have you on board the Citizen. Are you going to the movie tonight?"

"Movie?" River asked. He shifted his hips and leaned against the kitchen counter. "What movie is this?"

"They play outdoor movies in the park during the summer," I said, before Luke could answer. "Tonight they're showing *Casablanca* at dusk. I usually make up a picnic. And we like to go early and get a good spot close to the screen."

"Don't you need to attend to Sunshine or something?" Luke shifted his hips and leaned against the counter, in an exact imitation of River. "I was planning to steal some vodka from Maddy's house and drink it at the movie. Which sounds a hell of a lot better than a stupid picnic. What do you think, River? Shouldn't Violet stay home and let the men play tonight?"

River ran his hands through his dark hair and smiled. "Violet, why don't we join Luke on his walk back into town and try to actually make it to the grocery store this time. No stopping at tunnels and whatnot. Then we can buy some things for a picnic. And Luke, I've got a bottle of cognac in the back of my car, if you want it. I don't drink. Or rarely, at least. I was saving it for a special occasion, but you can have it."

Luke shook his head. He was mad at River for refusing

to mock me and my sweet little picnic idea. And for saying he didn't drink. All real men drank, as far as Luke was concerned.

"Nah," he said. "That's all right. You keep the bottle. I don't drink that much, either. I just wanted to tonight, because they always show old black-and-white movies, and those things are so damn slow. If I don't drink, I'll fall asleep."

"*Casablanca* is one of my favorite films, actually." River caught my eye, and the corner of his mouth flickered. "I've seen it a dozen times, dead sober, and never once fallen asleep."

Luke groaned, and I grinned. Hell, I *shimmered*. River was taking my side against Luke. Sunshine never did that.

Having River around was already a lot better than talking and praying to Freddie. Because Freddie was dead. And River was alive and kicking and standing up to Luke and about to go grocery-shopping with me, and I felt like a million bucks all of a sudden.

≈≈≈

Ten minutes later, tote bags back in hand, River and I followed a silent Luke down the path to town. This time when we got to the tunnel, we didn't stop. The boys walked on like the tunnel meant nothing to them, but I shuddered as we went by in the way that old phrase says you do when someone walks over your grave. And I kept my eyes focused on the path, afraid if I looked up, I'd see a dirty man grinning at me from the opening, brown, furry teeth snapping and gnashing like a wild dog's.

Our town had one café, and it was a good one. Right in the center, on the corner of two streets that outlined half the green-grassed, oak-treed town square. If you stood in the middle and spun around, you could see the library, the pizza joint, the café, the Dandelion Co-op, the flower store, Jimmy the Popcorn Man in his popcorn stand, the antique clock store, the hardware store, and the rare book shop run by the mysterious Nathan Keane—Nathan Keane was a century old, and he had long, unkempt hair, kept strange hours, and nursed a story of love gone wrong.

Echo had all the quaint white angles you'd expect in any American town older than most. It looked clean and sweet and timeless, especially in the bright yellow sun. And while I spent a good deal of time dreaming about leaving, sometimes I kind of liked my town.

The café was owned by the same Italian family who ran the pizza joint, so it was the genuine thing. On nice days, you could sit outside at one of the round black tables, and drink Italian joe, and stare at beautiful Gianni as he steamed milk, and feel like you were a little bit civilized.

I'd been drinking coffee at the café since I was twelve.

The summer Freddie died, I spent almost every day going back and forth between the library and the coffee shop, and could often be seen, I supposed, holding an espresso cup in one hand and a Brontë sister in the other. Adults would sometimes walk by and give me a look. But my parents wouldn't have cared that I drank coffee so young, even if they'd noticed, which they hadn't. Freddie wouldn't have let me, but my parents . . . my parents didn't like to intrude. It was one of the things about them. They didn't believe in rules. Not if those rules interfered with what they considered to be my own private matter—like the private matter of me drinking a height-stunting caramel-brown beverage if I wanted to.

Are they coming back? I asked, as I often did. *Freddie, are they ever coming back?*

Yes, came the answer. *Yes, yes, yes. You just hang on, Vi.*

We ordered lattes to go from Maddy, even though we just had coffee at the guesthouse. I smiled at her, but she was looking at Luke. She had round cheeks and long eyelashes and glossy black eyes, and I'm guessing she thought she was in love, or something close enough to it that she didn't care.

Luke pointed at her and smirked. "You staying out of trouble?"

She laughed. "No."

"That's my girl." And then Maddy smiled at him like he was the sun coming out on a cloudy day.

"You can do better," I said, but not loud enough for her to hear. Freddie told me that a person has to pick and choose her battles. And this wasn't mine, I guess.

River and I took our joe back outside and I sipped at mine and mused about how nice it was to drink coffee with a person you like. And I liked River. I looked at him from the corner of my eye, standing in his linen pants on the sidewalk, graceful and long and looking like he owned the town. In a good way. I liked how he narrowed his eyes before he sipped his espresso, as if he didn't know what to expect.

So I drank my coffee and looked around Echo's pretty town square, River at my side, until a gaunt man with thin gray hair appeared from around the corner and stumbled onto the green grass. He stood there, looking up, glaring at the sky as if the sun had insulted him. It was Daniel Leap, wearing the brown wool suit he always wore. He was drunk. He was always drunk. Usually I tried to feel sorry for him. But at that moment he was a dark splotch on the otherwise lovely view of my town, and so I hated him, suddenly, with the fast anger you get at a spill on a beautiful dress or a drowned fly in a perfect, cool glass of lemonade.

"Daniel Leap has ruined our view," I said.

"Who?" River asked.

"Daniel Leap. He'd be the town eccentric, except we already have Nathan Keane, the heartbroken man who runs the bookstore. So Daniel Leap is the town drunk."

"I like town eccentrics," River replied.

I smiled at that.

Daniel caught sight of me then. "Violet White," he shouted across the square. He didn't come over; just stood on the grass, swaying and pointing, his words slurring until they ran together like paint colors dripping down a canvas.

"Violet White," he said again, "is a snob who thinks she's better than the rest of the town, like all the Whites before her, and the Glenships too, until we drove them out of Echo. Snobs. Always was and always will be, living in that big mansion on the sea, knowing nothing, acting like they know everything, but I could tell them a thing or two . . ."

Daniel Leap had done this for years, every time he saw me, or my brother, or our parents, and I was used to it. His monologue always touched on the same themes: us being snobs, and him being able to tell us a thing or two. I asked my dad about him once, wondering if there was some bad blood between him and my family. But my father had just picked up his paintbrush, shrugged, and said, "Violet, who knows what motivates the lesser people," before going back to his painting.

So the snob description wasn't completely off.

I turned away from Daniel Leap, deciding I would just move along to the Dandelion Co-op at the end of the block. But someone grabbed my arm, and I stopped. River. I looked at him, but he was looking at Daniel Leap.

River was furious. His eyes were slits and his cheeks were red and his body was still. His grip tightened on my arm.

"It's all right," I said. I waved my free hand like I was shooing away a fly. "He always talks like this when he sees one of us. I'm used to it."

River shook his head once, fast. "You should never let yourself get used to someone talking about you like that."

Daniel Leap stopped pointing at me. He swayed and swayed, and then toppled over onto the ground.

"Look," I said to River. "He's passed out now. Let's just go to the grocery store."

River finally turned away from the drunk and looked at me. He smiled, and he seemed relaxed again, snap, just like that, all anger gone. "All right. Lead the way."

The Dandelion Co-op carried locally grown vegetables, and almond milk, and nuts and spices in bulk. Sunshine's parents had hooked me on natural food. Cassie and Sam had a plump little garden back behind the cabin, in the only spot that got much sun. They made coconut milk ice cream, and cauliflower fried in olive oil, and pesto pizzas, and on and on. They invited Luke and me over for holidays, since my parents had left. They even gave us presents last Christmas. I got a long, striped hand-knitted scarf that I wore all winter, and Luke got a book on artists of the Italian Renaissance, which he'd actually read. And it had been fun, cramped into their tiny living room, playing board games until midnight, pine needles from the too-big Christmas tree poking at everyone. Luke and Sunshine even forgot to flirt with each other, for a while.

My own parents rarely cooked. Or gave presents. I guess they wanted to spend their money and their creative urges on their art, not waste it buying gifts, or cooking a meal that would be eaten in twenty minutes by two semi-oblivious brats.

Shopping at the Dandelion Co-op made me feel European. Very Audrey Hepburn as Sabrina in Paris (that movie played a few weeks ago in the park). River picked out goat cheese to spread on crispy-crusted French bread for the picnic, and olives, and a jar of roasted red peppers, and a bar of seventy percent dark chocolate, and a bottle of sparkling water. He bought some things for himself too: organic whole-fat milk, another crunchy baguette, glossy espresso beans (which were roasted by Gianni's family and sold all over town), bananas, Parmigiano-Reggiano, fat brown eggs, extra-virgin olive oil, and some bulk spices.

I watched River as he shopped. Closely. I watched him breathe in deep the gorgeous roasted smell of the espresso beans before he ground them. I watched him open the egg carton and stroke the brown shells before closing it again. I watched him slip his slim fingers into the barrel of bright purple-and-white cranberry beans, unable to resist the urge, just like me. I always had to put my hands in the pretty, speckled beans. Always.

You wouldn't think a person could learn so much about someone by watching them buy food. But you can. Luke shopped savagely, throwing things into a basket like he kind of hated them. And Sunshine shopped slow and thoughtless, sauntering from one aisle to the next. She would look at foreign cheese for twenty minutes, and then just decide to buy the first bag of pasta she could reach on the way to the counter. Neither of them had ever smelled the coffee, or stroked the eggs, or stuck their hand in the cranberry beans. Not once.

"Where did you learn to shop for food?" I asked. "You're good at it. Not too slow, not too fast."

"I went to culinary school," he replied.

"No, you didn't. You're still in high school."

"Am I?" River asked.

He smiled, and it was crooked and sly and beautiful.

"Yes, you are," I said. And then I kind of scowled a bit. "Aren't you?"

River just shook his head and laughed.

When we got back to the Citizen, River helped me put the groceries away. Our kitchen hadn't been upgraded in decades, but all the appliances still ran well enough. It was a big, robust kind of room, with saffron walls, and high ceilings, and a long oak table in the middle. There were four windows on two sides, and an old yellow couch against the far wall that got all the afternoon sunlight. The windows had checkered curtains, and the floor was covered in dusky yellow tiles. Sometimes I slept in here, on the couch. Being in the kitchen at night made me remember things, like making Dutch Christmas cookies with Freddie—the hot cinnamon smell covering me like a blanket, and the sugary crumbs melting on my tongue like snow.

River kneeled down and began looking through the cupboards. His shirt lifted up in the back, and I stared at the tan skin that peeked out above his linen pants.

I wanted to kiss him there, suddenly, on his lower back. I'd never really wanted to kiss a boy before, to be honest.

Not the boys Luke and Sunshine locked me in the closet with, not any of the thoughtless, graceless, un-Byronic boys in our town.

But River was . . . River was . . .

"Violet?"

I blinked, and moved my eyes to meet River's. He was looking over his shoulder, watching me watch him. "Yeah?"

"Do you have a frying pan? Not Teflon, I hate that stuff. Cast iron? Or stainless steel?"

I found River an old cast iron pan in the cabinet by the sink. I put in on the stove, and I imagined, for a second, Freddie, young, wearing a pearl necklace and a hat that slouched off to one side, standing over that very pan and making an omelet after a late night spent dancing those crazy, cool dances they did back in her day.

"Brilliant," River said. He lit the gas stove and threw some butter in the pan. Then he cut four pieces of the baguette, rubbed them with a clove of garlic, and tore a hole out in each. He set the bread in the butter and cracked an egg onto the bread so it filled up the hole. The yolks of the eggs were a bright orange, which, according to Sunshine's dad, meant the chickens were as happy as a blue sky when they laid them.

"Eggs in a frame." River smiled at me.

When the eggs were done, but still runny, he put them

on two plates, diced a tomato into little juicy squares, and piled them on top of the bread. The tomato had been grown a few miles outside of Echo, in some peaceful person's greenhouse, and it was red as sin and ripe as the noon sun. River sprinkled some sea salt over the tomatoes, and a little olive oil, and handed me a plate.

I licked my lips. But not how Sunshine would do it. I did it like I meant it. I left the fork on the table, picked up the fried bread with my hand, chewed, swallowed, and laughed out loud.

"It's so good, River. So very, very good. Where the hell did you learn to cook?" Olive oil and tomato juice were running down my chin and I couldn't have cared less.

"Honestly? My mother was a chef." River had the half smile on his crooked mouth, sly, sly, sly. "This is sort of a bruschetta, but with a fried egg. American, by way of Italy."

I took another bite. My mouth was singing. I swallowed, and was about to dig in again, when I remembered something. I looked at River, in a hard sort of way.

"I thought you said your mother was an archeologist."

River's lips were shiny with oil, and his eyes were laughing at me. "Did I?"

"Yes."

He shrugged. "Then I must have lied. But the problem is, which time?"

I smiled, and then laughed. River backed you into a corner and crooked-smiled at you, until you felt too stupid to keep asking him things. And then he acted like it all mattered less than nothing, and so you started to think so too.

I realized suddenly, as I was biting into the fried egg bruschetta again, that I had only known River for a day. A *day*. That morning I had been River-ignorant, sitting on my front steps reading Hawthorne's *Mosses From an Old Manse* and unaware of his existence. Now I was shopping for groceries with him and liking that he did it like me. And I was eating his food and licking my lips, and everything seemed smooth and happy and one-of-a-kind wonderful.

But the truth was that I knew nothing, *nothing* about this boy at all. I wondered what Freddie would have said, about feeling so close to someone so soon . . .

"Now let me ask *you* something," River said, catching my eye and interrupting my thoughts. He shook his hair in the sunlight, and I saw a blond streak pop out among the dark brown. It fell back down into the side part, but stayed messy, in a good way. "How long has your brother been like that?"

I raised my eyebrows. "Like what?"

"The sexism, the insecurity, the drinking. Is it because your dad is gone?"

I set down the bruschetta on the white, chipped china.

"Yes. And no. Luke has always been sort of . . . aggressive. There's more to him than this, he just doesn't show it much. He needs something to believe in. At least, that's what my grandma Freddie always said."

"Freddie sounds pretty sharp." River wasn't looking at me when he said this, but was gazing off into the distance, with an odd expression on his face. And by odd, I mean it wasn't laughing and wily, but almost earnest. And sort of . . . stern.

"She was a lot of things." I paused, thrown by River's strange look. He didn't say anything, so I kept talking. "Luke's been worse since our parents left. They were always in and out when we were growing up, busy with artist things, but there was Freddie to watch us back then. Since she died, they've never been gone this long. It's like they forgot we're still kids, technically."

River didn't answer. Instead, he handed me a glass of sparkling water with ice. I took a long drink, and it tasted delicious after the salty meal. River kicked off his canvas boat shoes. He wasn't wearing any socks, and he had nice feet, especially for a boy—strong and tan and smooth and so beautiful, you almost couldn't call them feet anymore. He yawned, plopped down on the yellow couch in the corner, and yawned again. Then he leaned forward and grabbed my hand.

"Look, I was driving most of last night. I think I better have a nap before we check out this movie."

"We don't have to go, you know. You can skip it if you want." I was focused on River's fingers, covering my own. It was the first time anyone had ever held my hand. Any boy, I mean.

He shook his head. "No, I want to see it. *Casablanca* is one of my favorites. I wasn't just saying that to rile up your brother." He paused, and gave my hand a squeeze. His forehead crinkled as he did it, as if he was concentrating. "Do you have to check up on Sunshine? Or do you think you could lie down here and take a nap with me?"

I didn't answer. I didn't even think. I just slid myself onto the couch, pressed my back into River's torso, and let his arms wrap around me. I breathed in the warm, boy smell of him, the smell of leaves and autumn air and midnight and tomatoes and olive oil. His face nestled into my hair, and the last thought I had before I fell asleep was that I'd known River all of one damn day but who the hell cared, who the hell cared at all.

CHAPTER 7

I AWOKE WITH the sun on my toes. I had fallen asleep with it tickling my fingertips, so God only knows how much time had passed. I squeezed out of River's warm arms and got to my feet.

"What time is it?" I said, and rubbed my eyes. "We're going to miss the movie."

River's eyelids fluttered, then opened. "Aw . . . why did you leave? Come back." He patted the spot next to him.

I turned to look at the old clunky metal clock above the kitchen table. It was late. "I need go over to Sunshine's. I have to see how she's doing, and if she wants to watch this movie with us." I paused. "There's a picnic basket in the cabinet by the fridge. Do you think you can pack it while I'm gone?"

River stretched. He wiggled his toes in the fading sun, and smiled. "Violet, Violet. You curl up next to me, nap, and leave. What is this, some sort of one-nap stand?" He smiled. "Screw the movie. Get back over here."

I laughed. "You said you wanted to go. You said *Casablanca* was one of your favorite films."

"I was sleeptalking when I said that. It's like sleepwalking, except you do it with your mouth."

I laughed again. "Pack the basket. I'll be back in a bit."

I walked over to Sunshine's. The sun glowed behind the Citizen now, and the house cast its shadow over the dirty fountain girls. It was almost twilight.

The road that ran by Citizen Kane ended in a tangle of blackberry bushes that bordered the woods. I turned around at the end of Sunshine's driveway and stared at the trees. Sometimes, at dusk, I felt like they were edging in, slowly, slowly, so as not to be noticed, and suddenly, one day, I would look up and find myself, and my house, back in the middle of the forest.

Sunshine was sitting out on her porch, as usual, doing nothing. Her color had come back and she looked healthy and lazy, her face shining in the rust-colored slants of the late evening sun. I didn't know how she could sit there, with nothing to do, as the day waned. Like it or not, I had my parents' artistic temperament, and if left to themselves, my thoughts started to pace and circle and snarl. Things in Sunshine's head must be different. Maybe her idle thoughts were more like a trickling little brook. A trickling brook that ran by tweeting meadowlarks and pink teacups and talking squirrels and thatched cottages.

I was envious of her, all of a sudden.

"Hey," I said. "Do you want to come to *Casablanca* with me and River? It's starting in an hour."

Sunshine picked up a half-eaten tomato sandwich from the plate by her feet and took a bite. The tomato had been plucked from the vines by the porch minutes ago, no doubt. I'd noticed one of the big red ones missing when I walked up the steps.

"Is Luke going?" she asked.

"Yeah, but Maddy will be there too. So don't expect him to give you much attention. He's stealing some vodka and hoping to get to second base, whatever that means anymore."

Sunshine lifted her hand and waved it across her breasts. "I believe it generally refers to these girls. But maybe that was a hundred years ago, when our parents were kids. For all I know, second base now means reciting poetry together on a rooftop, naked from the waist up."

I raised my eyebrows.

Sunshine swallowed another bite from her sandwich

while shaking her head. "No, Violet, I don't actually know what the kids are doing these days. Haven't you noticed that I spend most of my time sitting on my porch or following you and Luke around?"

Sunshine kind of smiled at me, and I kind of smiled back. She drank the last sip of her iced tea, and set it on the nearby porch railing. "So what have you found out about the stranger living in your guesthouse?"

"I haven't asked to see his ID, and I won't, because it'll sound stupid now. And he's terrible at answering questions, so I know almost less than I did before. Are you still planning to get him drunk and steal his wallet?"

Sunshine leaned back in the swing and looked at me. Her eyes were sharp and honest—a rare expression for her. "River doesn't like me. And his liking me was a vital part of that plan." She paused. "Did you ask him if he saw the guy with the furry teeth too?"

I nodded.

"And?"

"He said that he didn't see anything."

"I figured. It doesn't matter. I know what I saw." Sunshine was quiet for a moment. "Look, you two go ahead to the movie. I'm going to stay here. Maybe a mysterious new guy will pull up and want to move into *my* guesthouse."

≈≈

River had the picnic basket ready to go when I got back to the Citizen. We took the path into town for the third time in the last eight hours.

The park was packed with people, and the sky was smoky and getting dark fast. We were late. The front spots were all taken, but the movie screen was big enough to see from the back of the square. We walked by a bunch of kids from school, but they didn't really acknowledge me, and I didn't really acknowledge them. It wasn't that any of us hated each other. There wasn't enough passion on either side for that. Everyone knew that our parents had been gone for a long time, but they didn't know whether to feel sorry for us parentless ex-rich kids or be envious of our freedom or make fun of us for having weird, artistic-parent problems. So people left us alone. I guess they thought we were snobs, like Daniel Leap.

Luke did better than me, socially. He was more attractive and a lot less sensitive. But that was all right. The only person I was ever easy talking to was Freddie, anyway.

And River, I realized. I was easy enough with River.

I threw the quilt I grabbed from the house onto the ground, far away from my classmates. I caught sight of Gianni among the group. He was tall, and dark, and he had mischief in his deep Italian eyes, which I liked. He worked at the café sometimes with his parents, when he wasn't working at their pizzeria, and he liked to talk to me about fair trade beans, and flat whites, and the perfect foam on a cappuccino. He tended to lose his temper over requests for artificial syrup flavors, like white chocolate, and it was pretty charming.

Gianni caught me looking at him, waved, and smiled. I smiled back.

On our right was a group of laughing little kids—they were playing with a bunch of red yo-yos and having the kind of wholehearted fun only kids can have. I wondered what they were doing at *Casablanca*. I supposed their parents kicked them out of the house after supper and they just headed toward the action at the center of town. I wondered if they would stay for the film, and chatter all the way through it. But then I decided I didn't really care.

River and I dug into the olives and the cheese and the baguette and watched the kids while we ate. There were six boys, all with yo-yos, and one girl with a hula hoop. I recognized one of the boys. He was maybe eleven, with dark red-brown hair, and pale, freckled skin. I'd seen him around town a lot and had been struck by how grave he seemed, for a kid. Sometimes he had a pack of boys with him, and sometimes not. Mostly he was just all on his own. He'd started coming into the café sometimes, drinking coffee too young, like me.

After a few minutes, an older kid crawled out of the dark beyond the town square and started bugging my yo-yo boys. He had shaggy dark hair and a mean look in his eyes, like a wild, half-starved dog. He was fourteen at most. He made fun of my boys for a while, but when they ignored him, he started pushing them around, taking their toys and holding them out of reach.

River popped the last juicy Kalamata into his mouth and then got to his feet. He went over to the shaggy-haired kid and grabbed his skinny white wrist in one hand. The bully dropped the yo-yo he was holding. River said something to him, and, just like that, the kid ran off into the night without another word.

River stuck around, and began to show the boys how to make their toys work. He was good with them, easy and natural, as if he'd shown millions of boys how to play with a yo-yo and could do it with his eyes closed. The kids were listening to what he was saying, so closely that some of them actually leaned toward him as if to hear better.

I stayed sitting where I was, watching River, and idly wondering what he was telling the kids, when the girl came over and handed me her hula hoop. She was a laughing little thing, with brown eyes and black curly hair. She held out her hula hoop to me with a grin, and I took it, smiling back at her. I got inside it and spun it around my hips, moving my torso a little this way, and a little that, until my body began to remember that hula-hoop feeling and the thing took off on its own.

The girl watched me. Everyone else was turned toward the screen, because the opening credits had started to play. My hips were moving and my yellow skirt was swinging and River glanced over at me, yo-yo in hand. The boys were still staring up at him like he was the greatest person ever—except my auburn-haired kid, who still looked serious.

I gave the girl her hula hoop and thanked her for letting me use it. She laughed, and ran back to the boys.

River came back and sat down next to me, and started fiddling with something in his hands, just as I spotted Luke making out with Maddy off to the side underneath an oak tree. He had a flask in one hand and was groping her back with the other.

Oh, Luke. You are such a disappointment, I thought. And then realized that was a stupid thing to say, even in my head.

"Here," River whispered, because the movie had started. He grabbed my hand, turned it over, palm up, and set something on it. "It's a bookmark, for your Hawthorne."

I looked down. "No, it's not," I whispered back. "It's a twenty-dollar bill folded into the shape of an elephant."

River smiled. "Origami is cool."

I nodded. "It is cool. But most people fold paper, not twenties."

River shrugged. "I didn't have any paper. Look, Violet, if you ever run out of groceries or something, and I'm not around, you can just unfold that and use it. All right?"

"All right," I whispered, because I wasn't too proud. I put the bookmark in my skirt pocket.

River nodded at me, and then he bent his knees up, threw one arm around them, and leaned back, ready to pay attention to the movie. He was so flexible and graceful, damn it. I was still haunted by all those boys in my junior high gym class with knees too big for the white legs sticking out of their shorts, their thigh muscles so tight already at fourteen that they moved like someone had taken them apart and put them back together wrong.

River was different from those boys. River made my insides slither and slide in that good way. River was . . . something entirely new.

CHAPTER 8

THE KIDS RAN off sometime during the middle of the movie. Back home to bed, I supposed. I got so caught up in Bogart's sad eyes and Bergman's pert little nose and the fresh night air and the never-gets-old novelty of watching a movie underneath the night sky that I was kind of stunned when River got to his feet at the first *"Here's looking at you, kid."*

He leaned his head down, so his lips were at my ear. "I'm going to go stretch my legs," he said. "I'll be right back."

What seventeen-year-old needs to stretch his legs during a two-hour movie? I thought, watching him go.

And he didn't come back right away. He was gone for almost a half hour. Tick tock. Tick tock. The minutes dripped by. And then, just like that, he was at my side again for the last *"Here's looking at you, kid."* He didn't tell me where he'd been, or why, but he did grab my hand. And he held it through the last scene of the film, which was all right with me.

The movie ended and there was no sign of Luke or Maddy. All around us people were drifting into the dark, repeating classic *Casablanca* lines to each other. River and I were the last ones left.

"So where is this town's cemetery?" River asked me.

"Why?" I packed the last of the night's supper back in the picnic basket and threw it over my arm.

"I want to see it. I like cemeteries."

"Me too. But I think it's illegal to be in them after sunset."

River didn't say anything, just slid the basket handle down my arm and took it from me.

"Okay," I said, caving, just like that. I didn't care that much about breaking cemetery laws, so it was pretty easy to persuade me. "It's sort of on the way home, anyway."

Echo had a gorgeous cemetery. It was big and old, with tall, ancient trees and a couple of mausoleums, one of them belonging to the ex-illustrious White family. I never visited it, although I should have, since Freddie was buried there. The cemetery spread itself out over a hill facing the sea, and had a view that rivaled Citizen Kane's. It was the kind of place someone like Edgar Allan Poe would want to rot away in . . . drippy green leaves and twinkling starry silence.

The cemetery was surrounded by a wrought iron fence, which I thought would be locked. It wasn't. The gate was wide open. We went inside, and River set the picnic basket down beside the first headstone he saw. Then he reached forward and took my hand. His fingers wove between my own, and mine tingled where River's wrapped around them.

"I like you, Violet," he said, in a low voice.

"You don't even know me," I said back.

River looked at me, and he was wearing his sly, crooked half smile that was becoming very familiar. "Yes, I do. I can learn all I need to know about a person in two minutes. And we've had hours." He paused. "You're careful. Thoughtful. Perceptive. More honest than most. You hate recklessness, but are impulsive yourself, when it suits you. You hate your brother, and you love him more than anything in the world. You wish your parents would come home, but you've learned to live without them. You like peace, but are capable of toe-curling violence, if pushed far enough."

River paused, again, and his hand squeezed mine. So hard, it almost hurt. "But the thing I'm really into—the part that makes you different—is that you don't want anything from me. At all."

"I don't?"

"No. And I find it . . . relaxing."

I had no response to that. I supposed I should have gotten nervous, what with River knowing so much about me already. But I didn't. I just took it in, and tried to figure out how to enjoy it.

We walked up a hill and came to a stop by the Glenship mausoleum. It was covered in ivy and so old that a person expected the stones to fall apart any second and drop a pile of bones on the ground. The moon disappeared behind a cloud and everything went pitch-black. I couldn't see anything, not even River. I felt him next to me, though. Heard him breathing. Felt his heat . . .

Something hard slammed into my back. I choked, and choked again, fell, rolled over, and suddenly there were shadows on top of me, all over me, everywhere, moving and grabbing at me—

"*River,*" I cried out. Cold hands gripped the skin of my legs, and hard palms pressed on my stomach. "What are they? They're all over me, *God—*"

"Its all right, Vi, it's all right. They're just kids. It's just a bunch of kids."

I stopped writhing underneath the hands and went

still. I held my breath and opened my eyes. Above me the clouds separated. The moon shone through, and I saw three boys. Their faces were white. And grim. They glared at me, streaks of pale moonlight sweeping across their cheeks. They looked somber and gruesome and not like kids at all.

I felt a scream building in the back of my throat, one I didn't want to release. I wasn't a screamer, I refused to be a screamer, that was for Sunshine and other girls, I was not going to—

Another white face popped out of the dark and bent over me. I recognized it. It belonged to one of the yo-yo boys from the park. The one I kind of knew. A makeshift wooden stake had replaced the yo-yo in his hand. Two twigs were tied together to form a cross, the ends sharpened into thick, splintered points.

I looked at the points, and shuddered.

"Please don't stab me," I said, looking into the boy's blue eyes, knowing that I was being scared stupid by a group of children and a couple of twigs, but not caring at all because, ah hell, I was still pretty terrified. There was something about their faces, their grim, shadowed faces, that made my skin shrink. I tried again to get away; I writhed and thrashed, but the hard hands of the other boys held me tight.

"Let her go," the serious boy said. He shook his head

with impatience, and his hair went flying. He stood, arms crossed and legs apart, like a *Seven Samurai* warrior. "I *told* you, the Devil has red eyes that glow in the dark. Did you check her eyes? Are they red?"

Three boys searched my face, and frowned.

"Right," the yo-yo boy said. "Her eyes aren't red. So let her go."

I took a deep breath as the boy sitting on my stomach slid off. The boys on my legs got to their feet and glided away into the dark. I sat up, rubbed some dirt off my face, and looked at River. Two boys were pointing stakes at his throat, but pulled them back as I watched. River stood up and came to me.

"Are you hurt?" he whispered.

I shook my head and brushed grass from my skirt. I'd scraped up my leg, and small beads of blood were popping out of the skin on my left knee, but other than that I was fine. River grabbed my hand and helped me to my feet.

The boy with coppery hair stared at us. "I'm Jack," he said, after a moment. His eyes were wide and unblinking. He looked at me. "I've seen you before, in the café. You're Violet White, and your brother's Luke, and you live in the big mansion on the cliff. Your family used to be rich, but now you're not." He shrugged. "You bought me coffee once, when I didn't have enough money."

I nodded, remembering. "Yeah, I did." Jack came into the café one day with twenty-nine cents in change, and tried to get an espresso. But I was standing right there, and bought him a con panna, since he didn't have enough money for either, anyway.

"You shouldn't be in here," Jack said. His voice was low and serious, like his face. "We're on patrol. The Devil stole Charlie's sister earlier. She was playing right beside us, and then the Devil came and took her hand, and they disappeared. And now she's just . . . *gone*."

His voice choked up a bit when he said that. I glanced at River, but his face was blank.

Jack cleared his throat. "I think he'll be back before dawn, to steal another kid. The Devil sleeps all day, like a vampire. That's why we have stakes. If he sleeps like a vampire, he can be killed like a vampire. Stake through the heart."

As Jack talked, the boys who attacked us began to form a semicircle around River and me, slinking in from the shadows like hungry wolves.

"Maybe we should stab him, just to make sure," said a short, thin boy with black curly hair and a stake pointed at River. "See if he bleeds. I've heard that the Devil doesn't bleed. So, one way or another, we'll know."

"Quiet, Charlie. I'm handling this." Jack gestured to

two boys. "Danny, Ross, and me all saw him. Isobel was playing with her hula hoop right here in front of the mausoleum and he swooped down and . . . and took her." Jack paused, looked up at the sky. "He had red eyes and he was dressed like in olden days and he looked like a normal guy, except for the red eyes and his Thanksgiving clothes and the snake stick. But I knew he was the Devil."

"Thanksgiving clothes? Snake stick?" I asked. "What?"

Jack squinted at me, trying to decide if I believed him or not. "He wore old clothes like they did at Thanksgiving, with a hat and a cape. And he had a stick. Like a cane, but it was taller."

"Like a walking stick?" This from River.

"Yeah, a walking stick. It was carved into a snake. He just swooped down from the sky and . . . and took Isobel. I thought the Devil would come up from underground, like, you know, like from hell, but he came from the sky, like an angel." Jack paused, and clenched his pale, freckled fists at his sides. "Then he disappeared. We're going to wait here until the Devil comes back. And when he comes back, we're going to kill him."

"Yes," the other boys said. "Kill him."

It was some kind of game. Some kids' game that had gone too far. I looked at their serious faces, the stakes gripped in each hand, the unnatural way each boy was silent and unmoving, as boys never are. I wondered about the little girl. Isobel. Had she gone home without telling her brother, and the game spun off from there? Or had someone really taken her?

River came up behind me. He slid an arm around my waist and tugged me back into him. "Let's get going," he whispered in my ear. "Leave the boys to their game. They're just having fun. They'll be fine."

The skin of my neck tickled where River's breath brushed by me. I ignored it. I slid back out of his arms and knelt down by Jack, who was on his knees now, using a knife to sharpen the end of another twig. "I hope you find your devil. Be careful, okay? It's getting late. You might want to go home soon. Your parents might get worried about you."

"I've got to make a bunch more stakes," he said, without looking up. "We have more kids coming to help. Isaac's been getting them, waking everyone up. I told Charlie he could be the one to stab the Devil, if . . . if his sister is dead. I said that he could be the one . . ."

His voice trailed off as he got caught up in what he was doing. River pulled on my waist, and we began to move away toward the gate. I threw one last glance over my shoulder at Jack, kneeling on the ground. There had been no glint of mischief, no pride over the creation of his game, no antsy joy at being out so late. He'd been as serious as a young soldier about to go to war. It was unsettling. Odd. I wondered if I should tell someone what was going on. Try to find some parents, or call the cops—

"Violet."

I stopped walking and looked at River.

"They're going to be all right. It's just a game."

I didn't answer.

River leaned his hips into mine and my back pressed against the wrought iron gate. His fingers curled over the back of my head, and my thoughts . . . ceased.

He kissed me. My lips met his and I just. Stopped. Thinking. I didn't think about the fact that River was still a stranger. I didn't think about the tunnel, or Jack, or the Devil, or anything. My lips melted into my heart, which melted into my legs, which melted into the earth beneath me.

Afterward, River walked me home in the moonlight. Neither of us talked.

And everything was damn near perfect.

CHAPTER 9

I SLEPT IN the guesthouse.

I had started the night in my own bed. But I woke up sometime before dawn, and found myself walking barefoot down the cold marble steps of the grand staircase, through the dewy grass by the wrecked greenhouse, to the cottage, to River's bed.

I don't know why. I just did it. River said he liked me, and I liked him. He reminded me of . . . me, somehow. Which might sound stupid in the daytime, but at night, when you're half asleep, it makes perfect sense.

River was turned onto his side. His sleeping eyes and his straight nose and his crooked mouth were glowing in a shaft of moonlight coming through the windows. I lifted the covers and slipped in beside him. He woke up, long enough to slide over, wrap his arms around me, and bury his face in my neck.

If he was surprised that I was there, he was too sleepy to show it.

So I spent the night with his body curled into mine. I fell asleep next to him, and woke up beside him. Twice, in twenty-four hours.

Morning.

River was one of those magical people who slept like a woodland creature or someone under a fairy spell. Sweet and pretty and quiet, with glossy eyelids and mouth in a soft pout. Next to him I felt rumpled and tangled and very, very real. I slid out of the bed and went to the window. It was a gray, stormy kind of day outside—stormy gray waves, stormy gray sky. The clouds were dark and fat and mean, and the air smelled of salt and expectation.

I couldn't see the horizon through the thick mist. I could barely even see the waves. This might make some people feel trapped, I suppose, but not me. I'd grown up with the sea in my front yard. It felt as comfortable as a white picket fence.

I stretched, and the ache started up in my knee where I had fallen on it the night before.

I had played night games as a kid, when my cousins visited. We played Burn the Witch in the trees behind the

Citizen, and my heart would race and race until I found a hiding spot. And then there would be the endless, terrified wait until someone found me, screams of "Witch!" and "Burn her!" ringing in the cool night air . . .

Still.

I was uneasy about those eerie boys with their stakes, and their strange description of the Devil. And their claims that a little girl disappeared.

I stretched again, and smoothed out the black silk nightdress I was wearing. One of Freddie's. I had gotten it out of the dresser a few days ago. It had still smelled like French perfume then, but now it smelled like River.

"What the hell happened here?"

I turned around and found Luke staring at me from the doorway of the bedroom.

River woke up at the sound of my brother's voice. He yawned, and grinned.

"Nothing happened, Luke," I said. "Not that it's any of your business. Don't you knock? This isn't your house anymore. River rented it, and you can't come barging in whenever you feel like it."

"I *did* knock, but no one answered. And you weren't around this morning, Violet. I was starting to get worried. If my twin sister isn't in her bed for the first morning in her entire life"— his eyes flicked around the room, resting for a moment on River before cutting back to me—"then I have the right to go looking for her."

I kind of smiled at that. "Luke, does this mean you care about me?"

Luke didn't smile back. "No."

"Good morning," River said, casual and calm as if he'd been expecting my brother to wake him up all along. Welcomed it, even. "Does anyone want some coffee? I bought some espresso yesterday."

Luke nodded his head. "Yeah, yeah, maybe later. But first, I've got news. I walked into town this morning because Maddy had an early shift at the café, and hell, the whole place is on fire. A little girl is missing. She disappeared from the cemetery last night. There are cops everywhere and search parties. Even a few reporters up from Portland. It's crazy."

I put my hand on my heart. Isobel. Charlie's sister. I looked at River. His face was relaxed, his eyes interested, but detached. I turned back to my brother. "A little girl? From the cemetery? Last night, River and I—"

Luke waved his hand at me. "Shut up, sister. I haven't even got to the best part. So some boys apparently saw who took the girl. And . . . wait for it . . . these boys are saying that it was the Devil." Luke laughed. "The *Devil*. Can you believe it? One of the journalists hanging out in the café was Jason Foster—he was that great runner in high school, Violet, you remember? Went to State and everything. Anyway, now he's a journalist, and man, was he loving this story. The Devil. What a town we've got here. Portland is going to eat this up. *Backwards No-Account Echo Kids See Prince of Darkness in Town Cemetery.*"

River stretched, long and slow, like a cat. "It seems that a lot of kids go missing in this town," he said, very casual and nonchalant, leaning back with his arms tucked behind his head and a smile on his face. "First Blue, and now the Devil?"

I opened my mouth to tell Luke about Jack, and his gang of stake-wielding boys, when Sunshine appeared in the bedroom doorway, long brown hair swinging over a white jersey dress that hugged her curves in the exact right way.

"Hey," she said, looking around at my rumpled nightgown and River, shirtless, still in bed. "No one was at the Citizen, so I came over here. Have you heard what's going on in town? I went in to buy some almond milk for breakfast and everyone was running around, talking about some girl that's gone missing and how the cemetery is full of kids with wooden stakes, trying to kill the Devil like he was a vampire. Did I miss the Apocalypse or something?"

The four of us went into the kitchen, and River made

coffee and omelets. He was pretty quiet, his attention focused on frying the eggs, so I was the one who told Luke and Sunshine about our visit to the cemetery the night before. I thought Sunshine might get upset, considering she hallucinated Blue in the tunnel not twenty-four hours earlier, and him being an accused child-stealer, but she seemed to have moved on. She just laughed along with Luke at the idea of Satan in Echo.

"As if the Devil wouldn't have a better place to spend his time than our cemetery," Sunshine said. "He could be roaming the seedy back alleys of Paris, or stealing souls in a New Orleans graveyard, or running around the red-light district in Amsterdam. But no . . . he chooses Echo, the fool."

Luke smiled, his eyes taking in the way Sunshine's second bases bobbed about in her dress when she laughed.

"Speaking of the City of Lights," I said, "Luke and I saw *An American in Paris* in the town square last week. It was—"

"Stupid," Luke said.

"Liar." I handed him an omelet. "You loved it. It was about a poor painter in Paris, and you were mesmerized. By the way, I saw that your information packet from the Sorbonne arrived in the mail a few days ago. Thinking of applying, brother?"

Luke pretended not to hear me.

I smiled, a River-smile, very sly. "Well . . . I don't know why you'd want to study in Paris anyway, when Italy was the true birthplace of art. Dad always said—"

"You and the Italian Renaissance, Vi. You're just like Dad. Both of your styles evolved from raping French Impressionism, no matter what you say about Italy. Mom knows it. I know it. End of discussion."

I smiled, not slyly this time. It always pleased me to get Luke talking about art. Seeing that Sorbonne packet in the mail had thrilled me to pieces.

I took a bite of River's omelet. It was delicious, salty and buttery, with a kick from a chopped-up onion and a little grated Parmecan.

I thought Luke might be pissed at River, because he found me in his bed. Last fall, Luke dumped me in the blue guestroom's closet with the square-jawed, over-confident Sean Fry. Luke and Sunshine laughed and laughed as I banged around, knocking hangers to the floor as I dodged Fry's fearless lips and expectant arms. But after Luke let me out, when Fry cornered me in the kitchen and tried again, Luke punched him in the face.

Luke didn't seem mad at River, though. He liked him, I think. He even asked him how he made the eggs. Luke didn't have the slightest interest in cooking. He could make a sandwich, and that was about it. So I took it as a good sign.

After breakfast I went back to Citizen Kane and took a shower in the large second-floor bathroom off Freddie's master bedroom. The walls were covered, ceiling to floor, in the square emerald-green tiles Freddie had chosen long ago, and the dusty chandelier cast shards of light across the room that made the dust dance.

I changed into an old cotton dress with flowers on it that Freddie used to do her baking in. It made me feel like she was right next to me, making ginger lemonade and keeping all the bad things away.

Sunshine talked to me while I got ready. She asked me about River, about being in his bed. I made vague responses, River-style, as my mind ran over all the things that happened the night before.

River. River. River.

≈≈

While I'd gotten dressed, I'd made up my mind to walk into town and help look for Isobel. And I wanted to find Jack, and talk to him too. I was pretty sure no one would be taking him seriously, and I wanted to ask him more about what he saw.

About the Devil with the red eyes.

Sunshine had nothing to do and wanted to come with,

and the next thing I knew, all four of us were heading toward town.

Echo was in chaos. Cop cars and people cluttered up the streets around the town square—everyone looked grave and furrowed and defeated in the thick fog that rolled in from the sea. I watched them move around in clumps, hunched under umbrellas even though the rain was mostly still mist.

The café overflowed with people, and there was a line almost to the door, but Sunshine and Luke went in anyway. River and I stayed outside. River had put on a clean linen shirt and pants, and looked cool and beautiful as a turquoise sea on a hot day, despite the fog. Behind me, I heard snatches of a tense conversation from a group of policemen:

"The whole thing gives me the creeps, all those kids with stakes . . ."

"Ideas can be contagious, like the flu . . ."

"It spread so fast—I think every kid in town is out there."

"Any word on the girl?"

". . . someone tells a story about a kidnapper and the next thing you know, you've got an epidemic on your hands—mass delusion, it's a documented fact . . ."

"Blue Hoffman, that story is still going around—"

"What we've got to do is get our hands on the punk who

started it all. *Trust me, it will all come back to one kid. We get him, this whole thing will crumble.*"

I grabbed River's hand. "Jack," I said. He nodded.

The cemetery was worse than the center of town. People were lined up outside the fence, thick as mosquitoes on a humid night, and the low buzz of voices made the air feel rigid, like it was wound up too tight. River and I squeezed by a woman with a worried expression and a death-grip on the wrist of a small boy. The boy held a stake of twigs, just like Jack's, and was pleading for her to let go.

River and I slid through the open gate of the cemetery, and my heart froze. Children were everywhere. *Everywhere.* Girls and boys, up trees and behind gravestones, small gray shadows in the fog. All held stakes. And all were ignoring the calls of parents to come home. Adults roamed around the graveyard like dazed sheep, shouting names like Zach, and Ann, and Jamie, and Charlotte, while kids darted in and out of the mist, not listening.

If the night before, the six boys had been serious, and un-kid-like, and scary, well, it was nothing to observing a whole damn *army* of kids brandishing stakes like guns. And the fact that all of them were united in the Devil hunt felt eerie and just plain *wrong*. Kids tend to faction out when they play. Some hit the swings, some the jungle gym, some beat up smaller kids, some pretend they're fighting dragons in a cave filled with gold. But *all* the kids were hunting the Devil. I couldn't wrap my head around it.

Goose bumps broke out down my arms. I looked at River. His face was dark. Dark and stormy as the sky. And, worse than the dark, his face looked . . . surprised. His eyes were wide, wider than usual, and a bit . . . lost.

It was a disconcerting look on him.

I turned to my left and saw a small girl crouching behind a big headstone. Her black hair was frizzing in the wet mist and her black eyes were shifting left and right, left and right.

I knelt beside her. "Hey," I said. "Are you here to kill the Devil?"

She nodded.

"Do you know where Jack is?" I asked. "I need to talk to him."

She nodded again. "He's up by the Glenship mausoleum. He's been there since last night." She talked fast and quiet, like she didn't want to be overheard. "Jack figures it'll be the first place the Devil will go, because that's where he saw him last. But it's been light out for hours. And I don't even know what I'm supposed to be looking for. All Jack would say is that he had red eyes and that he wore pilgrim clothes, but what does that mean?"

The girl looked over her shoulder, up at the gray sky, and shivered.

I looked at the gray sky too. I wondered what Freddie would have said, if she heard the Devil was a red-eyed man in black who flew across the night sky and kidnapped kids. I couldn't decide if she would have laughed at the story, or believed it.

Believed it, maybe.

I shifted my gaze to River, but he was watching a group of six policemen coming through the gates. A tall blond man in his forties lifted a megaphone to his lips and began to speak.

"LISTEN UP KIDS. EVERY LAST ONE OF YOU NEEDS TO GO HOME. NOW. WE'VE GOT A MISSING GIRL ON OUR HANDS, AND WE DON'T NEED ANY MORE TROUBLE. ANYONE CAUGHT LINGERING IN THE CEMETERY WILL BE ARRESTED. I REPEAT: GO HOME OR YOU WILL BE HANDCUFFED AND TAKEN TO JAIL."

It was an empty threat, obviously. But the kids believed it.

Dozens of small shapes started walking out of the fog and making their way to the exit. Their small faces looked upset and agitated, though, and I noticed that they took their stakes with them when they left.

I watched for Jack, but didn't see him. He was the least likely to believe the cop's bluff, anyway.

A white van pulled up and parked outside the gates. A short woman with long hair jumped out. She walked through the gate, and aimed a CHANNEL 3 NEWS TEAM video camera right at us.

"Ah, hell," River said. "That's all I need. Come on, Vi. Let's get out of here."

CHAPTER 10

THE SEARCH PARTIES continued looking for Isobel throughout the day. Luke and I joined one and hunted through the woods behind our house with a group of earnest retired people and a couple of old hound dogs. But nothing.

I prayed to Freddie that Isobel was okay. That everything would turn out all right. But I was pretty damn worried.

River disappeared. He walked me back from the cemetery, right after seeing that news camera, got in his car, and drove off.

I didn't know if he would come back. I didn't know anything. After I returned from the search party, I just sat on my front steps. Not reading, just waiting. Just waiting, and praying to Freddie.

Luke told me that I had scared River off, with my know-it-all gaze and my being-a-girl-ness, and thank God we had already gotten the rent in cash. But I ignored him.

The hours dragged by.

No Isobel.

No River.

The kids returned to the cemetery once it got dark. They crawled back when their parents were asleep. I knew this because I was there too. I scraped up the bravest bits inside of me and walked to the graveyard after night fell. I figured Jack would still be there, waiting for the Devil. But what I found, after I crept past the front gates, were dozens of kids returned to their posts—their pale faces shining through the dark. It was just silence and shadows, the dead buried below and the distant sound of the sea in their ears for all eternity. I crept from tree to tree, kid to kid, always keeping the ocean on my left side so I knew where I was.

Again and again, I would feel *him*, the Devil, breathing down my neck. I would spin around and no one would be there . . . except a quiet, creeping little kid, holding two sharpened twigs in his hands. I tried asking some of them if they knew where I could find Jack. I called up trees and knelt by headstones and asked and asked. But they were so hollow-eyed and *focused*. They wouldn't give me a straight answer, and after a while I started to think they were following me. Stalking me. Scaring me on purpose.

My heart started hitting my chest so hard, it drowned out the sound of the waves crashing against the rocks below. It was time to leave.

And then I heard something behind me. Feet. Small feet on stone.

I spun around, and there they were. Two boys, one girl. Standing in a line, ten feet behind me. They were holding the sharpened twigs. Staring at me.

"You don't have any stakes," the girl said. "The Devil is going to get you."

She took a step closer and the other kids followed. We stood face-to-face, not moving, just staring. A breeze lifted my hair as it brushed past my cheek. The salty wind was soft, but cold. *Cold*. Like swimming in the sea at night. Like clammy fingers crawling up your neck.

I shivered.

"Do you feel him?" the girl asked. "The Devil?"

I nodded.

"You'd better run," she said.

I ran.

When I got home, I shoved the huge front door closed behind me, and locked it. I slunk down, my back against the wood. I felt stupid and ashamed. But damn, the image of those kids in the dark, holding stakes, staring at the sky, following me from gravestone to gravestone . . . My chest hurt, and my ears ached, as if I'd been swimming deep underwater. I took three breaths. Then I started the search.

I did this sometimes, after Freddie died. Wandered Citizen Kane in the dark. I'd already searched through her bedroom countless times, and the library, and the kitchen, and the attic.

I started in the cellars this time, digging in corners dripping with mold, looking for loose bricks and trapdoors. I went upstairs into bedrooms that hadn't been used in years and pulled open dressers and wardrobes and crawled under beds. I tapped on walls, hoping to hear a hollow sound, and turned over paintings. I'd done this many times before. And would do it again.

I let the dust and the forgotten bottles of wine and the worn rugs and disintegrating curtains dig their way into my soul until I was as paranoid and as stirred up as Daniel Leap raving in the town square. I wanted to find Freddie's old letters, but I would have been satisfied with anything. A diary. A half-started cocktail murder mystery. Bits of bad poetry written on a yellowed napkin. Anything of Freddie's. Anything to bring her back, even for a second.

There had to be *something* left, besides the clothes hanging in her closet. No one lives a whole life and leaves not a bit of it behind but a handful of dresses. Had she burned all of her private things in those last weeks before she died? I refused to believe it.

There must be something.

And there was. But it wasn't what I wanted, because it asked new questions and gave no answers.

Citizen Kane had an attic that ran the length of the house. I used to spend hours up there as a kid, exploring all the odd old trunks and chests that came from who knew when. It's where I found the black trunk, the one with the empty bottle of gin and a small red card that, when opened, said: *Freddie—you were the first to know, and the last to judge. I promised I'd never burn you. I meant it then, and I mean it now. No matter what. Love, always. Me.*

It was written in a man's elegant, educated hand. Underneath the card were three white summer dresses, folded neatly, a black wooden cross, and two locks of hair—pale blond, and brown. But no letters from Freddie herself. Not one. I remembered that trunk well, because I had opened it on a hot summer afternoon a few days after Freddie had died, but the air inside the chest felt cool. I put the empty bottle and the red card back, pushed the trunk in the far corner, and left it alone.

But I'd tried everything else by now, so what the hell.

I was climbing toward the attic when I realized I'd

woken Luke up with all my noise. I could hear his feet tromping around above. He caught up to me on the third staircase—the one that had been the servants' back before I was born and we still had servants. It was narrow, with worn wooden steps and no banister. Luke stood at the top, looking down at me on the second-floor landing, his reddish brown hair sticking up. He looked tired, and younger, and more like the brother I'd known five years ago, when Freddie died.

"Violet," he said, blinking, "why on earth are you running around and slamming doors at three in the morning?"

"Exploring. I'm exploring." I climbed to the top step, sat down, and sighed.

"Exploring. Right." Luke sat down beside me, squeezing himself onto the narrow step. His bare feet lined up next to my bare feet, and both glowed an eerie color in the skinny shaft of moonlight coming through the window above—it didn't let in much light because half of it was blocked by the rickety spiral staircase that led to the attic.

"You were looking for Freddie's letters again. You're that upset over River's leaving?" he asked, when I didn't say anything.

I put my arms on my knees and let my hair fall over my face. "No," I lied. "I'm wondering where the little girl is."

I turned my head and looked at Luke. "But now that you mention it, River's leaving does make me kind of furious."

Luke laughed.

I caught his eye. "You know, River said I was capable of violence, if pushed far enough. Do you believe that?"

Luke didn't answer for a while. Then he shrugged. "I'd normally want to beat the hell out of some guy who shared a bed with you and then disappeared. But I like River. There's something about him."

I nodded. "There is."

A pause.

"I went back to the cemetery," I said. "The kids were in there again, and creeping up on me, with their stakes and their haunted little faces. It was terrifying. I couldn't stand it. I ran."

Luke laughed again, a soft sort of chuckle that I rarely heard from him. "It's been a long night for you, sister."

I smiled a bit at that, because it was true. "Are you always this nice in the middle of the night? Maybe I should wake you up more often."

"Please don't. Some of us get up early." Luke smiled back at me, and then stood, and yawned, and started walking back to his bedroom. "River will come back, eventually," he said, over his shoulder. "Count on it."

≈≈

My brother was right.

River drove into the driveway in the early stillness of pre-dawn. Which I knew because I was stupidly awake and waiting for him.

He got out of his car, swaggered up to me, and smiled his damn crooked smile. His brown eyes weren't as cool and easy as they had been that last time he met me on the steps. And his hair wasn't parted to the side, vintage-style . . . it was messy and tangled, like he'd been running his hands through it a lot. He was still River, nonchalant and graceful, but there was something odd in his expression, something that hadn't been there before.

"Hey, Violet," he said. His voice was as lazy as ever, though.

"Hey," I replied, just as lazily, though what I wanted to do was stand up, tilt my head back, and scream at the sky because of the kids and the cemetery and the Devil and the missing girl and the fact that River had taken off without a word when he was the first boy I'd ever kissed and damn, that gets to you.

But I refused to let River see me that . . . *moved*. I had the idea that he would like it, like seeing me get that mad. Besides, he'd already noticed the happy, traitorous sparkle in my eyes.

"Those kids go back to the cemetery?" River didn't waste time with chitchat. But that was all right, because neither did I.

"Yeah. Once it got dark again." I didn't tell him how I knew.

River held out his hand. "Well, I think it's gone on long enough, don't you? Want to help me put a stop to it?"

I nodded and grabbed his hand.

By the time we reached the cemetery gates, I still hadn't asked River where he'd gone, and why. And he didn't offer the information. But then, he probably would have just lied anyway. And his hand was all up in mine now, his long fingers weaving between my own and making my insides go from black-and-white to Technicolor.

Dawn was taking off its clothes, kicking up its pinks and purples on the horizon. I saw the girl again. The one with the frizzy black hair from before. She was curled up behind a headstone belonging to a young boy—a young boy who had *Drowned at Sea* so long ago, the letters of his name were almost eroded to oblivion.

River went down on his knees beside the girl, put his hand on hers, and gently took a stake out of her clenched fist. "Go home," he said. "We'll find Isobel. Your parents are going to wake up soon and be worried. Go home. There is no Devil."

The girl got to her feet, gave River a long look, and then took off at a run in the direction of the gate.

River broke the stake in half and threw it into the trees. We began to walk up the hill to the mausoleum. Early morning mist had started blowing in from the ocean again, and some of it was so thick it felt like walking through a wet, woolly gray sweater. Fog had never bothered me before, but for some reason I started to feel as if I was being suffocated. I focused on taking deep breaths of sea air, and the feeling went away.

There were some twenty boys by the tomb. They gave us tired, haunted looks as we neared, like a photograph of war refugees in the pages of a mildewed *National Geographic*.

I had looked for Jack in the cemetery six hours ago, but hadn't seen him. Yet, there he was now, standing on top of the Glenship mausoleum, a pile of stakes at his feet, his gaze trained on the sky. River called out his name, and he looked down at us but didn't move.

"Jack, can you come down?" River asked. "I want to talk to you."

Jack pointed a finger at one of the boys. "Danny, I'm leaving my post. It's your turn to watch."

Jack grabbed a handful of ivy and swung himself down. The blond-haired Danny then climbed up and planted himself in Jack's spot, head tilted toward the sky.

Jack rubbed his eyes and glanced around. He looked pale and tired. His russet hair was tangled, bits of leaves stuck to it like he'd been rolling on the ground. There was a streak of dirt blending with the tiny brown freckles that covered his face, and his thin shoulders sagged.

"Nick," Jack said, looking at a small boy with dark brown hair, "you can replace Jenny out in the southwest corner. Logan, go check on Holly, would you? She gets scared if she's left alone too long."

The boys darted off. Jack rubbed his red eyes again. "Hey," he said.

I nodded a hello. I was distracted by the small mountain of stakes at the base of the mausoleum. There were dozens. Hundreds, maybe.

Jack turned to River. "You're that guy we almost stabbed."

"Yes."

"You're the guy that taught us how to work the yo-yos. And the one that told us to go to the cemetery and look for the Devil."

I jerked my head up. I looked at Jack, and then at River, hard. But neither would look back at me.

"Well, what do you want?" Jack asked, in a soft, weary voice. "Are you going to try to get us to go home too? It won't work. The police kicked us out, but we just came back."

River put his hands on his knees so he could look Jack straight in the eyes. "Jack, do you know the old tree house? The one by the ocean, behind Glenship Manor?"

Jack's brow furrowed. "Yeah. Everybody knows that tree house. Why?"

"Go there, Jack. Now. And take Charlie with you."

They stared at each other for three, maybe four seconds. Then Jack shook himself and spun around.

"Tell everyone to go home," he called out to the group of boys behind him. "Tell them I know where Isobel is. Tell them . . . tell them *there is no Devil.*"

CHAPTER 11

WORD SPREAD QUICKLY. River and I watched small bodies fall out of trees and ooze out of shadows.

Fifteen minutes later, the cemetery was near empty. Only one boy remained. He had yellow hair and thin arms; he stood by the gate and fidgeted, as if unsure whether to leave. He eyed the sky, and the trees, and didn't move. But then River took the boy by the shoulder and gently pushed him out onto the road.

The fog had cleared and I could see the ocean far, far below the graveyard. It was bright and blue and full of promise. River and I stared at it for a while.

I wondered how he knew where Charlie's sister was. And how he got Jack to believe him so fast.

I wondered what Jack meant when he said that

River told him to look for the Devil in the cemetery.

I wondered where that beautiful, buttery, fluttery feeling I felt in River's presence had gotten itself off to.

Because it was gone now. Completely gone.

River pulled on my hand and we headed out of the cemetery and down a trail through the woods that skirted the main road. The woods were dark and silent, none of the dawn able to reach through the thick trees. Children wove in and out of the shadowed path in front of us, always keeping their distance.

Seven minutes later we were in downtown Echo. I turned to go to the café, which opened really damn early—but then I saw a group of the cemetery kids heading down one of Echo's side streets, with Jack leading the way. They were following River's orders. They were going down Glenship Road. And Glenship Road only led to one place. Glenship Manor, and the tree house.

Chester and Clara Glenship had been the wealthy folks in town, back at the turn of the last century, along with my grandpa's parents. They also built a big mansion on the ocean, closer to town than Citizen Kane, and threw rollicking parties for all their city friends up from Boston and New York, like characters in an F. Scott Fitzgerald novel. But the Glenships ran out of money before my own family. And, to make matters worse, Chester and Clara's charming, bright-eyed eldest son brought his young lover down to the wine cellar and slit her throat with a jackknife. For reasons unknown. It was lurid and the papers loved it, and the grand manor had sat empty and abandoned for decades, with overgrown ivy and broken windows, and an air of long-ago happiness.

I had a fantasy when I was younger that one of the Glenships would come back and fix the place up. He would be young and beautiful, and not at all insane like his throat-slitting ancestor. He would have slicked-backed hair, an expensive education, and a sharp tongue. The two of us would meet and fight and fall in love and live and have children and grow old in Echo's second mansion by the sea.

I was pretty stupid, when I was younger.

Behind the Glenship, spreading out to the edge of the woods, were the remains of the manor's extensive grounds. The lawn had grown wild in the last lonely decades, savage almost, with fountains covered in green mold and monstrous, untended shrubbery. The Citizen looked slightly better than this. But not by much.

To the back and right of the grounds stood the tree house. And it wasn't just any old tree house. Chester and Clara had a daughter, as well as a son, and they loved her more than life itself. So of course she had no choice but to grow up rotten to the core, or die young. She died young. Her parents built her a miniature mansion in the trees, where she played, pretty and spoiled and oblivious, until one day she fell out of the tree house, broke her neck, and died.

River and I followed Jack. We followed him and the other kids right up to the kid-killing tree house. The paint was long gone. The wooden boards were warped and gray, with rusted nails sticking out, dying to give someone lock-jaw. The gable roof was sagging in the middle, one strong wind away from caving in.

The kids fanned out around Jack, forming a circle around the tree. River and I drew close and rounded out the edges. Jack put two hands on the tree and scrambled up what remained of the wooden boards that had been nailed into the trunk as steps. We all watched, necks craned upward. Jack kicked in the rotted-out door of the tree house and went inside.

My heart beat once. Twice.

The door opened, and there he was again, Isobel next to him. She smiled a shy smile and waved at the crowd of kids below, as if the whole thing was nothing. As if kids went missing and spent two long nights in decaying, grandiose tree houses all the time, eating God knew what and sleeping on the hard floor and worrying everyone half to death.

Isobel hopped down the tree and was swallowed by the throng of kids. They shouted and whooped and congratulated her on not being kidnapped and possibly dead and taken to hell. I saw her brother Charlie give her a bear hug, their black curls blending into each other until you didn't know where one ended and the other began.

But Jack stayed where he was, up in the tree house. I squinted up at him and then looked at River, and saw that they were looking at each other.

My heart beat once. Twice.

We left the kids. We walked back to the town square and stood in front of the café. I fidgeted for a while, not saying anything. Luke and Sunshine were inside; I could see them through the café window, standing by the counter. They must have wandered into town while River and I were in the cemetery.

I didn't stand close to River, and he didn't stand close to me. I turned to face the square while he stayed at the window. A ray of sunshine broke through the gray sky, darted around a cloud, and hit me full in the face.

Silence.

Silence.

"So, is she going to be all right?"

"Who?"

"River, you know who. Isobel."

"Yeah."

"Should we tell anyone, like the cops or anything? Tell them that she's been found?"

"No. Word will get around fast enough."

I paused. "So . . . there's no Devil?"

"No."

I tried to catch River's gaze, to read his expression, but he was still facing the café and wouldn't look at me.

"How did you know where Isobel was? How could you possibly have known where she was?" I stepped closer, put my hand on his arm. "River. What did Jack really see in the cemetery? He wasn't lying. I know he wasn't. What's going on? And how did you become part of all this? What did Jack mean, when he said you told him to go look for the Devil in the cemetery?"

River just shook his head and continued to stare at the café window. "Look, I'll tell you about it later. I promise. But right now all I want to do is get Luke and Sunshine, and have a bonfire by the sea." He paused. "Yeah, that sounds like a great idea. I like to have a bonfire after exciting events. It calms people down." He caught my eye then. "Me included."

I looked down at Freddie's dress. I was wearing the

faded blue-flowered one. I gripped a bit of the fabric in my hand and squeezed it tight. Pushing River was only going to get me less of what I wanted, not more. "All right. Let's have a bonfire."

I turned and waved at Sunshine through the café window. She and Luke left the counter and headed outside. Gianni was working instead of Maddy, and he gave me a small nod and a smile. Which I returned. I could just make out a copy of *Fresh Cup Magazine* on the counter— the latest issue, no doubt. I wondered if Gianni hoped I would come in, so he could talk to me about it.

"Did you hear?" Sunshine said, sidling in between me and River. "Turns out the missing girl wasn't missing at all. She spent the last few nights in the Glenship tree house, drinking dew and eating nothing but wild strawberries, according to my sources."

River looked at me, one eyebrow raised in a cocky way that, for a second, reminded me of Luke. And I liked River a little bit less for it.

"How did you find that out already, Sunshine? It *just happened.* River and I were there, we—"

Luke interrupted me. "So I guess those boys made the whole Devil thing up. The one chance our town has at fame, and we blow it. Figures."

"Shut up, Luke. Maybe those boys really did see the

Devil." I paused. "Like how Sunshine saw Blue, in the tunnel."

Sunshine glared at me for a second. Then her eyes went sleepy again as she turned to River. "So where have you been? Luke said Vi's been doing nothing but wandering around the house, wringing her hands and wailing since you took off."

Luke grinned at me.

Sometimes I really hated my brother.

"Luke is lying," I said to River. "I didn't even notice you were gone."

River smiled. "And I thought I was the only liar around here." He stepped forward and put one arm around Sunshine's shoulders and the other around Luke's. "Enough about devils and tunnels and mysterious travels. The sun's come out and I've decided to have a bonfire on the beach. Everyone's invited." River's brown eyes were lit up like July fireflies. The serious, shadowed River from earlier was gone. Completely gone. As if he'd never even existed.

I was worried, I was. I felt a sharp tingle in the pit of my stomach that said All Is Not Right Here, even as I looked at River's smiling face and firefly eyes.

But he had come back, and the truth was . . . the truth was that it made me happy. Maybe it shouldn't have, I don't know. But then, who was I to slap a bit of joy in the face? We were going to have a bonfire together on the beach, and everything else could just go to hell.

≋

The bonfire. A steep trail led from the road by Sunshine's house to the ocean, winding down the cliff and ending in a small, secluded cove. There was a much bigger public beach down the coast a mile or so, but I liked my little private spot because it couldn't be seen from above, and so no one knew it existed. I often visited it by myself, just to read, alone, in the sand, the waves crashing nearby.

Luke and Sunshine and I swam down there sometimes too. The ocean was usually too cold and fierce for it, but some blue, calm days, it was all right, and we would take a picnic basket to the cove and splash around for a while. Sunshine had a slick white swimsuit that she loved to tuck her curves into and run around in. And I had an old, vintage suit of Freddie's, of course. It was navy trimmed with white, and it had a little belt. It covered most of me except my arms and legs.

I liked those swimming days. We were always cold and always laughing. Sometimes Luke held me under the water, or kissed Sunshine in the sand, but mostly we just had a really good time. For all that Luke complained to River about spending the summer with two girls, I think he actually kind of loved hanging out with us. At least, he never bothered finding anyone else.

It wasn't nearly warm enough for swimming now, but the sun had shoved the clouds away, and it was bright and blue again and barely past morning. Luke dug up a bottle of port from the Citizen's dusty Cask of Amontillado wine cellar, and took turns sipping from the bottle with Sunshine while River and I gathered dried-out driftwood into a pile and set it on fire. I'd found an old camping grill in the basement while Luke was looking for the wine, and River made grilled cheese, tomato, and mustard sandwiches for lunch.

Sunshine had taken some quilts from the Citizen, and after we ate, the four of us curled up on the blankets in the sand and watched the flames dance orange-yellow-red against the blue sea.

I had my own blanket, and River had his. We didn't sit near each other and I didn't even look at him.

Mostly.

River was lying on his back, knees bent, his pretty, bare feet tucked halfway into the sand. He must have felt me staring at him, because he turned his head and winked at me, slow and casual, as if he knew that I was beginning to distrust him a bit, and he wanted to show me he didn't all that much care.

There was something about sleeping next to a person that was . . . dangerous. More dangerous than sleeping *with* a person, maybe. Not that I would know. But being next to River, in the same bed, and waking up beside him, did bad things to my mind. I felt as if I *knew* him already. Like how I knew Sunshine, and Luke, and my parents. Like how I knew Freddie.

But I didn't. At all. And that knowing feeling, based on nothing, was dangerous. And, I felt, not quite sane.

"So Violet, get this."

Sunshine was all tucked up next to my brother, her elbow on his thigh, her hand on the bottle of wine, her long dark hair touching the sand.

"Get what?" I asked as I shoved her arm off Luke's leg.

"I had a dream last night. A dream about a giraffe."

I took the bottle out of Sunshine's hand and set it behind my back. It was almost gone. "A giraffe?"

"Yeah, this giraffe that I was friends with. You see, this giraffe had a party, and I helped her clean up afterward. I never dream about giraffes. Do little kids even dream about giraffes? But here's where it gets interesting. I read the front page of the Portland paper at the café and it said some giraffe at some zoo died yesterday. And I just realized that it probably means something. Don't you think that it means something? I think it means something."

Sunshine was drunk. She would never have talked about her dreams otherwise. Sunshine hated illogical things, like dreams and fairy tales and Salvador Dalí.

"Sunshine, you're drunk," I said.

She raised her eyebrows. "Didn't you hear, Violet? Boys like drunk girls." At this, Sunshine turned over on her side in the sand, lifted her arm, and let it fall in a gentle arc onto her hip. Then she wiggled. Just a little bit. Just in the exact right spot.

Sunshine continued to amaze me with her ability to draw attention to what she considered her most interesting parts. Without seeming to try.

Luke stood up, reached around me, and took the port bottle. "That's right, Sunshine. We *do* like drunk girls. What do you think, River? I bet you've had a few drunk girls in your time. Less fuss, I say." My brother paused and took a swig from the bottle. "Women are always making it so hard for us men to get the one thing nature intended for us to have. It's such a shame."

So Luke was at it again. I thought he might give up the man-love talk with River, but the wine had brought it back. River shook his head at Luke's comment and kind of laughed. Sometimes my brother said things that were so, well, *wrong,* in so many ways, it was impossible to do anything but laugh.

Luke grinned at River and drank down the last of the port in one long gulp. He reached his arm back and threw the empty bottle into the bumping, grinding waves of the sea.

"Luke, what the hell did you do that for?" I gestured at the water. "The bottle will break and someone will walk along the beach and cut their feet."

"Shut up, Vi. No one but us even knows about this spot."

"I can't believe you think throwing a bottle at the ocean makes you look cool. It's so dumb, I don't even have words to describe how dumb it is. It's speech-sucking dumb."

"Stop squabbling, siblings." Sunshine put her hands on the sand and pushed herself to her feet. "The fire's almost out and the wind is picking up. Let's go back. Let's, you know, go play in the Citizen's attic. Come on, Violet, we haven't done that in years. It'll be fun. Come *on*." She took my arm and began to tug on it.

"Okay, okay," I said to Sunshine. I turned to River. "Want to see the attic? It's big and dusty and scary."

"Yep," he said.

So we all climbed back up the trail to the road and walked home.

Jack was waiting.

CHAPTER 12

"I WANT YOU to show me how you do it," he said.

Jack was standing on the steps of the Citizen. He stared at River for a second, and then repeated himself. "Show me how you do it."

River tilted his head and smiled. "Do what?"

"The magic." Jack kept staring, and his expression began to match River's—cagey, and smart, and suspicious.

I looked at Luke and Sunshine. They were laughing and flirting with each other in a drunk, shameless way, and not paying attention.

But I was paying attention. I watched River closely. Very closely.

Because I knew. I knew that River sneaking away during *Casablanca* and the kids seeing the Devil in the cemetery weren't two separate things. I just didn't know how yet.

River leaned down and whispered something in Jack's ear. Jack nodded. Then River stood back up. "Jack," he said, out loud now, "do you want to explore a dusty, scary attic?"

Jack glared at River for a second and then shrugged.

So we all walked through the Citizen, up the marble staircase, down the second-floor hall, past Freddie's room, which was now my room, and up to the third floor, past Luke's bedroom, past the old ballroom that was now the art gallery, until we reached the rickety spiral staircase at the end of the hall that led to the attic.

The Citizen's attic was, objectively, breathtaking. The place was littered with trunks and old clothes and wardrobes and pieces of furniture and strange metal toys no one had played with in sixty years and half-painted canvases and on and on. There were several round windows to let in the sunlight, and I loved how it raked its way across the floor as I watched, dust dancing like sugarplum fairies in the bold yellow glow. If attics could make wishes, this one would have nothing to wish for.

"Will I find Narnia inside there?" Jack asked, pointing to a tall wardrobe against the wall. He was wearing dark jeans that were too big, and a faded brown T-shirt. Over the T-shirt he had a green army-style jacket, which was also too big but looked kind of cool on him. It had a lot of pockets, which was probably why Jack liked it.

Jack turned to River and me, and he was smiling about the wardrobe, his thin lips parting and his freckles shifting with the movement. "*The Lion, the Witch and the Wardrobe* is a good book."

So there was still a little kid inside Jack after all. A little kid that liked fantasy books and wardrobes.

River smiled. "There's no way Narnia isn't in that thing. I'm going in."

Moth-eaten fur coats began to fly as they dug their way to the back of the tall, deep cupboard. I went over to the old wind-up phonograph in the corner and began to sift through the yellowed record sleeves, occasionally stopping to push my hair out of my face so I could lean in closer. By the time the tips of my hair were covered with dust, I'd found what I wanted.

I put the record on the player and turned the crank. The rustling blues of Robert Johnson filled the attic.

After River and Jack disemboweled the Narnia wardrobe of all its old coats, it served as the attic's changing room. Sunshine put on a wrinkled saffron dress that was two sizes too small in the chest, which suited her fine. My brother found a dashing pinstriped suit, probably one of our grandpa's. When he came out of the wardrobe I wanted to say he looked good, and that he should dress like this all the time, and hey it's pretty awesome to wear your dead relative's clothes . . . but I kept my mouth shut, because I was afraid he would take the suit back off.

I pulled a black party dress and fake pearls out of a wooden trunk—very *Breakfast at Tiffany's*—and went into the wardrobe to put the dress on. When I came out, River took one look at me and grinned. A nice, kind of *appreciative* grin.

"You need to put your hair up," he said.

So I dug around in a small box of cheap jewelry until I had gathered a handful of bobby pins. Then River appeared behind me, and, with his long, tan fingers, started lifting my hair, one strand at a time, twirling it and pinning it until it was all piled on my head in a graceful twist. My hair was thick with dried salt from sitting on the beach, and tangled from the wind, but River made it look pretty damn elegant, all things considered. When he was done, I went over and looked at myself in one of the long dressing mirrors—it was warped and stained with age, but I could still see half my face pretty well.

"How did you learn how to do that?" I asked, putting my hand to my hair. "Wait . . . let me guess. Your mother is a barber."

River laughed, but his eyes didn't join in. "No. My mother is . . . invited to a lot of parties. While she puts on makeup and picks out her jewelry, we talk. She taught me how to do her hair when I was a kid. So that's how I know."

What River was telling me sounded personal. It sounded . . . real. As in, not a lie. So I was interested, and my tongue itched to ask some follow-up questions. But River walked away and started digging through a red trunk by the record player. Done talking, apparently.

I put my fingers to my hair and spun around so I could see myself in the mirror again. I pictured River as a little boy, with his straight nose and crooked smile, but also with soft, hairless cheeks and a small boy's body, like Jack's. I pictured him helping his mom pin her hair up for a party. It was a damn sweet image, and it kind of nullified the feeling I'd been working on since the cemetery.

Luke came over to the mirror and pushed me out of the way so he could see himself. He smiled at the way the pinstripes were pulled tight across his chest and arms. And then his smile faded, and his fingers flew to his forehead.

Luke had a deep widow's peak, and he was already worried about going bald. I would often catch him looking at himself in mirrors and window reflections, moving his head this way and that, trying to figure out if his hairline was receding.

"Vi, look," he said, pointing to his head. "*Look*. It's moved. I swear it's moved."

"No, it hasn't," I replied, without looking.

"Are you sure? I can't go bald, Vi. I just can't. I'm not a bald guy. I wouldn't wear it well."

I sighed, and kind of laughed. "Your hairline hasn't moved. I promise."

"Okay," Luke said. He took a deep breath, let it out, and turned away from the mirror. "I trust you."

I laughed again and then turned to look at River, who had just come out of the wardrobe in what looked like Italian peasant clothes, complete with a red kerchief around his neck. Something left over from my parents' bohemian friends, no doubt. He had even scrounged up a ukulele, and he sat down on one of the torn velvet sofas, strumming the chords to *Moon River*, in honor of my dress.

Jack searched around until he found a checkered vest and a tweed cap. He was smiling, and I think he was having a good time, but he was so quiet. I got the impression that he was used to keeping still and silent. He just didn't give off the feeling that other kids gave off—of recklessness and innocence and mischief. And I wondered why.

Jack took his costume into the wardrobe and came out

looking like a street kid selling newspapers on the corner in an old movie. It was damn adorable. And I don't consider myself particularly susceptible to adorable-ness. I had the urge to sit down and paint him, right there, on the spot. And I hadn't wanted to pick up my brushes in a long time.

Luke and I had been painting since before we could talk, and, while other kids had crayons, Luke and I had a box of acrylics. But after watching my parents prioritize art over us for so many years, I'd kind of gotten sick of it. I'd quit cold turkey last fall when they'd left for Paris. Luke hadn't painted in years, not since around the time Freddie died, as far as I knew. And he'd been a lot better than me too. He was good, really good, like our dad.

I remembered the damp paintbrushes in the guesthouse.

"Luke, are you painting again?" I looked at him, sitting in the dashing suit next to Sunshine on a pile of dusty old velvet throw pillows. He ignored me and began to nibble on her ear.

I kicked his leg. "Just tell me if you're painting again. It'll make me happy."

But he didn't answer me, just continued kissing Sunshine. Maybe he considered it too important to talk about. I kicked him again, but then let him be.

Jack sat down between River and me. It made me feel motherly, to have this kid around, even if the kid was kind of stoic and silent and hardly acted like a kid at all. Still, it made me think. It made me think about how, if I was a mother, I wouldn't spend all my afternoons with my artist friends, talking about Renoir and Rodin. Or take off for Europe, and disappear for months at a time. No . . . I would sit with my kid and make him maple syrup iced tea and tell him stories. It wouldn't have to be all the time. Just once in a while. Just so he would know I wanted him around.

Jack started yawning. Which made sense. He'd spent the last few nights in a cemetery, looking for the Devil. I thought about what Jack had said earlier, in front of the Citizen. About wanting River to show him how he did it.

River felt me looking at him, and looked back. His fingers were still on the uke and his eyes were open and happy and content.

I decided to go back to pulling a Scarlett and not think about the cemetery devil until tomorrow.

Freddie once told me that I was the worst sort of stubborn—because I wasn't stubborn at all. I was patient. Patient, but determined. A stubborn person could be distracted, or tricked. But not me. I just held on and on and on, never giving up until I got my way, long after everyone else stopped caring. I don't know if what Freddie said was true. Maybe she was just frustrated with me at the time for something.

Jack yawned again. He had high cheekbones that popped out when his mouth opened wide, and I thought he would be kind of an elegant-looking man when he got older—debonair, like a George Sanders–voiced movie star in the 1940s.

Jack closed his eyes . . . and fell asleep.

I turned my head and looked out the window. My gaze drifted, and my eyes followed a sunbeam to where it covered an old trunk in the corner, making the black leather look lighter, almost brown. I realized that it was the trunk with the gin bottle and the red card. I'd forgotten that I wanted to search through that thing again.

And I almost got up to do it right then, but Jack was leaning against me, and he looked soft and sweet. I didn't want to move and lose the peaceful moment by starting up my Freddie yearning again.

I would check it later. And I wouldn't forget this time.

"So there's this story by Faulkner. 'A Rose for Emily,'" I said, to no one in particular, after River finished the song he was strumming and everything was quiet except for the soft sleep-breathing of Jack next to me. I felt like talking, which was unusual—I had all these thoughts going through my head and I didn't want to think them. So I opened my mouth and just let it run. "It's about a woman named Emily who falls in love with a man, but he doesn't love her back. Then one day he goes missing. Disappears. Years later, when Emily dies, the people in her town find the decomposed corpse of the man in her bed, a strand of long gray hair on the pillow next to him." I paused. "Emily poisoned him with arsenic and then put him in her bed, to lie there, forever."

I paused again. "I know it's supposed to be a horror story, but I always thought the whole thing was sort of sad, and beautiful. She *really* loved that man. That's rare in life, I think. More rare than people think. Everyone thought she was insane, but I think she was just really, really in love."

River stopped fiddling with the ukulele and looked at me.

Then Luke stretched out his leg and kicked me in the shin. "*God.* Please tell me you don't go around saying crap like that to everyone. No wonder no one in town ever talks to us. Wealthy families always have a crazy person or two. Is that really the role you want to play, Vi?"

"We're not wealthy anymore. Remember? So if I'm insane, no one will care."

Luke turned to River. "What the hell do you see in my sister, anyway? I'm curious."

"Siblings, stop squabbling." Sunshine reached into her glass of tea, took out an ice cube, and started running it over her neck and upper chest. Slowly. "It's too hot up here for fighting."

"It's not hot," I said. "It's not remotely hot. It's sixty-five degrees at the most."

Sunshine stopped moving the ice cube, grinned at me, and then popped it into her mouth and began chewing on it.

I got up and started the record over. "You know, some people think Robert Johnson was poisoned," I said. "With strychnine. He was only twenty-seven years old when he died, and no one ever figured out what killed him, so who knows? Strychnine is a mean poison. Death is horrific and painful. Someone must really have hated him. Otherwise they would have used arsenic, or cyanide. If I was going to kill someone, it would be with cyanide."

I went through an intense Agatha Christie phase when I was fourteen.

Luke glared at me. "Now you're just pissing me off. Stop being eccentric, Vi. It wasn't cute when you were younger and now it's just plain disturbed. *This* is why you don't have any friends."

"Speaking of," I said, "can you clear some of your many, many friends out of the attic, Luke? It's getting so crowded up here."

River leaned back into the couch and put his hands behind his head. He was grinning. My fighting with Luke amused him, I guess, though I felt a bit ashamed about it myself. Not that it would stop me the next time.

"Wasn't Robert Johnson the blues singer who brought his guitar to the crossroads at midnight and sold his soul to the Devil for the learning of it?" River asked a moment later.

"Yeah, that's him," I answered. "Man makes a deal with the Devil. It's a Faustian myth—a classic. Johnson said it was true, apparently. But I guess the Devil collected early and dragged Johnson down to hell before he'd even reached thirty."

"*Faust.* We all know you're a smug bookworm, sister. Stop showing off."

"Stop *fighting*," Sunshine scolded again. "Both of you. It interrupts my flirting."

"I wish people would spread a Faustian rumor about me." I leaned over and knocked Sunshine's hand out of Luke's hair. "A Faustian myth," I repeated. "It's so much more interesting than just being that nouveau-poor blond girl who lives in a big house with nobody but her jackass brother with pecs bigger than his brain. Sunshine, if I ever disappear, please tell people that I ran after the Devil, trying to get my soul back."

Sunshine batted her sleepy eyes at me. "Whatever, Vi."

Next to me, River took off Jack's cap and rumpled his hair. Jack slowly opened his blue eyes.

"So . . . aren't you supposed to be somewhere?" River asked him. "You've been running around a cemetery for the last two days. Doesn't anyone care where you are?"

Jack rubbed one eye, not looking at River. "My mom left when I was a baby. And my dad is . . . working. Nobody cares where I am." Jack looked up at River then, his freckled face serious as usual. "Are you going to show me how you did the magic now?"

River stood up. "Time to take this kid home."

I nodded. River leaned over me, wrapped his fingers around my neck, and pulled my ear to his lips. "I'll make you dinner when I get back, and afterward, I'll be answering questions," he whispered.

River kissed my earlobe. And my whole body started tingling with something exotic and foreign and bittersweet and kind of world-shaking. I went speechless from it, as I suppose he knew I would.

CHAPTER 13

RIVER AND JACK left, and Sunshine followed Luke to his bedroom. I went outside to watch the night sky and wait for River to get back.

I sat out there, listening to the waves beat themselves against the rocks below, and the pine needles rustle on the trees, and tried to ignore the chill that was building back up inside me. A suspicious, River-lying, Devil chill.

And then a squeal pierced through the peaceful night sounds.

It sounded like Sunshine. And it was coming from the direction of Luke's bedroom window.

I contemplated going up there and putting a stop to the squealing, but I didn't feel like having my brother yell at me.

The minutes passed. My River chill grew worse. So did the squealing. I got to my feet and followed the sound of Sunshine's laughter to my brother's room on the third floor.

I opened Luke's door without knocking. I didn't even care that much what I would walk in on, which shows what kind of mood I was in. "What's going on in here?" I shouted, loudly, like some stupid character in some stupid play.

Silence. Luke and Sunshine were sitting on the floor of his bedroom, fully clothed.

"We found an old Ouija board in the attic," Sunshine said. She flipped her brown hair over her round shoulder. "Your brother is trying to convince me the Citizen is haunted."

Luke crossed his arms and glared at me. "Don't you knock? You hypocrite." But he wasn't really mad. I could tell, because his green-brown eyes were sort of laughing.

My anger fizzled.

Luke's bedroom looked like an Edward Hopper painting. It used to be our grandfather's study. The Citizen had plenty of spare bedrooms (seven or eight—I could never remember), but Luke liked the study the best. Probably because of its inherent manliness, what with the wood paneling and the bookshelves and the art deco black leather couch and the hint of cigar smoke that never seemed to leave. So when Luke turned fifteen, he and Dad replaced Grandpa's desk with a bed.

I sat down between Sunshine and Luke on the green Turkish carpet, right underneath a leather-bound row of Dickens novels (that I'm sure Luke had never opened) and in front of several blank canvases, all sizes.

I looked at the Ouija board. "Where was it in the attic?"

"At the bottom of one of the wardrobes." Sunshine shivered, in an obvious way. "We contacted a spirit. A girl. She fell into the sea and drowned when she was ten years old, and now she floats around the Citizen, watching all of us." Sunshine's sleepy eyes grew large. "Scary, huh?"

"Since when do you believe in ghosts, Sunshine?" I asked, allowing more contempt to sneak into my voice than I probably should have. Sunshine thought that boys liked girls who were easily scared. And hell, maybe she was right. If a boy could get a girl squealing, maybe she would crawl into his arms for comfort. And once she was in his arms, second base was probably right around the corner.

"Vi, isn't there a small painting of one of our dead relatives hanging in the ballroom, some blond-haired girl?"

I caught my brother's eye. "Yeah. Her name was True. She was Freddie's daughter . . . Dad's younger sister. Freddie never talked about her, but Dad told me that she drowned when she was a girl." I paused. "Dad must have told you too. Apparently."

Luke threw his hands up in the air. "I've never heard of her before now. I swear. She spoke to us through the Ouija board." He nudged it with his knee and the pointer shifted in an ominous kind of way.

I stared my brother down, but his innocent expression didn't falter. "Fine. Let's go to the ballroom."

The ballroom was now the family art gallery. No one had danced on the gorgeous hardwood floors in years, excepting the time my parents brought down the record player from the attic late one night and decided to teach me and Luke some of the flowing debutante dances my mother had learned, back when she was a coiffed, rouged, beautiful southern belle, and not my long-haired artist mother who never wore makeup but always had paint underneath her fingernails and Degas on her mind.

My parents started off teaching us the steps, but ended up dancing with each other, me and Luke sitting on the floor, watching them slide up and down the ballroom hardwood until dawn arrived.

That was one of my good memories.

"It's over there," I said, pointing to the portrait in the far corner. The walls were covered in paintings. Most had been done by my parents, or their artist friends, but a few had been around since the beginning. Freddie, being rich, intelligent, and charming, had known her share of paint-splattering people. There were over a dozen portraits of her, done by various men and women. Most featured Freddie when she was young, her bright blue eyes beaming with derring-do and looking like they'd shine forever.

But, of course, they hadn't.

My dad hung Freddie's portraits high up, almost too high to see. Probably because she was nude in most of them, and he didn't dig looking at his mother naked, day in and day out.

Sunshine, Luke, and I gazed at True's portrait. I hadn't turned on the ballroom lights, because the three chandeliers hadn't worked in years, but the moon came through the windows, and Luke had a small flashlight in his pocket that he'd found in the attic, and we could see all right. The portrait was a small thing, only some six inches square, and stuck between an early Chagall-esque painting by my mother and a stoic portrait of my grandfather Lucas White, complete with cigar and flowered lapel. True was very young. Just a girl, with yellow, yellow hair, like me, and fair skin, and pink cheeks, and a faraway, fairy-tale look in her eyes. The style was pastel impressionistic, down to the soft blue dress she was wearing, which exactly matched the color of her blue eyes, and which contrasted nicely with the two red poppies she clutched, one in each hand.

"She said she was watching out for you," Sunshine whispered. She took the flashlight from Luke and shined it on the painting. "The Ouija board spelled it out, plain as day. She said that she watches you and Luke."

I had goose bumps now. Big fat ones. Hell, I believed in Luke's ability to bullshit more than I believed in ghosts, but still. I glanced at him and back at Sunshine. "Did the board say anything else?"

River had found us by this time. He snuck into the ballroom like a shadow and came up behind me. "What's going on?" he asked.

I leaned into him, so my back touched his chest. "Luke's trying to scare Sunshine with a Ouija board. It's such a teenager cliché. I feel like I'm in an Agatha Christie mystery. Prepare yourself for the board to predict one of our murders next."

Luke turned around and glared at me. "I can't believe you aren't taking this seriously, sister." He pointed at the painting. "True spoke to us. She's trying to warn us. Something bad is about to happen."

Sunshine nodded, unable to take her eyes off the painting. "Yeah. The board spelled out: BE CAREFUL. SOME-

ONE IS COMING. That was right before you flew through the door, Vi, shouting. Pretty darn scary."

Sunshine pulled her gaze away from the portrait and shivered again. Luke put his arms around her. She smiled, tucked herself deeper into his shoulder, and winked at me.

I looked at Luke. "*Be careful? Someone is coming?* That's just vague enough to be terrifying. Good job, brother."

Luke shook his head. His eyes were sort of keen, and restless. "It wasn't me. I think we have a ghost, Vi. Seriously."

River looked down at me. "Maybe you *do* have a ghost, Vi. I think Luke's telling the truth. We'd better go talk to the Ouija board again."

I nodded. "All right. You guys win. I'm intrigued. Let's do this thing." I turned and headed back to Luke's bedroom. I had a couple of good questions for the Ouija board myself. I wanted to see how far Luke would take this.

River, Sunshine, and Luke followed me. The four of us sat down by the game, River by my side. We put our fingers on the wooden pointer.

And waited.

I fidgeted. Sunshine giggled. Luke had taken off his pinstriped jacket, and he began to flex his pectoral muscles in the way I hated. River sat, one lean arm around one bent knee, and looked amused. Nothing happened. I shifted onto my other hip, wishing my little black attic dress was longer. I looked at the ceiling, looked back at the board, looked at Luke, and told Sunshine to stop laughing. And still nothing happened.

"Is this True?" I asked, finally. I looked at Luke as I said it, but he was watching the board.

The pointer skidded to YES, so fast and hard, I fell onto my elbow.

I glared at Luke, but he seemed surprised. Was my brother this good an actor?

"Are you the girl in the picture? The girl who drowned?" This from Luke.

Again, straight to the YES.

A few seconds passed. And the pointer moved.

LOOK

FOR

ME

BY

MOONLIGHT

The hair on my forearms rose. I could almost hear the girl saying the words as I read out the letters—slow and deep like they were being said under water.

The pointer began to move again.

SOMEONE
IS
COMING

Luke and Sunshine were silent, staring at the board. River smiled his lazy smile and looked like this was all great fun.

"Who is this?" I asked the board one last time. "Who are you?"

The pointer shook back and forth under our fingers for a second, and then moved.

D

E

V

I

L

I put my hands on the Ouija board and shoved. It went flying into the wall.

"What the hell, Vi?" Luke punched me in the arm. "That game is vintage. It's probably eighty years old. Be nice to it."

"That crossed the line, Luke. Don't joke about the Devil."

Luke locked eyes with me. "I didn't. God, Vi, after all of Freddie's talk, do you really think I would make it look like the Devil was talking to us through a Ouija board?"

We stared at each other for a moment.

"Take it down a notch, siblings," Sunshine said, her voice relaxed and purring and completely unaffected by everything. She fell onto her back and put one foot up on Luke's bed. The vintage yellow dress hiked up to her white inner thigh, but she acted as if she didn't notice. "It's too late at night to fight."

"Fine," I said.

"Fine," Luke said.

I swept my hand in the direction of Sunshine's thigh. "I'll leave you to it then, brother."

CHAPTER 14

RIVER AND I walked to the guesthouse. He had picked
up more groceries in town after he dropped Jack off,
and had made me a late supper of Caesar salad and sweet
potato fries. The windows were open wide and the fresh
sea breeze drifted in and combined with the earthy,
clay-ish smell of old oil paint and good food to make
something pretty wonderful. River still wore his peasant
costume, and I was still in my black Audrey Hepburn
dress. The electricity in the guesthouse stopped working
for no good reason during dinner, so River lit candles and
placed them on little plates all over the kitchen, and the
atmosphere was so thick, you could taste it.

River and I were alone for the first time since the tree
house.

I was unsettled about what he was going to tell me—the answers he'd promised in the attic. And the good food and the sweet breeze and the thick atmosphere weren't really helping all that much, to be honest.

"You ran off during *Casablanca,*" I said. My fingers were oily with salad and sweet-potato fries, and I wiped them on the little lamb towel. "Where did you go?"

I had waited all through dinner for River to start talking. But nothing. I would have preferred not to push him, since it just seemed to make things worse. But hell. I needed to know if the boy who had just made me supper, the boy staying in my guesthouse, was the kind of boy who would run off into cemeteries and convince kids he was the Devil. And I needed to know it soon.

River picked up my plates and put them in the sink. "Later, Vi. Later."

He started to make some espresso, and the good smell of coffee added to the good smell of everything else. I sipped at mine. I was a night owl by nature, and had been since I was a baby. Some of my earliest memories were sitting up with my mother and father while they painted late into the night, Luke having been put to bed hours ago. My parents weren't perfect, even when they were around, but they did some things right, like let me stay up late if it was in me to do so. Anyway, I knew drinking coffee on the wrong side of the p.m. would make my night-owl side worse, so I stood on my tiptoes when I sipped.

"River, did you go to the cemetery, when you left?" *Pushing, pushing . . .*

He turned. "What on earth are you doing?" he asked, ignoring my question and smirking a crooked smirk at me as I wavered back and forth on my feet.

"Trying not to drink too much coffee." I put my heels back down on the guesthouse kitchen floor. "It's hard to gulp it down when you're on your toes."

River lifted his cup, and then his heels. He was barefoot again. He didn't like to wear his shoes. Which I liked because I liked his feet. He teetered, drank, came back down, and looked at me. "Vi. You are strange. Did you know this?"

I nodded.

"Did you spend a lot of time alone as a kid?"

I nodded again.

He smiled at me. "Well, I like strange. People aren't as strange as you want them to be. We're all pretty weird as kids, and then we grow up and . . ."

"River, are you changing the subject?"

"Yes."

"Don't," I said. I narrowed my eyes and hoped it made me look like I meant it.

"Just let me tell you this story first, before I answer your questions." River looked at his coffee, looked at me, sighed, and then looked at the wall. "There was this kid I liked to hang out with when I was younger. I guess you could call him my best friend. He was always in trouble, always in fights, always pissing off some kid a whole lot bigger than he was, and never thinking before he acted."

River paused, and his eyes went serious. Serious like when we were in the cemetery the second time. It scared me, that expression, because it looked so odd on his sly River face . . . but it kind of thrilled me too.

"People didn't understand him," River added, after a few seconds. "He wasn't trying to pick fights, he was just . . . honest. He would say what he thought, no matter what." River still wouldn't look at me. "I had his back in every fight. I spent my childhood covered in bruises. God, it pissed my dad off. I'd get beat in the fight and then again when I got home."

River kind of laughed. And then stopped.

"What happened?"

"What?" River asked, after a second.

"What happened to your best friend? Finish the story, River."

"What happened to the kid?" River's body tensed and his jaw tightened, so hard, a dimple formed on the left side. He breathed in, let it out. "I set him on fire."

"*What?*"

"I still get nightmares from it sometimes." River drank the last of his coffee and set the cup on the counter.

I put my hand on his shoulder. He finally looked at me. "Bullshit," I said.

River shrugged my hand off. "Well, I did. We were screwing around, having a bonfire on the beach. We were playing some game, and I tripped. I fell against him and he . . . went into the fire."

"But that was an accident. You didn't do it on purpose."

"Well, it still happened, didn't it? And I was the cause. He *burned*, Vi."

River's eyes glistened a bit. He looked, I don't know, sort of tragic.

And I was a goner, seeing him like that.

I reached up and hugged him. He went very still, and then relaxed. "I'm sorry," I said. "Truly. You don't have to talk about it anymore if you don't want to."

I felt River's hands go to my hips. He leaned down and kissed me. Slow.

He was good at it. Gentle. Not hard and fast like Sean Fry. River's kiss was more I've-got-all-the-time-in-the-world-because-I-know-you're-not-going-anywhere.

And I wasn't. This kiss came as less of a shock than

the cemetery one. I'd grown still as a statue from the neck down, that time. But not now. Now I moved. I kissed back. I didn't know what I was doing, but I *felt* like I did.

River's kiss tasted like coffee and storms and secrets.

And slowly, slowly, he began to move faster, and then faster . . .

And then he stopped.

River let go of me, just like that. Just about the time I'd forgotten who I was, just about the time I'd forgotten we were even two separate people anymore and not just one glowing, quivering, ocean of kissing . . . he let me go. He stepped back and took a deep breath.

"Are you going to stay here tonight?" he asked, his breath coming a little short. Like mine. He put his hand in his hair and made it stand on end in the way that was so sexy, it kind of pissed me off.

River looked out the kitchen window, at the purple-black sky and the purple-black sea. "I've been having nightmares since I turned fourteen. Always. But then I took a nap with you a few days ago, and, all of sudden, they're gone. I leave for a day, and *boom,* they come back, just like that." He paused. "You know what this means, don't you?"

I shook my head.

"It means that you're just going to have to sleep next to me, for the rest of my life."

A few seconds passed. Then River put one hand in my hair and the other on the small of my back, and tugged me into him. Tight.

"River?" I asked.

"Yes, Vi?"

"What was Jack talking about? What did he mean, about wanting you to show him how you did it?"

River's arms fell away. I felt cold, suddenly, and wondered if I should shut the window.

"Before I answer that, let me ask you something. Have you enjoyed the past few days with me? Have you been happy?"

I searched his face, sensing a trap. "Yes. No. Mainly no, I think. I've got a liar living in my guesthouse who tells kids to go looking for the Devil and then disappears after they find him. My neighbor is hallucinating in the town tunnel, and then I'm getting kissed in the cemetery. I wouldn't call that *enjoyable,* really. I'd call it unsettling."

River shrugged. "Ignorance is bliss. Why not just sit back and take what comes? That *is* an option, you know. You can just ignore all these questions that are taking up space in that blond head of yours, and come with me to bed. Let me wrap my arms around you, and we'll both sleep the sleep of the blissful. And ignorant. Me, without my nightmares, and you, without your answers."

I thought about it. I did. But only for a handful of seconds. "No. I want to know what's going on. I do."

River sighed. "Okay. But remember. You chose this." His brown eyes found my blue ones, and held. "I've got a secret, Violet. Something I can do, that other people can't."

"You've got my attention."

"It's—I call it the glow," he answered me, and his eyes were deep and open like they'd been before, in the attic. But his mouth was sly as always and I didn't know who to believe.

"Mostly," he continued, "because it . . . it makes me kind of *glow* when I do it. Inside. All over. It's like the feeling you get when you take a nap—you have a grand, epic dream, and then you wake up and the sun is shining and you stretch and your whole body tingles. It's like that, but a thousand times better."

He hesitated for a second, and then continued. "It's the same feeling I get when I'm kissing you, Vi. And nothing, *nothing*, has felt as good as the glow before. I just think you should know that."

He said this quick, almost as if he was ashamed of it. But afterward, his face slid back to its normal wily look so fast that I couldn't tell which part was real. Besides, my mind was still snagged on the word *glow*, and all my thoughts were tangled behind it. I put my hands to my head and pressed, because my brain felt as if it was bursting out of my skull, like the pulp of a too-ripe plum squeezed in a fist.

"The *glow*, River? What *is* that? What the hell is that?"

River grabbed my hand and brought it to his heart. I stopped talking. I could feel the beat, hot and strong, and, without my consent, it made me feel better.

"Here, I'll show you." His hand pressed against my hand, which was still pressing against his heart. River stared at me. Hard.

And then I saw him.

Jack's devil.

He stood behind River, tall body looming out of the dark, red eyes sharp as knives in his pale face. He was thin. Too, too thin. Just bones and shadows beneath a pointed black hat. I felt evil coming off him like a strong cologne. I didn't want it to get on me. I knew I had to move, but the demon was starting to lean over River, his upper lip curled back into a snarl, his white collar stroking River's ear, his white teeth gnashing, getting closer, closer to River's face—

I screamed.

River didn't move. He didn't even turn around. The

devil began to fade, fade, fade, until I was staring at the corner of the guesthouse kitchen, looking at nothing but dark.

"You gave me the idea for that one, you know," River said, voice calm, almost cheerful. "You were reading Hawthorne's short stories when we first met. Young Goodman Brown sees the Devil in the forest. Good stuff."

"Puritan clothes. *That's* what Jack was talking about." At first I wasn't even sure I'd said this out loud, because my brain was screaming at me and I couldn't hear if the words came out of my mouth.

But River nodded. "I wanted my devil to be dressed in sin, but I figured the kids wouldn't know what sin looked like. So I made him traditional Hawthorne—the *Scarlet Letter* clothes, the snake staff that's in the short story. I added in the red eyes myself. I thought it would be more vivid." He paused. "And Blue . . . that was you as well, Vi. The story you told us by the tunnel inspired me. Of course, I had to improvise, not having any idea what a mad, tunnel-living, rat-eating recluse would look like. Hence, the hairy teeth. I was proud of that. Nice touch, no?"

I snapped my hand out of River's and backed away. My hands were shaking, and I saw dark spots around the rims of my eyes. I thought of Sunshine, of her screaming, and falling to the ground in a faint. I knew exactly, *exactly* how she felt. This was fear. This was biting, scratching, howling, screeching, burning hot fear.

"What the hell are you? What the hell are you, River?" I was shaking my head and inching toward the door and biting back the urge to run, because it would look stupid, and I didn't want to look stupid in front of River, even then.

He shrugged. "A monster. A saint. Neither. Something in between. I've spent a lot of time thinking about this and all I've come up with is . . . me. I'm River. That's it. I can make people see things, ever since I hit fourteen, and I don't know why. All I know is that I'm not evil." He hesitated. "I don't know if I'm all that good, either. I'm just me. And using the glow on people makes me happy. It's kind of a . . . drug."

River looked away from me, back toward the sea again. "A drug I might be addicted to," he said quietly, almost as if he didn't want me to hear. Almost. He turned back to me. "Violet. Put your hand on my heart again."

River walked forward until he reached me. He took my shaking hand, and put it back on his warm chest. "Keep your hand there for a second."

River put his other arm out and pulled me to him. He kissed me. My neck, my cheeks, my lips. Beneath my hand, his heart sped up, and his skin went warm.

"See?" River whispered in my ear. "Kissing you stirs me, just like the glow. My heart goes fast and my skin goes hot." He paused. "And so it looks like I've found another thing I can't give up."

He leaned back, so I could read his face, and find the truth written there. But he wasn't giving anything away. His eyes seemed genuine and sincere, but his mouth was curled and tricksy-looking and I ended up with nothing.

"How does it work?" I asked him. "You just think of a monster and make someone see it?"

River shrugged. "Something like that."

I took that in for a second. "But why? Why would you do that?"

"Because I can." He paused again, and his face was blank, blank like the sea after a storm. "And because I have to."

"So you . . . you scared all those kids in the cemetery, my whole town—Jack, Isobel, Sunshine, everyone—just because you *can*? Just because the glow feels good, like kissing? Or do you do it because you really can't stop, like a drug? Like smoking and opium and gin? Which is it?"

He shrugged. "Both. I don't know. It's complicated." He grinned at me, and suddenly his face was alive again. Mischievous and carefree as a kid with a secret lying in a field of flowers under a blue sky. "I'm not going to bore you with the details. Not yet anyway. I'm too full and happy and sleepy and, damn it, turned on. Come to bed with me, Vi."

I stared at a hole in River's peasant trousers, at the brown skin of his thigh that showed through, and I didn't meet his gaze.

Monster.

Stranger.

God.

These were the three words that came to mind as I absorbed the things River told me. And I meant god in the Roman sense. As in River was one, maybe.

"Have you made anyone else glow?" I asked, finally. "Besides Sunshine, and Jack, and his friends? Have you made Luke see anything?"

"Not yet. I'm keeping my options open."

"Who else? Who else before you came to Echo?"

"Everyone."

I winced. "How many? How many people?"

"Hundreds." River paused. "Thousands."

"Oh." My heart started beating, faster, faster than it did when River kissed me. Nightmare fast. Running for your life fast.

"But not you," he said, as if he was reading my mind.

And then it occurred to me. "River, can you read my

mind? Because if you can get in there to make me see monsters, it only makes sense that—"

"No, Violet," River interrupted. "I'm not reading your mind. I can't read minds. Well, not *entire* minds. Tiny bits and pieces get through sometimes. Rarely, though. Children, they're easier. Like Jack. But not adults."

"Can you only do monsters, then? Does the glow only make people see monsters?"

River shook his head. He held out his fingers and placed them on the hollow of my throat, where my pulse beat. I took two breaths, and then River . . . shifted. And disappeared. And in his place stood my mother, clear as day.

My eyes filled with tears. I couldn't help it. *I* knew she wasn't real, but my eyes didn't. She was *there*, right in front of me, her flawless skin and her long straight hair and her too-wide smile, looking excited and stressed like she had the last time I saw her, right before she left for Paris with Dad.

And it had been so long ago. Months. And months.

"Mom," I said, and my voice cracked.

I heard a male voice say, *Damn.*

And then River was in front of me again.

"Sorry about that," he said. "I should have guessed that seeing your mother would upset you. See, *that's* why I stick to monsters."

I glared at River. Tears were dripping out of my eyes, and I was pissed. "River, that was cruel. I was over missing her, and then you brought her back and now I'm *not* over missing her anymore."

River moved closer to me, and his arm touched my arm in a comfortable way. I didn't shrug him off like I wanted to, though. Because suddenly I felt a little better, with our arms touching.

"Don't be angry with me," he said. "I won't do it again. I only did it to prove a point. It's easier to forgive someone for scaring you than for making you cry."

We were quiet for a while.

River gazed out the window, like he'd been doing all night, his hands on the cold counter tiles, and his hair in his eyes. "Jack wanted me to do it again," he said, not looking at me. "Show him the Devil. He liked it, my little trick. I don't know how that kid figured out what was going on, but he did. Before *Casablanca,* I told him that the Devil likes to visit the cemetery after dark, and he went there to check it out, just like I knew he would. He's a smart kid. And then I waltzed in later, conjured up the Devil, and, you know, fun, fun, fun."

"What about Isobel?" I asked.

"Yeah, Isobel," he said, still not looking at me. "When I got to the cemetery I found her with her little hula hoop, by the entrance. I asked her if she knew a good place to hide, and she told me about the tree house. Then I told her to go hide there for a while. I said it was part of a game. I didn't think she would stay there so long. I thought, maybe a few hours at most, but—"

"You glowed *Isobel*? But she's so *little*. You made her go to that tree house, all by herself? The other things, fine, they aren't so bad, Sunshine probably had it coming. But Jack, and *Isobel*? River, that's evil. Bad. Devil bad. Freddie would—"

River had me in a heartbeat. His arms were around me and his face in my hair and I calmed back down, way back down, calm, calm, calm.

"Vi, Vi, shh. What real harm has come from all of it, Isobel included?" He was whispering, his lips by my forehead and his fingers pressing into my back. "Your neighbor Sunshine saw a crazy man in a tunnel instead of getting kissed, as she expected. Your town had the most exciting day it's had since a rich boy cut his lover's throat in a cellar—your brother was loving it. And the two of us got to see kids running around a foggy cemetery, carrying stakes. It's just . . . fun."

"Just fun?"

"Yeah."

I was scared of him now. Really scared. What chaos had

this boy been causing in the world with his . . . with his *glow,* if that's what he thought fun was?

But still, I didn't step out of his arms.

The fingers of River's right hand were playing with the bottom of the long strand of fake pearls I was wearing— his knuckles kept grazing the area above my belly button, sending waves of good feeling through my insides. I should have pushed him away. I should have screamed, I suppose, or cried or tried to run. But I didn't. I just . . . let him.

River kissed me again. We kissed. And we kissed. I lifted my hands and put them on his back and he ran his fingers up and down my pearls and his knuckles touched whatever they touched.

We reached the bed.

River pulled his peasant shirt off, but left the red kerchief around his neck. He took off my pearls, and set them on the dresser. He pulled the bobby pins out of my hair, gently, so gently, and my hair fell past my shoulders. Then he reached around me and unzipped the back of my dress. It slid to the floor. I was naked from the waist up, and wearing nothing much of anything below. River took me in for a second, and I shivered in the moonlight coming through the window. One breath. Two. And his arms were around me.

I didn't know what was going to happen next, and I can't say I cared all that much. But River only tucked the both of us under the bed covers, kissed my bare back, up the spine, and then whispered good night in my ear.

He was asleep in seconds.

I was not.

CHAPTER 15

I WOKE UP a few hours later. Dawn was still just a twinkle in the night's eye, but the moon was full and bright, and my almost naked body was still curled into River West.

He hadn't let go of me in the night. He was still pressed against my back, his lips near my shoulder, asleep. I didn't move for a bit, just lay there thinking about things.

Like how the world was full of mystery and magic and horror and love.

Like how River scared the hell out of me. Because he was, I thought, evil.

He could have done really bad things with the glow. He'd *probably* done really bad things with the glow. Worse than scaring Sunshine, worse than scaring little kids.

Then something occurred to me as I lay there, listening to the waves crash far below. River made people see monsters. And missing mothers. What else? What else could he make people see?

Or feel?

I didn't want to think about that.

It would make River . . . worse than a liar. A lot worse.

And it would make me a fool.

I slid out of his arms. He didn't wake up. I put my dress back on, quiet, so quietly, and walked down the hall and out of the guesthouse. The cold night air hit me sharp. I shivered. I walked across the grounds, past the greenhouse, past the tennis court, past the maze, and in through the back entrance of the Citizen.

Inside my house, it wasn't much warmer. I'd left the kitchen windows open, and others too. I ran up the marble steps, my bare feet wincing from the cold stone, and down the second-floor hall to Freddie's bedroom. *My* bedroom.

Luke was sitting on the end of my bed.

His arms were crossed on his knees, his hands on his temples. He'd turned one of the lamps on, but it was old and weak and the hazy light barely reached past the pillows. His head jerked toward the door when I came in.

"Where have you been? Damn it, Vi. I've been waiting here for hours."

I grabbed a quilt from one of the art deco chairs and threw it around my shoulders. "I've been with River. Which I'm sure you knew. Why? What's wrong?"

I sat down beside him on the bed and threw the end of the blanket over his bare feet. Luke turned to me, and I saw that he was scared. Wide-eyed and about to panic and scared-scared-scared.

"*Look for me by moonlight.* That's what she said. And that's how she came."

"True?" I asked. And suddenly I had goose bumps on my forearms, and my scalp tingled like it does sometimes when I'm afraid.

"True," Luke said. And he shook his head and shuddered. "One moment there was nothing but moonlight coming in the window, and then I blinked, and there she was. This girl about ten years old with long hair and you could see through her like she was moonlight, like she was made out of it, and she smiled at me, and I think I screamed, maybe, but then—" Luke swallowed, his voice was going faster, and it was cracking too. "But then she was right in front of me and dragging her tiny moonlight fingers down my cheek and I couldn't scream anymore, and I just stared at her and her eyes weren't moonlight, but pure night sky black, no white edges, no color, and she put her hand over my mouth then and it felt like she was pouring moonlight down my throat and it was coming so fast and strong, I felt sure I was going to drown on it."

Luke took a breath, finally. His chest rose and fell as he breathed. I grabbed his hand and squeezed, thinking all kinds of things I couldn't focus on right then.

"I coughed," Luke continued, "and choked, and drowned on moonlight, which tastes like butter and steel and salt and mist. And then, just like that, just when I thought she was going to kill me, suck the air out of my lungs and make me a ghost too, she lifted her hand, and . . . faded away."

He tilted his head toward me, and his hazel eyes were kind of innocent-looking, trusting and overwhelmed, like a little kid's. "It was a dream, wasn't it, Vi? The scariest dream ever, but still a dream, right?"

I thought about River, and the things he told me, and how he said he was *keeping his options open* in regards to Luke, when in fact he'd already decided what he was going to do to my brother, was maybe even doing it while he was talking to me.

Liar.

He was such a damn liar.

I looked at Luke, at how scared he was, and I felt as if I couldn't breathe for a moment. River. *River.*

Breathe, Violet. Breathe.

Luke lifted the quilt and put it over his shoulders, so we were both tucked in it together. "Strange things have been happening ever since River showed up. It's weird, isn't it, Vi?"

"Yeah, it's weird," I said. I wanted to tell him. Tell him about River, and the glow. I did. But if I told Luke about the glow, about the kids in the cemetery, about Sunshine and Blue and the reason a ghost named True tried to drown him with moonlight in his sleep . . . Luke would probably kick River out of the guesthouse. I didn't trust River. I was even starting to hate him. But I didn't want him to leave, either. I didn't want to go back to just me and Luke and Sunshine and them kissing and me waiting. I wasn't sure what I wanted yet, but it wasn't that.

Next to me, Luke shivered again. "Sometimes I get this crazy urge to, I don't know, grab a pitchfork and chase the guy out of town. But the next time I see him, the feeling's gone. Completely gone. And then . . . you're doing things with him, and you've never been interested in a guy before, and I just don't know what to think."

"Do you want to sleep on the sofa in here?" I asked. And it wasn't just for Luke's sake. I didn't want to be alone, suddenly, in my big bedroom, in the damn dark.

"I used to sleep there, when this was Freddie's room," I said to Luke. "Whenever I would have a nightmare I'd run in here and she would give me a bunch of blankets and I would sleep on the sofa and everything would be all right."

"Yeah, I remember that," Luke said. He looked kind of embarrassed and solemn at the same time. "I can't go back to my room tonight. I just can't."

So I gave Luke three old quilts and one of my pillows and tucked him in and he fell asleep in ten heartbeats. I thought it would take him longer, a lot longer, but it didn't. And then my body hit the sheets and I slept the sleep of the dead too.

CHAPTER 16

WHEN I WOKE up in the morning, Luke was gone, but River was standing over me, looking clean and bright and wide awake, with fresh clothes on and a steaming cup of coffee in his hand.

"You left in the night," River said. "Why?"

"I had to absorb," I said. "I had to absorb the information you told me. By myself."

River nodded, like he expected this. He took a sip of espresso. I turned my head and saw that another bookmark was sitting on the nightstand beside me. A fish this time. A hundred-dollar-bill fish.

"I'm not too proud," I said, though I was starting to feel a bit like I was. "I'm not going to make you take it back."

"It's just a bookmark." River shrugged, and drank his

coffee. "So, do you think you've done enough absorbing to come with me into Echo? I want to check on Jack. Make sure he gets a good breakfast and has something to do today. I don't have any younger brothers or sisters, you know . . . I kind of like being responsible for someone."

Would the Devil care whether a grave, red-haired kid got a good breakfast? Would he?

Yes, Freddie's voice shot back. *Especially if he knew you would like him all the more for it.*

"All right," I said, ignoring what the voice said, shoving it deep, deep down to some dusty corner inside me where it could be forgotten for a while.

River had already showered and was wearing coffee-colored linen pants, a white James Dean T-shirt, black-and-white wingtip shoes, and a Panama hat—which might have been his and might have been something he found in the attic the day before.

I put on my mother's painting overalls. She'd found them in the greenhouse after she had to let go of the Citizen's gardener. They were covered in paint every color under the sun.

River and I walked into town. On the way, right about the time we reached the tunnel, I stopped walking and looked at him.

"So Luke had a nightmare last night" was all I said, because it was all I had to say.

River laughed. He tilted his head back, and *laughed*. "And how did he like it?"

"He almost choked to death on moonlight, at the hands of a ten-year-old dead girl. Yeah. He didn't like it much." I was starting to feel the tight, pinched feeling my face got when I was angry—searing, red-hot, fires-of-hell angry—and trying to hide it.

River noticed. He put his hands on me and drew me close to him. "I'm sorry," he said, and looked like he meant it, as much as you could trust him, which wasn't much. "I couldn't resist, after the Ouija board setup. It was just too perfect. Besides, I hate the way he talks to you sometimes. It felt good to send a little mischief his way."

I looked up at River. His skin was glowing in the morning sun, and it smelled clean and salty, like the sea, and his hair was still wet from his shower and looked almost black, and my anger . . . went away.

"So that's why you did it?" I asked. "To punish him? What about Sunshine then? Why did you do it to her?"

"I don't like the way she talks to you either."

"River, you didn't even know her when you glowed her in the tunnel."

"That's true," he said, and laughed again. "Look, Vi. The

thing is, I suffer from a deplorable need for justice. Yes, I like to feel the glow in me. Yes, I'm having a hard time stopping it. But I also can't just stand around watching people be mean to those who don't deserve it. It's a powerful thing in me. More powerful than the glow, maybe." He paused for a second, and the glint came back to his eyes. "But I'm also a fan of mischief. So between the two . . ."

My expression was kind of hateful, but River was pretending not to notice. "Is that why you glowed Jack and that little girl Isobel? Because you're a fan of mischief?"

River stopped smiling. "That . . . that I'm not proud of. Honestly. It went too far. I know that."

I didn't believe he regretted it. Not for a second. But I *wanted* to.

"Just don't do it again. Any of it. I mean it, River." He nodded. "I don't plan to," he said.

We stopped at the co-op and bought bananas and fresh pain au chocolats for breakfast. The woman at the counter smiled at us while River paid for the food. A nice smile. Genuine. River smiled back. And I thought about what Luke had said, in the attic. About no one in the town talking to us. And I wondered, for the first time, if maybe it was more our fault than theirs.

Were we snobs? We lived in a big house and had interesting ancestors, but our money was gone and we were holding on to the Citizen by a thread. Still, we kept ourselves apart. My parents had artist friends come to stay from the city, but they didn't mingle with the people in their own town. My father said once that the only thing that bored him was boring people, and that Echo had nothing but.

Thinking back, I wonder if he was just ashamed that we couldn't afford to pay the heating bill most of the time.

I took a deep breath and gave the woman a smile. She smiled back.

It felt good.

River showed me where Jack lived. The house was on a dead-end street near the big brick box of hate that was my high school. I let myself shudder as I walked past. I wanted to be tutored at home, like my father had been when he was a kid, but we couldn't afford it. I wasn't sure how I would face going back to school in the fall, if my parents didn't come back. Luke played sports and had sports friends, during the school year at least. All I had was Sunshine, and Sunshine . . . was Sunshine.

Maybe I should have joined things in school, like . . . drama. And the beekeepers club. Maybe I shouldn't have spent all my free time with books. Or following around a ninety-ish-year-old woman who liked to talk about the Devil.

I felt old suddenly. Really old. Freddie old. I put my hands to my face. But my cheeks were still smooth, still soft, still young.

River looked at me, and I put my hands back down. We'd arrived at Jack's house.

It was small, with a paint-peeling air of sadness about it, like a forgotten toy left out in the rain. We went up to the door and knocked. I had a smile ready, expecting the solemn face of Jack to greet me at the door.

A man answered instead. He was tall, and bone-thin. He had thin gray hair and dark hollows under his eyes, like the ones you'd expect to see on a half-starved train tramp in the 1930s. But his straight, even features had a kind of smooth, urbane grace, which still showed through the hollows and the bones. He would have been handsome, once, long, long, long ago. He wore a dirty yellow button-down shirt and brown wool pants. The matching jacket had been kicked into a rumpled heap in the hallway behind him.

The man was Daniel Leap, the drunk who bellowed his opinion about my family from every street corner in town, the man who had ruined my view that first day drinking coffee with River.

And suddenly I understood. I understood why Jack was alone. I understood why he was so quiet.

Daniel Leap held a glass of amber liquid in one long-fingered hand. Bourbon, I supposed. In his other hand he held a needle, with a tail of long black thread. His eyes were big, like Jack's, except that, instead of Jack's piercing sort of melancholy, they looked dazed, and lost.

"Is Jack around?" River asked. His expression echoed mine. Surprise. Confusion. Concern.

"What do you want with him?" The man's voice was soft, whispery. But there was an edge to it.

Before River could answer, Jack appeared in the doorway.

"Hey, River," Jack said. "Hey, Violet. This is my pa."

Jack's pa looked from his son, to River, to me. Then he leaned to the side and shoved Jack, just a bit. Just enough. "Be quiet, Jack."

There was a long pause. Daniel Leap drank from his glass and we watched him, not saying anything.

"So, what do you want with my son?" Daniel Leap asked again, and smiled. "Want to buy him from me? You rich people like to do that, don't you?" His eyes settled on me. "Yeah, I know what you're like, Violet White. My family's been in Echo nearly as long as yours. Only we don't live in mansions by the sea. No, my people live and die in the gutter." He laughed. It was soft and whispery, like his voice. "But look at you now.

Coming into my gutter, trying to buy my son. You want to rent him as a playmate, like in that Charles Dickens book? Yeah, I've read it. I can read."

He took a long swig of his whiskey and looked at me, up and down, from toes to eyebrows, until I started to fidget. Was he joking?

"No, I don't want to buy your son. We just want to . . ."

I looked down at Jack. He was half smiling, kind of cynically, which I didn't expect. He was used to this, his dad making a fool of himself. I looked back at Daniel Leap. I wondered if he knew how smart his kid was. I wondered if he knew that his son wasn't afraid of him.

Daniel started fumbling with the needle. He was trying to sew a loose button back onto his shirt while he was still wearing it, and while he was holding a drink in his other hand, and while both hands were shaking. "I've been trying to get this button on all morning," he said. He seemed to have forgotten all about Dickens and rented playmates for the moment.

"Can I hold your drink for you?" River asked, polite and quiet.

The man shrugged. He handed his glass to River. River tilted it back and took a deep swallow. My eyebrows shot up. Why would River want Daniel Leap's cheap bourbon? River didn't even drink.

Daniel, his right hand now free, stabbed the needle at the middle button on his yellow shirt. I flinched, sure he was going to draw blood. Jack watched for a second, then reached up and took the thread from his father's fingers. He led his pa to a chair near the door and gently pushed him into it.

River and I stood there, not saying anything, until Jack looked at River, hard. River turned the glass of whiskey over and dumped it onto the ground.

≈≈

River and I went looking for Luke when we got back. I had this notion of making River apologize to him. Though that would mean explaining River's glow, and I didn't know how that conversation would go down, exactly.

I noticed that the door of the shed was propped open. The shed was bigger than you'd think, considering it was called the shed. It was a little white building that had several square windows. Inside, there were cans of paint everywhere and little stools to sit on and easels and brushes and canvas cloths and still life props—pitchers and glasses and wine bottles, fake fruit and candles and a human skull.

Luke was inside, painting. He had two canvases set up—one had a base coat of white, and the other black.

"I'm doing a diptych," he said, and didn't look up

from the box of paints he was fiddling with. "A touch of impressionism with a streak of Victorian whimsy. The black canvas"—he gestured without looking—"is going to be a girl with deep, tired eyes, on the beach, on a bright, moonlit night. She'll be wearing an old-fashioned swimming suit, the kind with shorts and a belt, like the one you wear." He glanced up at me. "I'll throw in a few random objects, out of perspective, like some fish or a whale or something. And—this is *key*—she'll be holding up her own shadow, like it's sick and needs her support. I'm going to do the white canvas with the same girl at the beach during the day, same shadow. It's a metaphor. You know, the girl feels like she's a shadow, like she doesn't exist. Existential crisis, etc." He looked at me, real quick, and then turned back to the paintings. "You can help me with the white canvas, if you want."

I didn't say anything. But I was pleased as punch that my brother was painting again, and River knew it because he winked at me behind Luke's back.

I looked around, at the sun streaming in the little windows, at my parents' half-finished canvases, at the paint-splattered floor, at Luke, concentrating on the easel in front of him. I breathed in the faint, bitter smell of turpentine, the oily smell of the paint, the scent of fresh sea air. Maybe I'd been wrong to give up on painting.

My eyes caught on a half-finished portrait of my mother. It wasn't a self-portrait. It was my father's hand that had painted that long nose, those dreamy eyes. I could always tell. His lines were more crisp, more solid, his colors darker than my mother's. She was Chagall, Renoir. And my father was . . . well, he was himself. Of the two, he was the true painter, I supposed.

River was walking around looking at the old paintings. He was lean, and beautiful, and smiling. But I felt my sense of peace drain away, watching him. Our conversation from the night before hung over me, and it blocked out the very real, very warm sunlight that filled the room.

I pictured the Devil again, rising up behind River, with his red eyes. My scalp tingled and I shivered, like I was cold, though I wasn't. River saw. I know he did. But he didn't say anything. He just leaned over, grabbed himself a box of dried-out acrylics, put it under his arm, and then pointed at the largest canvas in the shed. "Is this guy available? My artistic talent is too big to be contained by anything but the largest of canvases. Canvii? I'm not sure on the lingo."

The huge canvas River wanted was supposed to be for a family portrait. My mother had talked about painting all four of us together since I was little. She brought that big canvas home years and years ago. And there it still sat.

"Sure," I said, not looking him in the eyes. "Take it."

River set down the box of acrylics and looked around until he found a can of house paint, which my parents sometimes used to prep a canvas. He popped the lid off, gave it a good stir, and then reached in a hand. It came up with a fistful of yellow.

"Jackson Pollock," he said, and smiled at me. "It's the only way to paint." He threw his fist at the canvas, opening it at the last second, and yellow paint went flying.

I picked up a brush.

CHAPTER 17

RIVER USED UP three cans of paint in his Pollock tribute. Blue, yellow, and black splotches covered the canvas. I stared at it for a while. River came up behind me and put his hand, still wet with paint, on my lower back, adding to the colors on my mom's overalls. "It's a painting of you, Vi. Blue eyes, yellow hair, black thoughts."

"That's why it's so ugly." Luke laughed. Loud.

"Don't take out your Pollock-hate on the new kid," I said, moving to rinse out my brushes in the shed's small sink. I looked at River over my shoulder. "Luke thinks abstract expressionism is, well, bullshit. Mom thinks the same thing. But it's just the natural descendent of—"

"Pizza." Luke stood up and stretched. "I need some pizza in my belly before I listen to Vi go off on art."

"Me too." This from Sunshine, who was standing in the doorway of the shed, a glass of iced tea in her hand.

"Where have you been today?" I asked. "We have been creating great masterpieces in here." I stood back and looked at Luke's painting. And then mine. And scowled. Why did my brother paint like me, and I like him? We were so different, in every other way. But my lines went the way his went, turned thin, then thick, same as his. My brushstrokes were short and quick like his too. It . . . bothered me. It made me think that Luke and I were more alike than I'd thought, as if . . . as if we were both headed in the same direction and just taking very different roads there.

"My parents made me drive the bookmobile around," Sunshine answered me, slow and breathy because Luke was there. "A lot of dried-up, house-bound spinsters needed their trashy romance novels."

"Sunshine, you're the kindest person I know. Have I ever told you that?"

She grinned at me, and then went over to ooh and aah at Luke's paintings.

"So where do you find pizza in this town?" River asked me.

"There's a great place right off the town square," I replied. "Want to come?"

"Yep," he said, a sparkle starting up in his eyes. "That will be perfect."

"Perfect for what?"

"You'll see," he said, and smiled the crooked smile.

≈≈

Echo had a great pizza place called Lucca, which sat on the main square by the café. It was run by the same Italian family—Luciano and Graziella, and their three sons. From what I could tell, the men in the family did all the cooking, and Graziella mainly went around giving orders and saying *allora, allora,* over and over. I asked her what that meant once, and she told me it was Italian for *now I think.* And I guessed from this that it must take Graziella a lot of thinking to make the pizza.

We were early and the restaurant was empty. Luke found us a booth near the large windows that overlooked the main square; they were half open and a nice breeze was drifting in. Sunshine had a pink, bottom-hugging summer dress on, and even I'd changed out of my painting overalls and put on a black silk shirt with a black skirt. I felt kind of pretty. The late sun was doing that slanting thing I found romantic, especially when it slanted off River and made his deep brown hair shine.

That will be perfect, he'd said.

I looked around the restaurant, and out the windows

into the town square, and then at River again. He was leaning back into the seat, his arms behind his head, as if to say: *Nothing to worry about here, Vi . . . I'm the most relaxed guy in the world . . . nothing on my mind . . . nothing up my sleeve . . .*

His nonchalance was annoying. It was. But then I noticed the yellow paint on his right forearm, and my irritation . . . melted.

I ordered pesto and margherita. The pizzas arrived in less than twenty minutes, and the crust was thin, black in spots from the wood fire. Delicious.

Graziella wandered over while we were eating, and made a long speech in Italian that no one understood. Except River, who actually did speak Italian, like I'd guessed. He said something back to her, smooth and fast, and she laughed. Then she called out, *"Gianni!"* and her dark-haired son came over. She sent him off to the kitchen and he came back with a bowl of pistachio gelato for each of us.

In sixth grade I stood next to Gianni while we had our class photo taken. And the whole time I couldn't take my eyes off the long brown sleekness of his arm, next to my white one. Even when we were supposed to be looking at the camera, I kept starting at Gianni. But he just smiled at me, when he caught me staring, and I'd kind of liked him ever since. It helped that he always said hello to me, when the other kids in my class didn't.

Gianni squeezed into the booth next to Sunshine and Luke, so now all three of them were sitting across from River and me. He put his elbows on the table, and Sunshine pressed up next to him, smiling.

But he was looking at me. "The new issue of *Fresh Cup* came out," he said. Gianni's English was perfect, since he'd grown up in Echo, but his voice still held the low, emphatic speech patterns of his native Italian.

I nodded. "I saw it in the café. What's the latest news?"

Gianni's eyes lit up. "Pour-over coffee, still, *molto bene, molto bene.* But Ma won't let me serve it, even if we just roasted juicy, tropical Kenyan beans that would be perfect for it. It's traditional espresso only. Because we're *Italiano.* I did order the special kettle, though, so you'll have to come over and try it, after hours sometime. It should arrive in the mail this week, so we could—"

"I'm River." He held his hand out across the table. "New to town. I'm living with Violet."

"He rented the guesthouse," I added, a bit too quickly.

Gianni let River's sudden rudeness roll right off him. He reached forward and shook River's hand. "I'm Gianni." There was a pause, and River looked at me, and Gianni looked at me, and I turned to the open window and tried not to look at anyone.

Luke was staring out the window too, fingers to his scalp, checking his auburn hairline in the reflection. But he stopped when I caught him.

"So have you all heard the news?" Gianni asked, after a few seconds of silence.

"What news?" Sunshine asked. She put her ice cream spoon in her mouth and pulled it back out, nice and slow. "I don't like to read the newspapers. They make my head hurt."

I kicked her leg under the table, but she ignored me.

"Something strange happened in Jerusalem Rock. Everyone's talking about it because it's kind of like what happened here, with the kids in the cemetery. Only worse."

"Where the hell is Jerusalem Rock?" This from Luke.

"It's a small town about two hours south of here," Gianni answered, and his eyes were sort of shadowed and unreadable. "Two days ago a group of people in Jerusalem Rock met in a field outside of town and accused some old woman of witchcraft. They tied her to a stake and threw rocks at her until she passed out. And then they set her on fire." Gianni paused, and took a deep breath. "They said she was a witch because she had red hair. *Red hair.* What's going on with the people around here lately? Did someone put LSD in the well?"

"What . . . what happened to the woman?" I asked, in

a whisper, because all the air had been sucked out of my lungs. "The red-haired woman. Did someone rescue her? Was she all right?"

Gianni looked at me and shook his head. "No, Violet. She died. And they put a little girl up on the stake next, a little redhead, and were shouting accusations at her. Their hands were full of rocks, ready to throw, when the police finally arrived. She was just nine years old. Scary, no?"

None of us said anything. River just kept staring at Gianni, and Gianni was looking at me, kind of worried, and I was watching River, and suddenly my hands were shaking and then I was shivering a little all over and I felt sick.

River. The glow. He left. He could have gone to Jerusalem Rock, that day he disappeared, he could have done it, it could have been him, who else would it have been?

"Gianni," Graziella called from the kitchen. "*In cucina. Subito.*"

Gianni shook his head again and slid out of the booth. "Consider getting yourself some San Pellegrino, is all I'm saying. Probably best to be on the safe side, and get your water from Italia for a while."

Gianni disappeared through the kitchen door. Sunshine and Luke started talking to each other, but I couldn't pay attention to what they were saying. River refused to look at me. He just turned and stared out the windows. The part of my leg that was touching his felt hot, suddenly, burning hot, so I started inching away from him in the booth.

River tensed. His shoulders jerked backward and his head snapped up. I stopped moving and followed his gaze.

Outside in the town square, two dark-haired girls sat underneath a tree, one reading a book out loud to the other. A skinny kid with shoulder-length red hair and a cowboy hat sat on the swings, watching a mother with twin toddlers as they walked by. Jimmy the popcorn man sat in his popcorn cart, chin on his chest, asleep. It was a happy scene. I breathed deep, and felt a little better.

And that's when I saw him. Daniel Leap. Jack's father. He was drunk. Really drunk. He staggered, one unsteady foot after another, into the middle of the village green, and stood there, swaying side to side, sucking the sweetness out of my town.

I felt River fidget beside me. He was also watching Jack's pa. His eyes had narrowed into tight slits, and his face looked . . . eager. So eager, his jaw was clenched tight with it.

That eagerness scared me. Sitting there in the booth next to River, fear began to claw and claw at me like water claws at a drowning man, until my throat constricted and

I half choked. Something was going to happen. Sunshine and Luke were busy flirting, and not paying attention. River's hand gripped mine underneath the table, but his skin felt cold and my fingers went limp inside his. I watched Jack's father, swaying in the square. I watched as he put a hand into his pocket. I watched as he pulled out something silver, something that sparkled in the fading sun.

I watched as he lifted it to his neck.

I watched as he slashed it across his throat.

Nothing happened. One second. Two seconds. Three.

And then the blood poured.

It gushed down the front of his yellow shirt, and his shirt went slick, and crimson.

Jack's pa turned white, stark white, against the dark red of his shirt. He looked at the silver thing in his hand as if seeing it for the first time. He threw it from him. It hit the sidewalk and skidded a few feet.

The mom with the toddlers screamed. The two dark-haired girls screamed. Jack's father fell down to his knees. One second. Two. And then tipped over on his side, and didn't move.

Sunshine jumped up at the screaming and looked out the windows. Her mouth opened, and a weak little wail dribbled out of her lips. Luke sprang to his feet. He followed her gaze. His hands went to the table and gripped it tight.

A man killed himself in front of me. In front of the town. And River made him do it. I knew it. I knew it like I knew I was near the sea by the taste of salt in the air. I knew it like I knew the sound of Luke's steps as he walked around the Citizen.

I knew it like I knew the feel of River's arms around me, when he was fast asleep.

Sunshine kept wailing her weak, drooling wails, and I was shaking all over, my fingers, my legs, my head . . .

River's face was blank. He didn't look guilty. Or ashamed. He didn't look like anything. His hand still squeezed mine underneath the table. I shook it off. I pushed myself out of the booth and ran out of the restaurant.

I stopped running when I reached the screaming woman with the toddlers. She was quiet now, staring and silent, her hands covering the eyes of the two twin boys so they couldn't see what lay at her feet.

I looked at the gaping slit in the man's throat, and the front of his shirt, covered with blood, at the ground beneath him, also covered in blood. The grass was black with it.

Something caught my eye off to the left.

A razor.

Sunshine was beside me now. She let out another weak scream. A crowd was forming around the body. The two girls. The popcorn man. The cowboy kid. Luke. Graziella. Gianni.

I took one more look at the body on the ground. And then went back into the restaurant.

River still sat in the booth. He saw me, and smiled, like it was nothing. Like it was all *nothing*.

I left. I took the path through the woods toward home. But when I got halfway, I turned around and went back.

I walked through town, past my high school.

I found Jack in his plain, bare kitchen, in the dark, staring into space like he was waiting for something bad to happen. Which it had.

"I decided to run away once, after my dad had been drunk for a whole week straight," he said, after I entered without knocking. He was sitting on a rickety chair by a cheap wooden table. I wondered if the lights were off because he liked it that way, or because the electricity bill hadn't been paid. I was familiar with both.

"I tried to fake my death first, like Huckleberry Finn," Jack went on. "With the pig's blood. I even went into the butcher's, and asked about getting some. But the guy started to ask a lot of questions, so I left."

I glanced around the kitchen. Its sad walls were covered

in faded wallpaper, and you could taste the rotting optimism of the sweet pink-flowered print, now coming off in strips. There were empty bottles of liquor in the sink, and the smell of smoke, and dust, and unchanged garbage. And I compared it to the Citizen's kitchen, with its high ceiling and big windows and yellow couch and good food in the fridge for once.

"You want to get out of here?" I asked.

Jack nodded. He got up and walked down the hallway that led off the kitchen, and returned a few minutes later with a backpack. He followed me out of the house.

We avoided the main square, the sound of an ambulance siren echoing in our ears, and walked to Citizen Kane in silence.

I supposed he would find out soon enough, about his pa. No doubt he'd already guessed. Flashes of Daniel Leap's white face and blood-drenched shirt kept hitting my brain like a fist. I didn't know much about kids. Especially smart kids who noticed everything and looked at me with big smart blue eyes under reddish brown hair. The tips of my fingers were still shaking and my heartbeat was hard and irregular and *off*, like all my shaking had shook my heart out of position and it couldn't find its way back.

So I took Jack into Citizen Kane's kitchen. He sat down on the yellow couch and watched me while I grated fresh ginger into two glasses of homemade lemonade. Freddie used to do the same thing whenever I was unhappy.

Jack and I sat on the yellow kitchen couch, in the weak evening sun, and sipped the spicy, sweet, tangy stuff, and felt better. Or I did, at least. And whether it was the ginger or the memory of Freddie, I didn't know. But my fear dissolved a little. Maybe it shouldn't have, but it did.

Afterward, I brought Jack to one of the guest bedrooms on the second floor. It was dusty, but the sheets were clean . . . or had been once, when they were put on the bed, which I hoped wasn't that long ago. It was kind of a manly room, with olive-green wallpaper and dark curtains and carpet and a black brick fireplace.

Jack took a look around. He didn't say anything. But I think he liked it.

He put his backpack down on the bed and then leaned his thin body against the carved fancy-pants bedpost. "Was it Pa?" he asked, looking straight at me, thin lips pressed hard together.

"Yes," I said.

"Is he dead?"

I stared back into his dark blue eyes. "Yes."

I went over to the old lamp by the bed and turned on the light. It was thick and yellow, and filled the guestroom with a fuzzy sort of warmth. I could see the brown freckles on Jack's nose and cheeks now. And his dry eyes. I cleaned the dust off the nightstand with my palm.

"Did River do it?"

My heart stopped. And then started again. "What do you mean, Jack?"

"Did he use the glow and make Pa kill himself?"

I swallowed, and took a breath. *River had told him about the glow?* "No. Yes. Mostly yes, I think."

Jack didn't say anything for a few minutes, just gazed at the fireplace, though it didn't have a fire in it.

I looked at the ceiling. Citizen Kane had high ceilings in all its rooms, and it usually gave the house a sense of air and space. But tonight the ceiling didn't feel nearly high enough. This bedroom, and its old satin bedspread, and big wood bed, and six shrouded windows, was stifling.

"I'm sorry, Jack," I said finally. "I'm going to make River leave the guesthouse. I'll make him go far away. I will."

Even as I said it, I knew it was a lie.

I wouldn't do anything of the sort.

"River was just looking out for me," he answered.

"It doesn't justify what he did," I said, kind of sharp. But then I put my hand on his thin shoulder. "What did he tell you, about his . . . about what he can do? What did he tell you about the glow?"

Jack shrugged, his hair shaking around his ears as he

did so. "Not much, just that he could do things, like make people see monsters. I don't think it's the whole story, though." Jack looked me direct in the eyes. "River is a liar."

"Yeah," I said. "I know."

Jack started to unpack his bag. He'd taken a lot of things, probably because he hoped to never go back. And I hoped that too. I helped him put away his stuff, and fetched him toothpaste and whatnot. When he got to the bottom of his bag, he reached in and pulled out a small, square painting, maybe nine inches tall.

"It was my grandpa's," he said as he leaned it against the wall above the nightstand. "My dad sold the rest of his paintings off, because he wanted to be drunk all day instead of working. But I saved this one."

The painting was done in oils, and it was a self-portrait. The painter had painted himself, in front of a canvas, brush raised, while a blond-haired woman lounged on a couch off to his right.

The painter looked like somebody. Somebody familiar. Maybe Daniel Leap, without the drunk in him.

Or maybe not.

And the lounging woman looked exactly like Freddie.

I tucked Jack in, went down to the kitchen, and waited for River.

Chapter 18

Luke came home first.

"*Daniel Leap,*" he said, and threw himself down on the couch beside me. Dust motes flew up and swirled around in the last bits of the day's sunlight coming through the kitchen window. "*Damn.* And you saw the whole gory thing, out the damn pizzeria window. How are you doing, sis?"

I just shook my head. Luke didn't know the half of it.

Luke sighed. "He's been our town drunk for as long as I can remember. God, I hated the way he would scream at us . . . but still. He was almost an Echo landmark." Luke slouched down into the couch and crossed his arms. "Wonder what finally pushed him over the edge?"

"He was Jack's pa," I whispered. "Daniel Leap. That was his *father.* River and I met him this morning."

Luke rose out of his slouch. *"Fuck."*

"Exactly." I paused. "I brought Jack home with me. What was I supposed to do? I couldn't just leave him in his house all alone, waiting for a government official to show up and toss him in some godforsaken facility. So I put him in the green guestroom."

Luke leaned over me suddenly, and gave me a hug. I didn't know what to do at first. But eventually my arms floated up on their own and hugged him back.

"Our father's an ass," he said, letting me go, "who ran off to Europe and never calls or even sends postcards. But at least he didn't kill himself in the town square." Luke let out another little sigh, and his shoulders slumped forward.

I gave my brother a sad kind of smile.

He smiled the same sad smile back, and it was so different from his usual arrogant grin that he barely seemed the same person.

Luke got up, went to the fridge, pulled out the iced tea, and poured both of us a glass. Then he sat back down on the couch. "What's going on with the world lately? Devils, kids in cemeteries, witch burnings, drunk men suiciding themselves in the town square. Are we living in the end-times, sis? Is the Apocalypse nigh?"

Luke took a long drink of tea and shook his head. "Like I said last night, it all started when River got here. Which could be a coincidence, like most things in life. But what are the odds that a man kills himself in the center of town, *and* you have a front-row seat when he does it, *and* the suicider's kid was hanging out with you in the attic the day before? *God*. I'm not going to get the image of his bloody shirt out of my head, not for *years*."

I shivered. The shiveriest sort of shiver, the kind that starts in your heart and spreads down your legs, all the way into your toes.

What was making me shiver, though, wasn't the image of Daniel Leap's bloody shirt, or the gaping slit in his throat. It was River, looking eager as Daniel raised the razor to his neck.

The last of the light slipped from the window. A blue twilight settled over the kitchen.

"Jack has a painting," I said. "I saw it when he unpacked. It's of Freddie. He said it was his grandfather's."

Luke's eyebrows shot up.

I nodded. "Yeah."

He got up from the couch and stretched. "Well, add that mystery to the growing list. Look, I'm going to bed. Jack will probably be up early. And since it looks like he's moved in, we'll need to start taking caring of him."

The right way, his face said, *as in, not like our parents.*

Luke walked out the kitchen door, and a minute later I

heard his feet moving on the second floor above. He was probably going to check on Jack.

I sat in the empty kitchen and drank my tea. It was dark now. Most of the room was in shadow. The windows were wide open, and suddenly I had the feeling that someone was watching me, looking in from outside, hidden by the darkness—

The front door banged open. I heard footsteps cross the foyer, go past the marble staircase, through the formal dining room we never used, and stop at the doorway to the kitchen.

I clanked the ice cubes at the bottom of my glass and looked up.

River.

I sat there and looked at him, and he looked at me. And I got an itch, looking at him, a *burning* itch, to shove him out the front door of Citizen Kane, into the dirt, and kick him in the face until he lost the lazy look in his eyes.

Maybe River was right, about me and the toe-curling violence.

"Remember the time we napped on this couch, Violet?" He sat down next to me.

"I do, actually. It was Monday." I turned and stared at the fat, mean butcher knife that was sitting on the kitchen table. Luke sliced bread with it, though I'd told him more than once to use the serrated bread knife instead. I thought about picking up that knife, about how it would feel in my hand as I shoved it into the soft part between River's ribs. I let my mind linger on that feeling for a moment, let the toe-curling part of me sing out.

"Monday? Monday was a lifetime ago."

I ignored him. "So. Tell me how you did it. And try not to lie, liar."

River stopped smiling, but his face was calm. "I made him think the razor was a silver pen. And then I made him draw a line across his throat with it." River gave a sort of low, quiet laugh.

Hearing River admit what he did, actually say it out loud and make it real and true, made my heart seize up tight, like someone was digging their fingernails into it.

He had lied about not planning to use the glow again. Straight to my face.

I hated him.

Part of me hated him.

The other part . . . That part didn't really care.

Which scared the hell out of me.

River grabbed my hand and held it to his chest. I yanked it away, and he grabbed it back . . . and a heartbeat later my fury disappeared, fast, like cold water down the throat on a scorching hot day.

"Just because you didn't hold the weapon doesn't mean it wasn't murder, River."

He continued to hold my hand. I tried to pull it away, but it was halfhearted and he just held me tighter.

I reached down inside myself. I tried to muster my previous anger. But there was nothing there. River's hand was hot on mine and it felt good and I had nothing left.

"Don't worry, Vi. I'm not in danger. That's the beauty of being able to do something no one else can. No one would believe it. There's no way for me to get caught."

"*Damn it,* that's not what I meant." I threw his hand off of mine, and dragged myself into a standing position so I was hovering over him. "This isn't about you getting caught. This is about you committing murder. *Murder.* Don't you think there was anything wrong with what you did? At all? Daniel was a drunk, and he shouted insults at me, and he wasn't taking care of his kid, but he was also pathetic, and lost, and sad. You don't murder people like that, River. You don't murder *anyone.* You show them compassion, for God's sake."

Go ahead, Vi. Get mad. He deserves it. Even seems to want *it. That lazy look . . . it's a challenge, rise to it . . .*

River shrugged. "Who has the time? Murder is pretty ambiguous, morally speaking. Be a little more philosophical, Vi. What kind of person would I be if I let Daniel

Leap go on living? The way he talked to you, that day in the square—that was just wrong. And Jack's life with him was miserable. You could argue that Daniel *wanted* to die. Why else would he get drunk so often? And here I could help him get what he wanted, as easy as a thought. Some people don't deserve to live. And, to go a step further, some people *need* to die. Why was I born with this gift if not to make the world a better place? Sure, I do the monster stuff, for fun, and because I like to feel the glow in me. But Jack's father—that wasn't fun. I did that for Jack. And for you. Yes, it was a bit messy, and far from perfect. But hey, you're both better off." He put his hand to his mouth. And yawned. This conversation was boring him. "You can't deny it, Vi."

I stood there, silent. "Yes. I can," I said, at last. But River was . . . River was starting to make sense. At least, what he said *sounded* logical. Some part of me, some sharp, noticing part, didn't buy it. Not entirely. Something about it felt . . . wrong.

Didn't it?

River reached forward, put his hands on my waist, and pulled me to him. "I have no regrets. The only thing I wish is that it wasn't getting more and more difficult to predict the results of my glow. I was really good at it, even just a few months ago. But lately, I can't seem to stop using it, and then when I do, it doesn't go how I plan."

"Wait . . . *what*? You can't predict the results? What the hell does that mean?" I squirmed in River's grasp, but my heart wasn't in it and he ignored me.

"Oh, it's nothing. I just seem to be losing a little bit of my control. Kind of surprising, is all. It seems to have taken on a mind of its own, almost as if it's controlling me, rather than the other way around. I'm sure it's not a big deal, though."

I stopped squirming. I was starting to feel better. River was right. Some people *did* deserve to die. An uncontrollable glow *wasn't* a big deal.

"You know, Violet, when I'm right next to you, I can pick up small drops of all the Violet things going on in your big brain. For example, I can tell that you hate beets. The idea of beets has an ugly brown haze around it, in your head. I saw it when I held them up at the grocery store. Needless to say, I put them back. Unlike tomatoes. Tomatoes have a nice rosy Violet halo around them."

I put my hands on my head, instinctively, as if I could block River from reading the bits that were leaking through. But then I felt stupid and lowered them.

"What else can you tell?" I asked.

"I can tell that you like me, despite yourself." River

smiled, and part of me melted at the smile, like chocolate in the mouth and ice in the sun.

But the other part wished I had a brick in my hand, so I could hit him, right in the middle of his lovely, crooked mouth, until his blood flowed and flowed and covered his shirt, like it had Daniel Leap's.

"Vi, you should have seen the black cloud surrounding Daniel Leap in your head this morning. Wow. And I thought you hated beets. You had the bastard in a black hole. An *abyss*."

"There's a world of difference between wishing someone was dead and making them so, River."

A thought occurred to me then, a black, evil, oozing thought. What if for River, there wasn't any difference? Is that what he meant by not being able to predict the results of his glow? Was all his talk about moral ambiguity just a way to justify something he couldn't control?

And then I remembered what Gianni said, about the poor red-haired woman. The witch. I had forgotten, with all the horror that came afterward, I had forgotten—

"River, where did you go that day you were gone?"

He shrugged. He lifted the edge of my shirt with one hand and began to kiss my stomach. His hands were covered in dried paint.

"Did you . . . did you go to Jerusalem Rock?" *Focus. If*

you let him smooth away your anger, if you feel no anger, then you're no better than him.

River kept nuzzling my torso. "Where is Jerusalem Rock?"

"It's the town Gianni was talking about, where they burned that woman. It was you, wasn't it." I felt nothing, saying this. Only River's soft kisses on my skin, like a cool breeze on a hot day.

"I." Kiss. "Have." Kiss. "No idea what you are talking about." Kiss, kiss, kiss.

"So you didn't go to Jerusalem Rock?" It was getting really hard to concentrate. River's kisses . . . I was feeling so good, so dreamy, so happy, suddenly. "Where did you go, then?"

"Somewhere else. I just had to get away for a while. I drove south. I don't really remember where I went."

"That sounds like a lie, River. You're so mysterious, always mysterious, I like it, I do, but I want . . . I want to know if . . ." *Focus.* "But have you . . . have you ever . . ." *Damn it.* "Have you ever killed anyone else? I mean, have you made anyone else kill themselves, besides Daniel Leap?"

"Yes," River mumbled into my skin.

"How many?"

River turned me around in his hands, and began to kiss my lower back. "A lot, Vi."

My eyes closed. "How many is a lot?"

"I don't know. As many as needed to die. Maybe twelve, I guess. Maybe a whole lot more. I'd have to think about it. I've had the glow for four years, you know."

"So . . . so you don't even know, off the top of your head, how many people you've murdered?"

River stood up. His palms were stroking my back, slow and confident. He nestled his face into my neck. "No," he said. "Once it's done, it's done. I don't really think about it afterward."

His lips followed the line of my jaw. His hair smelled like sand and salt, as if he'd been swimming. Maybe mine did too. Living by the ocean did that.

We were kissing now. Deep, long kisses. I felt the River thing start coursing through me, like it had that first time, at the cemetery. It flowed and flowed, like water flowed down a mountain. Like time flowed by on a summer day. Like blood flowed down a razored neck.

"River, are you using the glow on me?" I asked.

"Maybe." He paused. "Do you care?"

I didn't. Or, if I did, I wouldn't know it until later.

"Screw it," I whispered, and brought his lips back to mine.

CHAPTER 19

I AWOKE TO a hazy male shape looming over me. The sunlight streaming in through the window made a halo around him, like a golden angel in an early Renaissance painting. I blinked, and closed my eyes again. I was in River's bed in the guesthouse. I put my hand to my head. I felt dizzy. Thick.

"Don't you ever knock?" I asked, closing my eyes again.

I yawned, threw back the covers, and got to my feet. I had a moment of panic, wondering if I was naked, but I looked down and saw that I still had my black clothes on. I looked at my brother.

Only it wasn't Luke standing by the bed.

It was a stranger.

He was young. My age, or maybe a year younger.

And he was tall, with blond hair lighter than mine, but more bleached-white-in-the-sun than having-a-Dutch-grandma. He had a fading purple-blue bruise on the cheek under his right eye, big as a fist, and a slight bend in an otherwise perfect nose that said *I've been broken.*

"Well, hello there," the stranger said, and gave me a grin. "I'm sorry to burst in on . . . whatever this is here. I was looking for . . ." He turned, and locked eyes with River. "My brother."

River slowly sat up in bed, stretched, and scratched his head. "Hey, Neely. Nice face bruise. How did you find me this time?"

The stranger threw a newspaper on the bed. "It made national headlines, jackass. Kids running around a cemetery with stakes." He threw another newspaper on the bed. A local one. "And last night. A man takes himself to the town square and slits his own throat. Good one, River. Subtle."

He threw one last paper on the bed. *The Jerusalem Rock Review.*

Silence.

I put my hands to my hair, and my clothes, and tried to straighten them out while my mind raced around inside my head.

River has a brother named Neely.

River said he didn't have any siblings.

Was anything he said true? Ever?

I realized that River and Neely were looking at me. I took a deep breath. If I didn't calm down, and fast, my cheeks would turn red and everything I was feeling would write itself across my face.

"This is Violet," River said. "She lives in the big house with her brother, Luke. But I guess you know that already."

Neely grinned at me again. The same crooked smile as River's. It was strange to see it on this stranger's face. Neely's eyes were blue, not brown like his brother's, but they had the same glint. The one that said *I'm up to no good.* River's glint was lazy, though, and cocky. Neely's was . . . I don't know. Good-natured, energetic, looking for mischief—like a hell-bent little kid, or a damn Jack Russell terrier.

"I met Luke in Echo," Neely said. "I was asking around for my brother, and someone pointed Luke out to me at the coffee shop. He told me that River was in the guesthouse here, and the *American Graffiti* car in the driveway confirmed it. Luke failed to mention that there might be a pretty girl in my brother's bed, though." He pointed his thumb at me, but didn't look in my direction.

My cheeks were turning red and there was not a damn thing I could do about it. "Yeah," I said. "I was here. In

River's bed. Nothing happened, though. Not that you asked. We were just sleeping together. *Next* to each other. I was upset last night, and then River calmed me down, and he has these nightmares, so . . ."

My voice trailed off. I wasn't sure what went on the night before, after River and I started kissing in the Citizen's kitchen. I remembered hating River for what he did to Jack's pa, really hating him, and then . . . the hating stopped. And then we were in the guesthouse, and then the bed . . .

Neely lost his smile. He looked at his brother and his eyes went hard. "Tell me you didn't use it on her. God, River. You've reached a new low. I didn't think it was possible."

River sighed and got out of bed, picking his shirt up from the floor and slipping it over his head. "Violet knows all about the glow. I told her everything. And if I did use it last night, it was only recreationally." River glanced at Neely and away again, fast, almost—*almost*—like he was ashamed, for a second. "Whatever we did, it's between us. Violet and me, and no one else, all right?"

Neely stared at his brother, but said nothing.

"Look," River said, calm and lazy again, "let's move into the kitchen and I'll make breakfast. There's no point having a big talk on an empty stomach. And with you, Neely, it's always a Big Talk."

We all went into the kitchen. No one spoke. The only sound was the clanking of pots and pans and the pissed-off sighs coming from River's brother. After a few minutes of this, I decided it might be wise to let the two of them have some time alone, so I left them in the guesthouse.

I went back to the Citizen to check on Jack, but he was gone. Damn. I should have gotten up earlier, like Luke said. I shouldn't have gotten into River's bed again. Damn. I couldn't think straight. I wasn't myself around that boy. And it was scaring me. But then, everything lately was scaring me, though I'd never considered myself a coward.

I went back outside and saw Luke painting in the shed, the door open to let in more light. He was bent toward the easel, his face determined but content. It was an unusual expression for him.

"Hey," I said, walking over to the door. "Know where Jack is?"

Luke pointed to the corner table without looking up. Jack was there, leaning over a canvas, applying black and white acrylics in jagged, thin lines.

I saw red eyes, and small hands gripping gravestones. He was painting the Devil in the cemetery.

"He's a natural," Luke said. "He told me he's never painted before, but he's as good as we were at his age. He's got an eye for color and atmosphere . . . and dimension . . ." Luke trailed off, his eyes back on his work.

Jack looked up and flipped his coppery hair out of his freckled face. He grinned. "I guess it runs in my family."

I smiled back at him. "Ours too."

And something clicked then, in the back of my head. Something important. Something I knew I should pay attention to—

"River's brother find you?" Luke set his brush down and turned to face me.

"Yeah. In bed. With River."

Jack looked up again when I said this, then bent back over his painting.

Luke lowered his voice. "What's going on with you, Vi? You show no interest in boys, minus a bit of coffee talk with Gianni, and suddenly you're spending every night in bed with a stranger?"

He was right. Dead right. What *was* going on with me?

River. The glow. That's what. Still, I didn't feel like getting scolded by a brother who spent his summer either fumbling toward second base with a round-cheeked café girl or getting to know our next-door neighbor's thighs with his hands. "Who are you to talk," I said. I sounded bitter and I hated myself for it. "Maddy. Sunshine. *You* don't keep your hands to yourself."

Luke shook his head. "It's different. You're . . . You

need to be more careful than me. And no, before you interrupt, it's not because you're a girl. It's because you're . . . you're passionate. More than Maddy, and Sunshine, and me, all put together. River will break your heart. Count on it."

"He won't."

Luke met my eyes.

"He won't," I repeated. "Sometimes he seems all right, when he's nice to Jack or he makes me supper or he tells me sweet stories from his past. And I like that he's different. I like that he's . . . mysterious. But mostly I don't trust him. At all. I just . . . forget that sometimes. I'm not letting him near my damn heart, Luke. I'm not."

Luke sighed. "So what did the brother want? I see he left his BMW parked in the driveway. Must be rough. What kid drives a new BMW?"

"He wanted to see River, I guess."

"So, is BMW boy moving in too? Because then we can charge them more rent."

I shook my head. "Just go back to your painting, Luke."

Luke frowned. And he looked so much like our dad, right then, in front of a canvas with a paintbrush in his hand, that it bothered me. I looked from him to Jack. Their red hair glinted in the sun as they leaned over their paintings. They both held their brush in the same odd way, squeezed between their thumb and third finger, at the middle rather than the base.

I left. I walked back into the guesthouse without knocking. River was in the middle of poaching six eggs and Neely was drinking a cup of steaming espresso. Neither was talking. The air was thick and awkward. I stood in the doorway and wondered what to say.

Finally, River shoved a plate of eggs into my hand, and we all sat down at the table to eat. Silently. I dipped warm toast in drippy orange-yellow yolks, and tried not to notice the clumsy quiet. Neely was a serious coffee drinker, like his brother, and they both downed three cups of espresso by the end of breakfast. They drank holding the cups in the palms of their hands, rather than grasping the handle. They both narrowed their eyes before sipping. They drank like brothers.

After we were done eating, River and Neely moved around each other, cleaning up, and still not talking.

I watched them, fascinated. Neely was at least six inches taller than River, and slightly leaner. But he had the same light, healthy tan, and he wore the same expensive-looking, not-quite-normal clothes—dark linen pants that hung low on his waist, paired with a white Windbreaker that was zipped all the way to his chin. I wouldn't have thought a Windbreaker could look expensive, but his did, somehow.

Neely was about as beautiful as River, with a face that looked sort of sweet and open in the places that River's looked dark and secretive. When they drank coffee, they looked like twins. But when they moved around the kitchen, they seemed like strangers. River's gestures were slow and lazy. Neely's were quick and smooth. They wore the same scowl, though—it cut right across both their tan foreheads.

"River told me he didn't have any siblings," I said, deciding to break the silence by calling River a liar. It felt good. I looked at Neely. "Are your parents really archeologists?"

Neely tilted his head back and laughed. *Laughed*. It was something to hear. Deep and kind of contagious. He looked at River. "You lie more than our dad sleeps around. And that's saying a lot."

River shrugged. "Lying makes life more interesting. Not to mention easier, for the most part."

Neely laughed again. And then his eyes met mine. "River thinks life should be easy. But then he creates more mischief in one night than the Devil does in ten. Which I guess works out fine for him because he has a little brother to clean it all up."

Neely came closer to me and lowered his face toward my ear. "Can I tell you a secret?" he whispered. "It's all bullshit. River talks big when he's scared, just like our dad.

The question is . . . what is he afraid of? Have you figured it out yet?"

Neely backed away again. I rubbed my ear where he'd been whispering in it. River was watching me closely, but I didn't meet his gaze.

"What did you say, Neely? What did you tell her?"

River looked . . . worried. I took joy in that.

Neely put his hands on the table and leaned forward. "No siblings. What bullshit. We have at least two half brothers and one half sister, that we know of. As I said, our dad likes to sleep around. Luckily they're all just little kids still, so they probably don't yet know what it means to be part of our family. They'll find out soon enough."

"A sister?" River's worried expression slid away and mild surprise took over his face. "No one told me about her."

"I just found out myself, jackass. I was digging through some of the accounts and found out he was supporting another one, somewhere in Colorado. Why do you care anyway? Dad will never officially adopt them, and you told me, quote, that you 'never want to meet the spawn of our father's cheating loins.'"

River shrugged, all lean and graceful. "Maybe I lied."

"River, shut up." Neely caught my eye. "Violet, did he happen to tell you what his last name was?"

"West," I said. "He said his name was River West."

Neely laughed, and it shook his blond hair into his eyes. "River's last name—my last name—is Redding." He paused, to let that sink in. "Neely is short for Cornelius. And River is a nickname. His real name is William."

I blinked. I looked at Neely, and then at River, and then back to Neely. River's face was shifty and narrow and not meeting my gaze, but Neely's eyes were directly on mine and still open and laughing. He grinned at me, like he knew I knew what that meant.

And I did. The Reddings were one of the great old families of the East Coast. If my family was once upon a time wealthy East Coast mansion-building industrialists, they were nothing, *nothing* to the Reddings. The Reddings had mansions up and down the entire thirteen original colonies. They owned ships, and railroads, and presidents. They had ties to the mafia, and the Masons, and the Beatles.

Freddie had mentioned the Reddings in her stories. She pulled out a piece of jewelry once, when I was ten or so, an emerald necklace that we sold after her death. She said she wore it to a depraved Redding party when she was young.

So. I had been sleeping with a Redding. *Next* to a Redding.

"So I've been sleeping with a Redding," I said. "*Next* to a Redding." My thoughts were all coming out of my mouth.

"I've heard of your family." I looked at River. "Freddie said she went to a wicked Redding party in New York City once."

"That sounds like us," River replied, giving me an odd look I couldn't quite decipher.

Neely ran a hand up and down his right forearm in a thoughtful gesture. "Echo. What a nice name for a town. It's perfect. An echo of all the things that came before it. How many places is this now? Eight, nine?" Neely noticed what he was doing with his hand, and stopped. "When are you going to quit running away, River? Because I'm thinking if you don't stop soon, I'll have to beat you. Bad. With my fists. And I'd rather not."

"It's eight. Eight towns. Unless you're counting Archer, which you shouldn't. No one even died that time."

Neely laughed again, a darker laugh—it had a bitter streak in it now. "So the towns without death counts don't even register. Good to know. Jesus, River. I'm not sure whether to put you out of your misery or worship you."

So River had run away before. And people had died then too. I felt an ache deep inside me, as if I'd been bitten by sharp, frigid cold . . . though the morning was warm enough. I looked back and forth between the two boys and wondered what the hell I'd gotten myself into.

River reached over and put his hand on Neely's arm.

"I've got everything under control this time. I promise."

Neely shook his brother's hand off. "You always say that." His cheeks were red. It had started in one small spot on each side, when River said Archer didn't count, but now the blush covered him from neck to scalp.

River's mouth tightened, and I saw the dimple in his jaw, where he clenched it too hard. And his eyes . . . the last time River's eyes went narrow like that, a man killed himself in the town square.

"Cornelius, don't pick a fight with me. It won't end well."

"Dad is the only person allowed to call me Cornelius," Neely said. His voice was wound tight and the laughter was gone from his eyes, and I felt creepy, witnessing this brother fight, like some kind of verbal Peeping Tom.

"And how *is* Dad these days? What's it like, playing the good son all the time? Does it ever get old?" River and Neely stared at each for a second. "I'm trying to stop, Neely," River said finally. "I am. If I go back home, it'll start all over again. And I'm not as good as I used to be. The glow is changing—"

"You're trying to stop?" Neely let out a short laugh. "Some job you're doing, River. Every place you go erupts into chaos within hours." Neely closed his eyes, put his fingers to his flushed temples. Then he opened them and looked at me. "Ask him about Rattlesnake Albee."

"River, what happened in Rattlesnake Albee?" I asked, sort of quiet, and realizing halfway through that I didn't really want to hear the answer. I wanted to walk out the door and go hang out by the ocean and not come back until I'd figured out how to raise Freddie from the dead.

River unscrewed the moka pot and began to fill the small cup inside with espresso. He didn't look at me. "Nothing happened in Rattlesnake Albee. Neely is blowing things out of proportion, as usual. It's just a small town on the prairie that I stumbled across, once upon a time. I thought it would be fun for some of its citizens to believe that they were in the middle of an Indian attack, pioneer style. How was I to know that everyone in town had a shotgun?"

Neely glared at his brother. "The entire town of twenty-three people. Dead. In one hour. How exactly am I blowing that out of proportion? How would a person blow that *into* proportion?"

"Look, no innocents died. The whole town was past retirement age and mean as villains in a Shakespeare play. I'd been in the place all of five minutes and I saw a man beat his horse with a whip and a woman throw a cat out an upstairs window. A sign at the church said *All women are the Devil's concubines, all children, his pawns.* The town held an annual celebration in honor of the black plague for ridding the world of filth. Need I go on? I did the world a favor."

"No," Neely said. "You played God."

"I am a god."

Neely threw an arm in the air. "Well, there you go. What can I say to that? How do I reason with a *god*?"

"Why didn't I hear about this? A whole town up and shoots itself to death. Why didn't that make the news?" I went to stand between Neely and River. A black, furry dread was growing in my belly. River wouldn't kill a whole *town*. That wasn't just mischief, or vengeance. That was evil. *Devil* evil.

"Because Rattlesnake Albee was in the middle of nowhere, so no one cared." River paused. "And because me and my father made *sure* no one cared."

There was a long silence.

"You know, you and Dad are more alike than you think," Neely said. "Things would get a lot easier for you if you'd start seeing that."

River whipped his gaze toward his brother. "And you wonder why I keep leaving. Don't you think I know how much I'm like him? And don't you think it scares the hell out of me? Go home, Neely. We're done here."

Neely didn't move. He blinked a few times. "I read about those teenagers. What you did to them. Making them think they were on fire. For two hours. Two *hours* of screaming. Writhing in agony while their parents looked on, helpless." Neely gestured to the bruise by his eye. "I found myself a frat bar and got into a fight with a trust-fund dick after I read that. And every time my fist hit his face, I wished it was you."

River took a step back and put his hands up. "Kids on fire? Neely, what are you talking about?"

"The teenagers at that park in Texas a few weeks ago. I've got the newspaper in the car. Did you think I wouldn't find out?"

River shook his head. "I've never even been to Texas."

Neely slammed his fist down on the table. *"Stop lying."*

"Neely, I swear that I have no idea what you're talking about. I. Have. Never. Been. To. Texas. You're my *brother*, Neely. If you don't believe me anymore, then who will?"

"I *want* to believe you, River. You have no idea how much I want to believe you. I love you. I love you more than anything in world. But you. Are. Killing. Me. I hate the things you do. I *hate* them. I hate them so much, I have to punch strangers until they bleed, just to keep from going crazy. It's driving me mad. *Mad.* I feel like I'm losing it, really losing it, sometimes . . . and it scares me, River. I'm *scared.*"

River looked from his brother, to me, and back again,

and his look was hurt and bitter and sharp as the razor that sliced up Daniel Leap. "You know what?" River said, after a moment of silence. "Go to hell. Both of you."

And then he walked out the door.

I made to go after him, but Neely blocked my way. "River needs to be alone for a while. He'll be back to his old self in a few hours. It's always like this, at first, when we see each other."

I leaned against the door frame and watched River until he disappeared into the woods. "Yeah. I have a brother too." I glanced toward the shed. "I know about fighting."

Neely looked at me then, really looked at me. And grinned. The red had started fading from his face, and I noticed his broken nose again.

"Hello there, Violet White," he said. "It's nice to meet you. I'm Cornelius Redding of the East Coast Reddings, and I've got a magical, murdering brother and one hell of a temper." He laughed.

I laughed right back, and Neely and I stood there, looking at each other and laughing somehow, after all of that, and the ocean wind blew in and I could smell Neely. Chamomile shampoo and clean clothes and dirt and forest and midnight.

No . . . not midnight. Noon. High noon.

Sun, not stars.

CHAPTER 20

"WHAT ARE YOU doing?" Sunshine walked into my bedroom without knocking because everyone had decided not to knock anymore, I guess. "Luke and the kid are painting," she continued. "I heard about the new guy in the guesthouse, and I went over there to see if he wanted to meet me, but it was empty. And I'm bored. So I went looking for you. What's that on the nightstand? Is that a frog? A frog made from a hundred-dollar bill?"

"Thinking," I replied, in answer to her first question. "I'm just lying here, thinking." I moved my legs so Sunshine could sit down on my bed, but she walked over to the full-length mirror and began admiring her breasts and her long brown hair instead. "And yes, it's an origami frog. River keeps leaving them for me. I'm not too proud."

Saying it makes it true.

Sunshine just shook her head. "I'm hearing all kinds of things about you these days, Violet. Sleeping in River's bed. And now this." She waved her hand at the frog. "Wow."

"He's worried I'll run out of money and I'll need to buy groceries, or something."

"That's a justifiable concern." Sunshine pushed her long hair behind her back and faced me. "But leaving you frog money on your nightstand is still . . . weird."

But I didn't want to talk about River. My laughing with Neely had released something. I wasn't sure what it was. But I felt . . . better. Clearer. And without River in my head, I could think about other things, like Freddie, and Jack's painting, and the thing that stirred in me when I saw Luke and Jack working in the shed together, and stirred again when I saw River and Neely drinking coffee.

I sat up. "Freddie told me something, once. She was getting ready for Christmas dinner—we'd prepared the meal all by ourselves because we'd had to lay the cook off a few months before—and she'd put on an old, slinky black dress and looked kind of far away and sad. Not because we were running out of money, which she didn't care about. It was because she thought it might be her last Christmas. And it was."

I paused for a second, and blinked, fast, a few times. "She was brushing her hair in front of that mirror. I was watching her reflection, and admiring the way her black dress matched the cross on the wall behind her, and thinking how good they would look lined up against the moss-green wall. I wondered if I should try to paint it. But then she put the hairbrush down and turned to me. She said, *Hide your letters, Vi. Hide your letters, but not so well, your loved ones can't find them after you're dead.*"

Sunshine's wispy brown eyebrows went up. She came over and sat next to me on the bed.

"I've been looking for those letters ever since," I said. "I've got to find them, Sunshine. Soon. It . . . feels important, for some reason."

"Well, I've got nothing better to do." Sunshine stood back up, went over to my dresser, and started pulling out drawers and looking behind them.

I smiled. Sunshine was a good sport sometimes.

We tore through the two dressers in the bedroom. Nothing. We looked behind the seven paintings in the room, hoping to find something taped to the back. Nothing. We dug around in the closet, and under the bed. I'd done all of this before, but I did it again.

And still, nothing.

Until. Until I pictured Freddie again in my mind. I

pictured her turning away from the mirror in her black dress, catching my eye, and then turning her gaze to . . .

I went over to the dark wooden cross on the wall, and took it down. It was heavier than it looked—two inches thick, with the simple cut of a medieval monk's. I turned it over. I pressed the back with my thumb. And it moved.

The back of the cross slid open. There was an empty black compartment, about twelve inches long and three inches wide. I put the cross back.

"Follow me," I said. And Sunshine did.

We walked to the guesthouse. No one was there, as Sunshine said. Neely had probably gone in search of River.

I went into River's bedroom and opened the top drawer of the dresser. The cross was still there, right where I'd seen him put it. I picked it up, turned it over, and pressed in the exact same spot with my thumbs.

The back panel slid open.

"Here we go," Sunshine said, because, as the panel opened, two sheets of folded paper fell out and drifted down to our feet.

I smiled.

June 21, 1947

Freddie—

Last night was a mistake.

I've been in love with you since the first moment I saw you, since the first moment I moved into your guesthouse, since the first moment you snapped your fingers, and then took off all your clothes in front of me, shameless and free as the hoochie coochie girls I saw in the dance halls of Europe.

I loved painting you. I loved tracing the sharp curve of your elbow with charcoal, loved bringing the pink sheen of your skin to life on canvas, loved mixing the perfect blue for your eyes. I loved it when you draped yourself over my sofa, in nothing but your white skin, relaxed as a kitten in the sun. I loved how you drank sloe gin from a flask like a drugstore cowboy. I loved how you never wanted to know who I was, or where I came from, because it didn't matter to you. The only thing that mattered was what you saw in front of you. And you liked it. Liked me. I think.

But you have a husband. And I . . . I have nothing. Nothing but a handful of brushes and an itch in my fingers to draw.

I'm packing my things now. And by the time
you wake up, by the time the decent, stoic Lucas
returns, I'll be gone. Back to the city. I left you
two of my paintings. They were your favorites.

—John

I knew. I knew even before I read the next letter.

February 27, 1950
Freddie—
It's been a long time. Three years, I think, this
summer. You could have told me a long time ago.
You should have told me a long time ago. But I
forgive you. I suppose you thought I would come
back and cause trouble . . . go howling into the
night or fight a duel. But you should have known
it's not my way. I've never had the fiery artistic
temperament that made my fellow painters
notorious.

I married recently, a girl from Echo. Ann
Marie Thompson—yes, the pretty blond girl that
worked for you as a maid, some time back. We ran
into each other at a dance in New York, a few
months ago. She's a ducky shin-cracker, Freddie.
You'd never believe it. She's almost as good as you.

We will be moving back to Echo in the next
few weeks. As I said, I won't cause trouble. We
will be like strangers.

But it will make me happy, to see the boy, once
in a while, just in passing.

—*John*

P.S. You named him after me. That was kind.

"Does this mean what I think it means?" Sunshine and
I had walked back to my bedroom in silence. Now we
were sitting on the bed, the letters handed back and forth
between us as we read them over and over and over.

"Yeah, I think so," I said, but my voice wasn't working
right. I cleared my throat.

"Your dad's name is John," Sunshine said. She was
watching me closely, trying to figure out what I was going
to do—if I was going to stomp around or throw things, or
what, though I knew that she knew I wouldn't.

"Yes, I know what my dad's name is, Sunshine."

"And this 'John' was an artist, and your dad is an artist,
and you and Luke are artists."

"Yes, I *know*. So what?"

Sunshine threw her arms up in the air. "Rich people."

I gave her a sidelong glance, and I supposed my so-what expression was kind of fragile-looking, because she stood up and went to the door without another word.

But then she stopped and turned around, and her face was . . . sad . . . and thoughtful, and very un-Sunshine. "Vi . . . I think you'd better see if Freddie hid any other letters." She watched me a moment.

I nodded.

She left.

Freddie had looked at me like that sometimes. Sad. Thoughtful. Mainly when she was worried about Luke beating on me, or my hating him, or my parents being gone too long.

I went to the ballroom. I sat under my grandpa Lucas's painting until the sun set, just thinking about things and feeling like I could probably start crying, if I let myself.

But I didn't.

CHAPTER 21

THERE WAS ANOTHER movie in the town square that night.

Luke and Jack were still painting. I wanted to talk to them about the letters, both of them, but didn't have it in me yet.

Besides, there were more. I was sure of it.

But where?

Where had I seen another black cross?

River was still nowhere to be found, which meant a kind of ache was starting in my insides. I didn't know what it meant, or why it was there. I tried to ignore it.

Sunshine invited us for supper. Her parents had cooked up a roast chicken with fingerling potatoes and crème fraîche. Luke and Jack went, but I stayed behind. I didn't feel like small-talking. What I felt like doing was sitting on the front steps and staring at the sea, which is how Neely found me.

"Want to go to an old movie?" I asked.

"Yes," he said. "More than anything."

I packed a picnic for Neely and me, just like the one River had packed for me and him and *Casablanca*. But it wasn't the same. Now there was a devil, and a ghost, and a murdered man, and twenty-three dead people in a nowhere town called Rattlesnake Albee.

I considered telling Neely about the tunnel when we passed by it on our way into town. I considered telling him what River showed Sunshine while they were inside it together. But I didn't say anything, in the end. I figured Neely would either laugh, or get into a fight with someone. I wasn't sure which was worse.

"So River's run off before?" I asked, after a few minutes of silence.

"Yep," Neely said. He slid his arm under mine and took the handle of the picnic basket from me.

"And you always have to come get him?"

"Yep."

"And then the two of you get into a fight, and he disappears for a while, and then you both go home."

"That's the way it works." Neely glanced at me. "He won't

stay, Violet. I don't know what he's told you, but he won't stay. He never stays anywhere, not for very long. Including home."

I tried to look like I didn't care. I kind of hated River, so I should have been better at it.

"You're the first girl, if it's any consolation," he said, noticing my expression. He stopped walking, grabbed my hand, and turned it over. Then he leaned over and kissed my palm.

I sucked in my breath, stunned. He'd done it as natural and easy as smiling in the sun.

And I'd thought River was smooth.

Neely laughed when he saw my expression. "I've never caught River sleeping next to someone before. Look, there's no doubt that he's fed you some lies. That's what River does. My brother has . . . problems. But, as far as I know, you're the first girl he's ever noticed. And it's got to be a good thing. So . . . thank you."

"You kissed my hand to say thank you?"

"Yep."

I'd spent the last few days with a rich boy who had a glow he couldn't stop using and an inclination for vigilante slaughter. But all I could think about, the rest of the way into town, was how I could still feel Neely's kiss in my palm.

I looked around the park after we arrived, my eyes peeled for River. But nothing.

The night had gotten cool, and I could feel the warmth coming off Neely where he sat on the quilt next to me. On the screen, a train went by, and Rachmaninoff began to play. The movie was *Brief Encounter*. I'd seen it before, last summer in the town square. Crisp British accents and a damn heartbreaking end.

To my left, two girls whispered in each other's ears, while a little kid shared a dripping ice-cream cone with a very polite border collie. To my right, a tall, skinny boy with deep red hair—almost purple, in the fading light— cut an apple into slices with a small, thin knife, and offered it to a blond girl sitting with her family nearby. A bearded man stepped over a pile of dirt and threw a blanket down beside it. I knew why the dirt pile was there. Someone had dug up the bloodstained grass where Daniel Leap . . . fell.

"Are you a philanderer?" I asked Neely, under my breath, as the horrid, chatty woman with the hatbox interrupted the doomed lovers on the screen in front of us.

"A what?" he whispered back, throwing me an amused, puzzled look.

"A . . . a man who has many love affairs."

Neely's laugh burst through the movie-night stillness.

People turned around to look at us, but he didn't stop, not for a while.

My face turned red. Thank God for the dark.

"I get it now," Neely said, whispering after his outburst. "River. You. I get it. River's always been so picky about girls. But this"—he pointed at me—"this makes sense. *You* make sense."

And then he smiled at me, and it was crooked like his brother's, and I thought about how I'd been sitting in this same spot, doing this same thing, with River, just a few days ago.

≈≈≈

Halfway through the movie, right after the rowboat scene, I felt a hand on my elbow. I looked up into Gianni's brown eyes.

"Come, Violet" was all he said. "I need to talk to you."

"Okay," I whispered. I was curious, but not all that worried. He probably just wanted to show me his new coffee pour-over thing.

I got to my feet. Neely looked up at me, his eyebrows raised, but I just pointed at Gianni and shrugged my shoulders. "Neely, this is Gianni," I whispered. "I'm going to go talk to him."

Neely frowned at him, then at me. "Hurry back," he whispered.

I followed Gianni away from the square. He stopped under the oily yellow glow of the streetlamp near the Antiquarian Bookstore, and shook a black curl out of his eye. He had a scratch on his right cheek that looked fresh.

"Gianni, how did you hurt your face?" I asked.

He ignored me. "Violet, I want you to see something."

A cool sea breeze hit me out of nowhere. I began to button up my yellow cardigan. "All right. But can it wait until after the movie?"

"No. You have to see it now."

It was strange. It was. And if I hadn't been so distracted, thinking about River, and Neely, and the Devil, and the suicide, and Jack, and the letters, and the glow, I would have noticed it at the time. But, instead, I just let Gianni slip his fingers through mine and pull me down the street. Down, down, into the dark dead end.

I should have told someone that I was following Gianni into the great unknown. Like Neely. The bearded guy. The kid with the apple. Anyone. But I didn't. I trusted him. Hell, I'd known him since sixth grade.

So I let him lead me, calm and serene as a nun saying her prayers.

We came to a stop on the road outside Glenship Manor. Gianni pointed. "The thing I need to show you is in there."

Finally, the first tingle of fear rustled inside me. "But

the Glenship is boarded up," I said. "We can't go inside. And I wouldn't want to. No one has been in it for years. There must be rats, and bats, and ghosts, and . . . other things."

Normally I wasn't such a coward. But the night was dark, and Glenship Manor looked big and black and imposing and haunted as hell. And Gianni was staring at me in an odd way. His bright brown eyes looked different in the moonlight . . . kind of dull, and blank. He reached into the pocket of his jeans and pulled out a small hammer.

"Come," he said.

He led me over to the Glenship, and his fingers didn't release mine, not for a second. I saw that two planks of wood were lying on the ground. One of the Glenship's floor-length windows was exposed, and I saw a dim light flickering inside the building, low to the ground. Gianni ripped another plank back, one-handed, and threw it on the ground. The window was broken, but Gianni made sure all the sharp glass was clear before he pulled me inside after him.

He dropped the hammer and picked up the lantern. It was the kind that needed oil. Using the moonlight that streamed in through the now un-boarded window, he found the knob on the side and turned. The room filled with light.

I was standing in the dusty, ramshackle library. Peeling wallpaper, a lonely leather chair, ripped and ragged, all the books gone, and the shelves looking naked and empty. I fought an overwhelming urge to run around and explore. I hadn't wanted to come inside, but suddenly I wished I would have broken into Glenship Manor years ago. I was dying to compare it to the Citizen, to see what things had been left behind, to dig in drawers, oh, all sorts of things. Gianni was still looking at me strangely, but damn, I wanted to see the bedrooms, and the kitchen, and the cellar where the girl was murdered. Freddie said once that the Glenship had an underground swimming pool, and six secret passageways, and—

Gianni tugged on my hand. "Come, Violet. He's up here." He motioned with the lamp toward the staircase.

My eyes stopped scouring the room and focused on Gianni. "Who's up where, Gianni?"

He blinked at me, his fingers still wrapped tight around mine, his eyes still holding that eerie, lifeless look. "The witch, of course."

Even then, after he said *that*, I wasn't really scared. I thought Gianni was joking. Poorly, and in bad taste, after that Jerusalem Rock story. But still. I let him pull me out of the library, across a black-and-white tiled floor, up the grand Glenship staircase, so like the Citizen's, up and up past the second floor, past the third. The staircase got narrower and narrower, and then we were in the attic.

I caught my breath. The Glenship attic looked so much like my own sweet attic that for a moment I forgot where I was. The full-length mirrors, the wardrobes, the trunks, the cobwebs.

Who had left all these things behind? Was there anyone still alive to claim them?

My fingers itched to dig into the dust and see what I could find; I imagined photographs and old records and maybe even a mention of Freddie in some letter—

Jack.

His auburn hair was tangled and dirty, matted with dust and God knew what. His skinny arms were raised above his head; his hands were tied with ropes that hung down from the support beam stretching across the slanted ceiling. He had on a pair of jeans, no shirt, and his bare feet looked small and porcelain-white against the dirty floorboards.

His freckled face was turned to the side. I could see tracks through the grime where he'd been crying.

"Help," Jack said, his voice cracking. "He keeps saying I'm a witch. What does he mean? What's wrong with him?" He pulled on the rope above his head. His wrists looked impossibly small, pressed together underneath the knots.

I turned to Gianni. All the fear that wouldn't come before, it came bursting through me now. "Gianni? What is this? What are you doing?" But my throat closed up as I spoke and my voice got smaller and smaller until I wasn't even yelling, only whispering.

Gianni smiled and nudged me with his elbow. "Someone tipped me off that you had cornered a witch at Citizen Kane. So I went to your house and tempted him out of your lair. What do you think, Violet? *Look at that red hair.* What wickedness. Red-haired Devil-loving monster." He paused, bent down, and picked something up. "I had to show you, Vi. It is a rare kind of girl that could appreciate what I am about to do. And you are rare, Vi."

"What are you going to do, Gianni?"

That's when my eyes caught sight of what Gianni had in his right hand. I reached forward, yanked the lantern out of his left, and shined it around the attic.

There was a pile of rocks in the shadows to my left. Next to a wheelbarrow-red can of gasoline.

Gianni looked at me with his dead eyes. "Make him confess, of course. You can watch. Or help, if you want. I've got the rocks over there. But if they don't work, I found a rusty old jackknife in the cellar. That will do the trick. We just have to make sure to leave a little juice in him, at the end. He'll need to feel the flames. I've heard that you've got to burn the Devil out of witches, and you can't do that if they are already dead before you put them in the fire."

Jack was screaming by this time. Writhing against the ropes and screaming.

And over his screams, I could hear someone else. Someone behind me, laughing, in the dark. I lifted the lantern, but it didn't penetrate the far corners. Laugh, laugh, laugh.

"River?" I cried out, my voice a whisper that couldn't cut through Jack's screams. "Please don't be River," I said to no one, because no one was listening.

Freddie, help me. Gianni's going to burn him, what should I do, what should I do? Something's wrong with him and he's not himself and I think I know why, Freddie, help me, help me, Freddie, please . . .

Gianni picked up the gasoline can. "Might as well get him good and drenched before the confession. Saves time."

And he lifted the can over Jack's head.

Freddie wasn't going to help me. How could she?

She was dead.

I threw myself into Gianni's side. He let out a strange, guttural yell and dropped the can. It went sprawling onto the floor. Thick fumes filled the air.

Gianni jumped to his feet. His beautiful face was scrunched and twisted and he was howling and shaking my arm and I dropped the lantern—

And then came the flames.

And then came Neely.

Smoke and fumes were everywhere, and I couldn't see, but I heard laughter, and then Gianni was rubbing his eyes next to me and yelling *Where am I?* and the smoke cleared a bit and Neely was throwing old quilts and clothes on the fire until it was dead-dead-dead and I was trying to get Jack free and finally the last knot came loose and Neely was pushing us out of the room and down the stairs.

We climbed through the broken window in the library and everything was jumbled and confused and my knee hit the windowsill and I fell to the ground and felt grass under my hands. I got back to my feet, keeping my eyes on Gianni, who didn't look angry anymore, just confused and terrified and so damn lost.

Jack wrapped his arms around me, and I held him. Tight.

Gianni was still rubbing his eyes.

"Gianni," Neely said, his voice low and hard. "Gianni, look at me."

Gianni moved his hands away from his face. "Why am I here? What happened?"

Neely reached out and grabbed a fistful of Gianni's plain white T-shirt. He shook him, not rough, but not gentle, either. "Quiet. Be quiet, damn it."

"Did I start that fire?" Gianni kept looking from Jack to the Glenship attic windows and back again. "I . . . Something's wrong with me, I—"

Neely hit Gianni. In the jaw. Gianni went down in the dirt. He lay there for a second, not moving. Then Neely reached over, gave him a hand, and helped him to his feet.

"Gianni, *focus*."

Gianni's lip was bleeding, and the blood was running down his chin. But he met Neely's eyes and nodded.

"Here's what you're going to do," Neely said. "You're going to forget this all ever happened. You're not going to think about it, you're not going to ask questions." Neely reached into his pocket, pulled out his wallet, and took out a pile of green. "Take this and keep your mouth shut."

Gianni just stood there, mouth open. Neely grabbed Gianni's hand and shoved the bills into it. "Gianni. Go home. Someone might have seen that fire and the cops are probably on their way. So *go*. Get out of here. Now."

Gianni tightened his fist over the money. He nodded. Turned. Cast a look back over his shoulder at Neely, and then his eyes met mine. Held. Broke away. He took off into the dark.

Neely grabbed my arm. "We need to get going too, Violet."

I shook my head. "He's up there. In the attic. We have to go back—"

A police siren ripped through the still air. Neely pulled on my arm. I grabbed Jack's hand. We ran.

CHAPTER 22

"GIANNI SAID YOU were looking for me." Jack and I were sitting on the floor in front of the fireplace in the green guestroom. I gathered some wood from the garage when I got home, and started it up, thinking a warm fire might help after all that, if anything could.

Jack had stood near me as I got it ready, as if not wanting to let me out of his sight. He'd been shaking, and was pale under the dirt still streaked across his face. But he was doing better now. The shaking had stopped. I'd given him an old black sweater of Luke's to wear, and his cheeks were red from the heat. So he was warm, at least.

"I'd left Sunshine's, but Luke was still there and Gianni found me alone in my room and said you were waiting for me in the Glenship attic," Jack continued. "It was weird, and he was acting weird, but I don't know . . . I fell for it. It was stupid. I won't, next time. Next time I'll be smarter."

Jack's hands clenched and unclenched. "He made me take off my shirt, and my shoes. He tied up my hands and said he was going to burn me alive."

I put my arms around Jack and hugged him.

"I heard the laughing too," he said. He tilted his head up at me. "Was it River?"

I didn't answer, and we were quiet for a while.

"I found something today," I said, figuring now was as good a time as any. "Some letters. You know that painting you have over there on the nightstand? Well—"

"Is this about my grandpa?"

I sighed. "So you know already."

Jack shifted and got to his feet. He went over and got the painting from the nightstand. "This is her, isn't it? Your grandma? My dad told me things, when he wasn't drinking. Things Grandpa told him."

"Yeah. It's her. And that's John Leap, your grandfather. He looks like your dad." I stopped and took a deep breath. "And mine."

We looked at each other for a heartbeat. Two.

"I found the paintings of your grandma in the ballroom," Jack said, putting the canvas back on the stand. "That's when I knew for sure."

"Show me."

I followed Jack, down the hall, and up the marble stairs to the third floor. I wanted to stop in Luke's room as we passed, but I could hear Sunshine laughing inside.

Jack walked to the far left of the ballroom, by the windows, and pointed at two small nude paintings, both of Freddie, both lost amidst the sea of bigger, fatter canvases that covered the walls.

Now that I was looking at them closely for the first time, I could see that John Leap's paintings had been done in the guesthouse. Same sofa, same wallpaper—there were even cans of paint on the windowsills. Freddie was white and naked and shining.

Jack and I stared at the portraits for a while. And then we went back to the green guestroom. I pulled out Freddie's letters, which I'd been carrying in my pocket all day, and gave them to Jack. He read them by the fire.

And when he was done, his blue eyes met mine. And he smiled. "So our dads were . . . brothers."

I nodded. "Half brothers, it looks like."

"So I can live here now? Because we're related?"

"If Luke and I have anything to say about it, then . . . yes."

And he grinned again. Even after the night he'd had, the kid could still grin.

I stayed with Jack until he fell asleep. I sat by his bed and read to him from *The Lion, the Witch and the Wardrobe* until his eyes closed. But then I woke him up before I left, and made him lock the door behind me. And I made him promise not to let anyone in, except Luke or me. Not for anything.

I walked to my bedroom, closed the door, and sat down on my bed. Now that I was alone again, I felt empty, all through my insides. As empty as Montana, which I heard was the emptiest of empties, next to Wyoming. I went to one of the windows. They were black with the black night, which matched my black, empty sort of mood.

There was an origami penguin sitting on a pile of books on the floor.

I went downstairs to the kitchen.

Neely was there, right where I had left him when we got back from Glenship Manor. He'd lit the two candles on the table, and things looked medieval. He was sitting on the couch, whistling Rachmaninoff.

"Did you follow me and Gianni to the Glenship, Neely?" I asked him.

"Yes."

"Why?"

Neely didn't answer.

"Any sign of River?" I asked.

He shook his head.

"Why did you hit Gianni?"

"Because I had to. We were running out of time and I needed him to listen to me."

"So you just hit people? That's what you do?"

Neely grinned. "No, I'm a philanderer. I . . . philander."

I laughed. I didn't mean to, but I did. I gestured to the fridge. "Do you want some lemonade with ginger?"

"You bet I do," he answered.

I made up another batch of Freddie's feel-good juice while Neely watched, and then poured out two glasses. He took a sip, and sighed. "I feel bad about punching Gianni. It wasn't his fault, what happened to him. Don't get me wrong, I like a good fight. But that was . . . an unnecessary evil." Neely put his hand in his hair and messed it up. He looked so much like River that I stopped breathing for a second.

Neely put his hand down. His hair stayed tangled up. "It was just, the thought of him hurting a kid, hurting you, hurting whoever else, I just lost it . . ." His voice drifted off.

I leaned against the table. "River doesn't feel all that sorry for anything he does."

"My brother's not as bad as he seems." Neely looked up at me. His bruise was a darker purple in the candlelight, as if it had gotten worse throughout the day rather than better.

"I know he's not," I replied.

"He's living with a gift. A powerful gift. And he's alone. He has no one to talk to about it, no one to help him figure out right from wrong."

I drank my lemonade and didn't say anything. I put my hand to the back of my neck. I'd gotten that tingling feeling, the one I'd felt before in the kitchen at night, the one that said *Someone is watching you*. I turned around. No one. I looked out the dark kitchen windows, into the night. Nothing but Neely and me, reflected back in the glass.

I thought of the laughter in the Glenship attic. Shivered.

Neely stood up and took off his Windbreaker. He wore a black T-shirt underneath, but that wasn't what caught my eye. I was looking at the long pink scar that ran from Neely's neck down the length of his right arm.

"Damn," I said. And instantly wished I could take it back. Still, I wanted to reach out and touch that scar. I wanted to take my fingernails to it, peel it off, and see the clean, smooth Neely skin underneath. I fought the urge.

"It's okay," he said. He grinned. "Sometimes I still lose my breath when I look at it in the mirror. You can touch it, if you want."

I did. I ran my fingers down his neck and then down his arm. The scar ended at his wrist, and the pale skin there was hairless and soft. Softer than it should have been.

"It's a challenge, keeping the thing hidden," he said. "Especially when you're a yacht brat who likes to take his shirt off in the sun like every other person."

"How did it happen?"

Neely laughed. It was a quiet little thing, but still, a laugh.

"River was fourteen," he said, the corners of his mouth still twitching, "and I had just turned thirteen. My brother didn't know about the glow yet. He was beginning to suspect something, though. He was beginning to suspect that he was . . . different. River and I were out on the beach one day, having a bonfire. River likes to start a fire whenever he's upset about something. And, before long, the two of us got into a fight. When I wasn't fighting other kids, I was fighting River." Neely paused and smiled a little bit. "Me and my fights. Usually River knew how to handle me, how to talk me down while avoiding my fists. But that time, he lost control."

I knew this story. I knew what was coming. I closed my eyes. So River didn't lie. Sometimes he didn't lie. Not entirely.

Neely's hand brushed my arm. "It wasn't his fault. That time it really wasn't. He was mad and thought something at me. We all do it, think bad things at a person when we're mad at them. But River's thoughts aren't just thoughts. They're *weapons*. We were fighting in the sand, and I had him pinned, and . . . he made me see something. The bloody corpse of a girl. Floating in the ocean by my feet. Very morbid, very River. He didn't mean to. He just thought it, and it . . . happened. But I got scared, and started running. Then I tripped. And fell. Right into the fire."

I opened my eyes.

Neely put a hand on his scar and shook his head. "I fell right into the flames, Violet. I was on fire. River pushed me onto the ground and threw sand on me to stop the burning. He was yelling out my name and crying. Then I passed out, and that's all I remember. I spent the next month in the hospital. The world's most expensive doctors did what they could. And this is what is left."

Neely looked down at his arm. He was still kind of smiling, but his eyes looked darker.

I put my fingertips on the puckered white-pink skin of Neely's forearm. "I'm sorry," I said, because I couldn't think of anything else.

"Look, I know that River's done . . . bad things." Neely

paused. "I know about the old vintner. And the Spanish twins. And that little Scottish girl. I know about all of it, all of the others. And I hate it. I hate it so much. But River is my brother. He was there every time I shot my mouth off as a kid, every time my temper took over and I was suddenly fighting three kids at once, all of them bigger than me. He never backed down, never ran, never told our dad, never even asked me to stop, or try to change. He's broken his right hand six times. He's always been there for me. Always."

I wanted to ask about the vintner, and the twins, and the Scottish girl. I wanted to hear more about River as a kid, before the glow.

But when I opened my mouth, what I said was: "I heard laughter." I let out a breath I hadn't realized I'd been holding. "I heard laughter in the attic. Before you arrived. It wasn't Gianni. There was someone, back in the shadows, watching and laughing. And it wasn't sane. It was hysterical. And terrifying. And—"

"Hey, just forget about all that." Neely took my wrist for a second. And then let it go. "Just don't think about it. I'm going to take my brother home and this will all stop. Okay? River . . . he isn't himself."

Neely sat back down on the couch and rested his head against the wall. "I think he's gotten himself addicted to the glow, like it's some sort of drug. He keeps running away, and maybe it *is* because he wants to stop using it. I don't know. But my brother gets bored, or meets someone he doesn't like, or gets fired up by some injustice, and . . ." Neely looked at me. And smiled. But it was sad this time. A sad crooked smile that matched his crooked nose, and it looked good on him. "And people end up dead. Always."

I sat down on the sofa, right next to him, and we stayed like that for a while, our arms touching. I smelled the ocean, like always, and Neely's high noon-ness, and I felt . . . better.

And then the back of my neck tingled again.

I wished I could see, suddenly. The kitchen corners were full of shadows, and I hadn't turned on any lights. Was River out there in the night, watching us? Or was I still just spooked? Maybe I'd imagined the laughter in the attic.

Maybe I'd been scared insane.

Was that possible?

I suspected that it was.

But no . . . Jack had heard the laughter too.

"I don't know what to do, other than make him come back home," Neely said finally. "Even though he'll just run away again."

I didn't meet Neely's eyes. I didn't tell him about the

damn, stupid ache I felt at the thought of River leaving. I didn't trust it.

Neely got to his feet again, put his Windbreaker back on, and zipped it up to his chin. "Violet, I've got a favor to ask."

"Okay . . ."

"I think it's great what's going on between you two. You and River." He looked at me, and I knew from the glint in his eyes that he was thinking about how he first saw me, rumpled, in River's bed. "But. I think you need to stop letting River touch you. Hear me out. I have a feeling, an intuition, that the only way for River to get better is to stop using the glow. Except when he absolutely needs to. So you have to stop letting him touch you. Can you do this for him?"

I shook my head. "Neely, I'm lost. What does River's touching me have to do with the glow?"

Neely just stared at me. "You mean you don't know? He didn't tell you?" He pounded his fist on the table, hard and fast and loud. One of the candles fell over and went out. Half the kitchen fell into shadow. I was still sitting on the couch and he loomed over me. I got to my feet and he *still* loomed over me. He was just so *tall*. Even his voice sounded tall. "River needs to touch people to use the glow. He can't make you see something unless he's had some kind of physical contact in the recent past. There used to be a glow window of about an hour or two but now he can make it last for days sometimes. His glow is . . . changing. Becoming stronger. Or weaker. Who knows."

He smacked the table again, and the other candle went out. The kitchen was dark now. I could still see Neely, but not well.

"I can't *believe* he didn't tell you. He had you in his bed, touching you, making you see, making you feel . . . who knows what, and he didn't even tell you how his glow worked?" Neely tilted his head back, and I thought he was going to laugh again. But, instead, he let out an anguished, frustrated kind of yell. I jumped back, startled.

Neely's yell started my thoughts running, running wild—

River, wrapping his arm around Sunshine. River, showing Jack how to use his yo-yo, hand on his shoulder, River, wrapping his arms around me in the cemetery, kissing me, River shaking Gianni's hand at the pizza joint, River taking the glass of whisky, River's fingers next to Luke's on the Ouija board pointer, River kissing me, touching me, touching me, touching me . . .

"It's wrong. It's bad for you, Violet. He can make you think things. Things that aren't true. I love him. But I'll be the first to say that he's unstable. And dangerous. More dangerous than anyone I've ever known, or will ever know. *You have to stop letting him touch you.*"

But I was barely listening because my brain was all smashed up and my thoughts were shattered and broken and bloody on the floor. And I knew that Neely was sensing it, sensing the sad, sick feeling that was coming off of me. But I didn't care. I didn't care if he saw.

I hated River.

I *hated* him.

CHAPTER 23

NEELY LEFT. HE didn't want to. I could tell. But he was mad at River too. We both needed to cool off. I sat alone on the edge of the kitchen sofa for a while. In the dark. Long enough for my anger to shift into exhaustion. Long enough to feel the hairs on the back of my neck begin to rise. Someone was in the room with me.

I felt a warm body slide onto the couch beside me.

I sighed. "River."

Relief. And anger. Comingling together. I wanted to shove him off the couch, make him hit the floor. But my hands wouldn't move. And then River got up anyway and lit a candle. He watched me for a second. Then nodded. "So Neely showed you the scar."

"Were you eavesdropping?"

"Sort of." He paused. "You know, every time I look at Neely, the image comes back to me. My brother covered in flames. Because of what I did. Because of what I can do."

River reached down for my hand. He put it to his heart. I yanked it back.

He sighed. "I'm hurt, Vi."

"What do you mean?"

"Well, the pink rosy haze that always surrounded the thought of me in your mind—it's gone. Now my color is more blood red, with streaks of black in it. Which in my experience usually means fear. Or hate. Which is it, Vi?"

"Both," I said, in a tired voice.

"Was it the Rattlesnake Albee story?"

I didn't say anything.

"The suicide?"

"Do you know where I was tonight, River? Do you know what happened to me? Do you want to know why I smell like smoke?"

"You went to the movie with Neely. Did you have a bonfire afterward?"

"No. Gianni came and found me while we were watching *Brief Encounter*. He wanted to show me something. It was Jack, tied to a beam in the Glenship attic. He was going to throw rocks at him, River. Cut him. *Set him on fire.*"

I stood up. Talking about Jack tied up and scared was making me lose my apathy. My cheeks felt flushed and my anger was coming back, fresh and tall and strong.

"Get out, River. Leave. *I mean it.*"

River didn't move. His eyes were dead serious for once, and hurt, and even a little . . . betrayed. Could his eyes lie? Could they lie as well as his mouth?

"Violet, that wasn't me. I would never use the glow to hurt an innocent kid. How could you think me capable of that?"

"You made Jack see the Devil. And you made his father slit his throat in the town square."

"True," he said. He put his hands in the air, as if he was pushing away the truth. "You're right. You're right. Damn it. Look, I'm not sure what happened at Glenship Manor, and I don't know what's wrong with Gianni, but it had nothing to do with me. Are you okay, Vi? Is Jack?"

"I heard you laughing, River." My cheeks were on fire and the fury was flowing through me now. "In the attic. I *heard* you. And then I find out from Neely that you have to touch people to make them glow. How many lies is that now, River? How out of control is this glow of yours? Because part of me thinks I should save the world and brick you up in the cellar. And I haven't made up my mind

not to do it yet. You had better say something convincing. Soon."

River leaned his back against the kitchen door frame and sighed. He looked different, suddenly. Not sly or catlike. Just young, and sad, and kind of hopeless, which threw me, because that was *not* how River looked.

"You want to know why I love Neely?" he asked me. "We fight and fight, and yet, his color of me never changes. I'm always a bright yellow. No matter what I've done. And I've done a lot. He's never been afraid of me. Never hated me. You got to love a person for that. Unconditional devotion is blue-moon rare."

I watched him leaning for a bit, and didn't answer.

"Do you want to come up with me to the attic?" River asked, at last, in a soft voice. "I'll stop lying," he said. "And I'll start talking."

"All right," I said. Just like that. Because . . . because what the hell. River was leaving and it was for the best. One last night talking wouldn't hurt. Besides, there was a part of him, the non-glowing part, that I still liked, despite everything . . . the bonfire, his taking my side against Luke, and cooking good food, and the origami animals, and the sleeping with his arms around me . . .

Ten minutes later, River and I sat on opposite ends of the old velvet couch in the attic, listening to Robert Johnson. I loved the static crunching sound that ran on in the background of all these old-timey recordings. I breathed in deep and smelled salt on the breeze, and, underneath that, the smoke that still clung to my hair. The sea wind blew in through the round windows, which opened sideways like a coin spinning on its side, and it made the candles flicker with the regularity of a heartbeat.

River slipped a few purple-black grapes into his mouth. I had brought up some food from the kitchen, knowing that he probably hadn't eaten all day. And knowing that I shouldn't care. But damn it, I did anyway. River grabbed the triangle of Gouda, cut a slice, and handed it to me. I took it from him, careful not to let our fingers touch. And then River put his arms behind his head and leaned back into the couch.

"I heard Neely tell you not to touch me."

I looked at him. "River, I don't remember what happened last night. I don't remember anything after we kissed in the kitchen. I woke up in your bed this morning feeling dizzy, and not even knowing if I had any clothes on. I don't trust you, River. I don't. You're a liar. And an addict." I paused. "Why couldn't I remember going to sleep? Or anything that might have happened before that?"

River shrugged. "Look, yes, I used the glow on you

at first, to calm you down. You were upset about Daniel Leap. I was *helping* you. I didn't intend for you to forget what happened. The glow just does that sometimes."

I absorbed this new information for a minute. "So first you confessed to me that you're having trouble controlling your gift. And then Gianni *went mad and kidnapped Jack tonight and I heard that laughter and you say it wasn't you.*" I gritted my teeth and slowed down. "Well, I guess I have to believe you. You're a liar. And yet I have to believe you. If I don't believe you, then I have to do something about it. Like get you drunk and then drown you in the ocean before you get Jack killed."

River lifted a hand shiny with olive oil, stuck it into his hair and looked at me. "That's pretty much the way of it, Vi."

"*You shall love your crooked neighbor with your crooked heart,*" I said.

"What?"

"It's from a poem by Auden. It's something Freddie used to say sometimes."

"What's it mean?"

"That nobody is perfect, I think."

"Well," River replied. "That's the truest thing said round the world today."

We sat by each other, not talking, and not touching. Robert Johnson began to sing "Between the Devil and the

Deep Blue Sea." He played the song slow, and melancholy, nothing like the Cab Calloway original.

I looked at River and listened to the waves crash outside, and figured that Robert was singing right to me, right then.

The air started feeling heavy, and thunder burst into the quiet like a drum roll. A storm was beginning. The record stopped, the wind got even colder, and the feeling in the attic changed. It became freezing and black, all in the span of a hundred heartbeats. It was like a dream shifting into a nightmare. Usually I loved thunderstorms. But I wasn't in the mood for one just then.

"Neely is right, though," River said. His face had become dark and raw, with the beginning of the storm, and I wondered if I could trust it. "Neely's right, and I should keep my glowing hands off of you. He's always right, the bastard. Violet, can I tell you something?"

"Yes."

Thunder crashed.

River flinched. "I hate thunderstorms. I ditched my uptight private school and ran off to New Mexico a few months ago. It didn't rain. Not once. I didn't dream about burning up Neely. I didn't dream about anything. I haven't slept that well until . . . until I got here. And met you.

"My mother wasn't an archeologist, or a chef," he continued, after a few seconds of silence. "She was a big-hearted socialite who died five years ago. She drowned at sea, like a character in a poem. Fell off a yacht in the middle of a storm. I was there. I watched her go over the side, watched as she hit the black water and disappeared."

Freddie died five years ago too. I knew about missing and I knew about death. "I'm sorry," I said. And I meant it.

"She used to tell me that I didn't have to be like him. Like my dad. She said I should be compassionate, even to people who didn't deserve it. But Neely takes after her, in that way. Not me. He . . . he took her death hard. That's when he starting fighting—really fighting. It was every day, for a while." River ran his hands through his hair and leaned back into the couch again. "But he didn't get punished for it. I did."

I didn't say anything. I didn't touch him. And I didn't let him touch me.

"A year after my mom died, I got the glow," River said. His eyes were closed. "I got the glow, and then I did something stupid. I had the best intentions, but you know what they say about those."

River opened his eyes, sighed, and closed them again. "It was my father's birthday. My father, well, he'd loved my mother. *Really* loved her, despite all his affairs. Despite all the times he got distracted by the young pretty things that threw themselves in his path, because of his money. My parents had been best friends since they were children. High school sweethearts. Her death about killed him. So I came up with what I thought was a brilliant idea for a birthday present, stupid kid that I was. I found him in his office, sitting in the sunshine and staring at the wall. I went up to William Redding II and put my hand on his. I let him see my mother. I let him see her for . . . for a long time. Until he was crying. And then I pulled my hand away."

Thunder boomed, and River flinched again. He leaned forward and put his elbows on his knees. "He beat me for it, once he figured out what happened," he continued. "My father took a paperweight from his desk and hit me with it until he broke two of my ribs."

River said this without a trace of self-pity, as if he were reading a recipe or giving directions.

I could hear the raindrops on the roof above, pounding, pounding, as if they were trying to get inside.

"And for all that my father kicked the hell out of me, he made me do it again," River said. "He made me do it over and over until he went half mad with it, seeing my mother in front of him, ripe with life like the day before she died. And he didn't stop there. From then on, if anyone disagreed with him, he called me in to fix things. I did what I could. Like I said, I was better at controlling the glow when I was younger. But it wasn't enough. It was never enough. I killed my first man because my father demanded it. Or made him kill himself, at least. Just because he had the nerve to refuse an offer from a Redding. Dad likes himself a good pinot, and wanted to buy this man's vineyard. The guy was Italian, and brought the vines all the way from the home country when he was a boy. He refused to sell. Well, guess who won, in the end? The kind, stubborn old vintner went down, and my father, William Redding II, now has his own wine label. And damn me to hell, I helped him get it."

I wrapped my arms around River. I didn't think about it. I didn't think about the glow. I just did it. We stayed like that for a long, long time, all tangled up in each other, until the storm died away, and the wind quieted down.

Then River wiped his eyes on the sleeve of his shirt, and blinked fast. "Dad wants me back because he's grown addicted to it, to what I can do. He needs to keep seeing my mother, even though it's driving him mad. He can't let her go. I swear, it's worse than a drug. I know Neely thinks I have a problem, but my father is much worse. 'A Rose for Emily'—was that the name of the story you told us?"

I nodded.

"I've been thinking about that a lot. About Emily, and how she couldn't let the man she loved go, and she went crazy from it. I don't think my father is completely...sane." River put his face to my neck. His hands were on my back, his fingers aligning with my spine. "Neely is the peacemaker. Which is hilarious considering how many fights he gets in. He thinks he can convince our dad to change. To stop. Or let me stop, at least. But he's wrong—my brother has no idea what he's up against. Besides, he never quits fighting long enough to help out anyway." River shook his head. "Neely seems open and sweet, and he is. Mostly. But he's got a temper. Just like our dad."

"And you," I said.

"And me," River answered.

We sat for a bit longer, in each other's arms, both done talking. Eventually River began to run his thumb up the inside of my arm, bare skin on bare skin. Neely's voice was in my head, telling me to make River stop, but I ignored it. I wanted to see what would happen.

River had his hands on my cheeks now. My skin tingled, and I felt that River-thing starting. The good feeling, flowing through me, calming me down.

I wondered, in the far back of my mind, if River was

using the glow on me a lot more that he'd admitted. I wondered if he was, in fact, using it every time he touched me.

He had touched me a lot.

I might even be getting addicted to it. Like him. And his father.

Maybe he couldn't help himself. Maybe he genuinely wanted to touch me, and didn't know he was using the glow. But that didn't change anything. Maybe it made it worse.

I put two hands on River's chest and shoved. River opened his eyes and looked at me. His face was flushed, and I supposed mine was too. I got to my feet, and then River got to his feet, and we were both standing there, looking at each other with our flushed faces.

"Daniel Leap was my uncle," I said, because now seemed like as good a time as any. "My half uncle. And you killed him. Before I got to know who he really was. That cross you took down off the wall in your bedroom had letters hidden in it, written from my grandfather, who was not Lucas White, but John Leap. Painter."

River shook his head. He looked a little taken aback.

"Let me read them," he said. He was serious. As serious as when he talked about his dad and the paperweight. "Now."

I pulled the letters out of my skirt pocket and gave

them to River. He read them, twice, and handed them back.

"I'm sorry," he said simply. "I didn't know. He was a drunk that insulted you and neglected his kid. I couldn't bear it."

"Yeah. I know, River. But at some point you're going to have to learn how to deal with injustice, like the rest of us non-glowers. It's part of life. You can't punish everyone."

"I can try."

"Well, maybe you could think of a way that doesn't involve people shooting each other. Or cutting their throats in the town square. Life isn't a gritty Western novel, River. We're trying to be civilized here, and you're acting like it's Deadwood."

River laughed. "That's because I wish it was."

I didn't laugh with him. But, damn it, I knew what he meant. I'd read enough Zane Grey and McMurtry, seen enough Sergio Leone, that the words *lonely gunslinger* and *vigilante justice* sent a sweet burst of excitement through me.

"Are there more letters?" River asked, after I didn't respond. "Are these the only letters of Freddie's that you've found? I . . ." He hesitated and got that strange look on his face, the one I'd seen before. "Because I'd really like to read anything else you find," he finished, soft and quiet.

"No, I haven't found any others," I said, looking at him closely. "Why? Why do you want to know?"

And then River's strange look went away and he just kind of laughed, soft and gentle like a summer breeze. And that laugh was so different from the one in the attic, so one hundred percent in every way different. It couldn't have been River up there.

But then . . . who?

And a thought occurred to me, a thought so big, it pushed all my other thoughts—like the letters and Daniel Leap and River's Deadwooding—off to the side.

Why hadn't River been curious about who was *actually in the attic, glowing Gianni, and laughing? He hadn't asked any questions. Hadn't speculated on any answers. Why?*

A terrible, cruel little voice inside me said there was a good reason River wasn't curious. River said the glow made people forget things sometimes. If it could make me forget, it could make River forget too.

River already suspected himself. And that's why he didn't want to talk about it.

I felt tired, suddenly. Old and worn out and used up and fit for the fire like a cheap pulp novel that was missing pages and bad to begin with anyway. Here I was, dealing with River and the glow, and devils, and a tied-up Jack in an attic, when my life a few days ago had been nothing but iced tea on Sunshine's porch and trying to find some money for groceries.

That Violet seemed far, far away.

"I'm sleeping in my own room tonight," I said, in a flimsy, frail little voice that I hated. "And damn it, River, I'm letting you off easy. So don't touch anyone. Don't touch Luke or Sunshine or Jack. Just go back to the guesthouse and go to sleep. I mean it."

"Don't, Violet," he said. "Please don't leave. The storm . . ."

But I did leave. I turned my back and walked out.

CHAPTER 24

I TRIED TO read, though it was well after midnight. I grabbed seven books from the Citizen's substantial library and spread them on the bed around me. But I didn't open them. Not even the thousand-page book with the footnotes and the two magicians, which I was always in the mood for.

I just sat and looked out my window into the dark, running my hand through the fringe on the lampshade near the bed.

The skin on the back of my neck prickled.

I got out of bed, threw a yellow Freddie shawl over my shoulders, and left.

I walked by Luke's bedroom door. I could still hear Sunshine's voice inside, and other shuffling, rustling noises as well. When had Luke and Sunshine progressed from kissing to piss me off to kissing for the sake of kissing?

I felt creepy, suddenly, standing outside my brother's door, hearing something between them that, for once, I wasn't supposed to be hearing. I felt my face go hot. Just like that, I knew. I knew that all their groping and kissing in front of me, to make me mad . . . it was bullshit. I was just the excuse. Because Luke and Sunshine liked each other. *Really* liked each other.

I turned away, a little bit stunned.

But I didn't move. I wanted to leave, but I didn't want to go back to my room, back to staring at the books and feeling like I was being watched.

And then, before I could even comprehend what they were doing, my feet started moving. Down the hall. Up to the attic.

River was gone, and I wasn't sure if I was pleased about that or not.

I stared into the attic's shadows, again getting that watched feeling, like I had in my bedroom, and the kitchen, and at the Glenship.

At least no one was laughing this time.

My eyes fell on the black trunk. It's why I'd come back—I just didn't know it until I got upstairs. I went over, knelt down, and opened it. I took out the empty gin bottle, the dried rose, the red card, and the dresses. There it was.

I pulled the dark wooden cross out, pressed the back, and slid the panel open. When I turned it over, creased pages of paper drifted to the floor. There were five in all. Five pages. Five letters.

My eyes scanned down to the bottom of the first. I expected to find John's name again. But the first letter was signed by someone else. I flipped through all five pages, reading fast, and then faster—

January 11, 1928

Dear Freddie,

How can you say you're going to marry him?
You don't mean it. Lucas is kind, and steady, but
he's not for you. And yes, I know he's building you
a très grand house by the sea, but you will never
live there. It can't happen. It won't happen.
You are so young, still. We all are. We're children.
Don't grow up, Freddie.

A plea from a friend,
—Will

February 18, 1928

Freddie.

Marry me.

You know me better than anyone. You were there, when it first happened. The first burn.

We gave each other our innocence, in that Manhattan cellar, while the party raged above. To this day, whenever I hear footsteps on ceilings, I think of you.

We tell each other everything. We've given each other everything.

I know what you will say. What you always say.

So fine, don't marry me. But, if not me, marry Chase. He, at least, has passion. Nerve. Heart. He's traveled. He can hold his own in a conversation, and he's tried to read Joyce. His parents adore you. They've never been the same since Alexandra fell out of that tree house and died. His family could use some of your easy charm. Your laughter. Your zest for life. Please don't marry Lucas. He will bore you and you will be unfaithful. Spare him. Spare yourself.

Love,

—Will

June 10, 1929

Dear Freddie,

It's not what you think.

*I was getting better. I had it under control.
You made me promise never to use it, after the
church burned. And I tried. I did. It was only
supposed to be the once.*

*Rose. And Chase. I'm sure you knew. Our
families have been visiting each other for years,
and Rose had been enamored with him since she
was in braids. It was bound to happen, I suppose.
I should have guessed. And then to find them,
the way I did, in his bedroom . . . it was a shock.
She's only sixteen. They . . . they weren't right for
each other. Rose is too sensitive, too innocent, for
a playboy like Chase. I couldn't believe he seduced
her. I was angry, so angry. I only meant to scare
him off a little, make him think her unfaithful, so
he would leave her alone, and let her go free . . .*

*It wasn't supposed to happen this way.
I thought it would just make him stop loving
her . . .*

*I gave him that jackknife, on his fourteenth
birthday. It was for our fishing trips. For cutting
nets and lures and fish and things.*

Instead he used it on my sister's throat.

I'm quitting. I'm done. Forever.

You remember that time we smoked opium, up in the Glenship attic? Chase said you wouldn't and you had to prove him wrong. Well, this thing I have, it's worse than opium, Freddie. So much worse. I may need to go away for a while. But I will overcome this.

I love you, Freddie. Forever and ever and ever and ever,

—William

December 15, 1942

Dear Freddie,

You are the only person who understands me. You are the only person who knows besides my family. Your silence these last years has been . . . unbearable.

Someday I might have sons of my own, sons who share my hair color. And may selfishness. And my burn. I worry, Freddie. Remember how scared we were, when I first grabbed your hand and made you see your older brother in his lieu-tenant's uniform? You slapped me so hard, my nose bled for an hour.

And afterward you took me in your skinny

arms and told me everything would be all right,
over and over again.

I went to Echo, five years ago. Just to see it
once more. I didn't tell anyone I was going. I just
drove there one day. I went to Glenship Manor.
It's boarded up, on its way to becoming a ruin.
It nearly broke my heart.

We made love once, in the library, late one
night, behind the green velvet curtains. Do you
remember?

I went to see Rose too. You had her buried in
your family's mausoleum, so she could rest forever
in the town she loved. I never thanked you for
that.

I saw the film Citizen Kane *the other day.*
It made me think of you.

> *You are my Rosebud, Freddie.*
> *—Will*

March 13, 1958
Freddie,
John tells me True drowned. Yes, I have one of
your old lovers keeping an eye on you. Don't
blame him. He's still in love.

John said you stopped wearing makeup and
drinking and sponsoring artists and throwing

parties and all the things you used to adore so
much. All the things that gave you life. He said
you've holed up in your mansion, and spend your
days staring at the ocean, or the sky.

People die, Freddie. Even children, sometimes.
It's not your fault. God's not punishing you for
being wild. Just like he's not punishing me for . . .
things I've done. It's just life.

You always said I had the Devil in me, when
we were young. But people can change. I've
changed. I'm not the Devil, Freddie.

Write to me. Please.

—Will

I got dressed and went to the guesthouse. I picked my
way over the dark, wet grass, shuddering with each cold
gust from the sea. River was still awake, sitting in the
kitchen drinking coffee. If he was surprised to see me, he
didn't show it. I told him to go wake up Neely, because I
had something to show them. He didn't say a word, just
went down the hall and did as I'd asked.

I started down the path into town, River and Neely
behind me, nothing dividing us from the dark night except
the watery white beam from the flashlight I carried. It had
stopped raining, but the path was slick and muddy.

"Where are we going, Vi?" River asked, finally, after we'd passed the tunnel. Neely still hadn't spoken.

"To find proof," I answered. "At the White mausoleum."

"Proof of what?" River asked, and it was nice, that he was asking the questions for once.

I ignored him. "Jack was on top of the Glenship mausoleum when he was looking for the Devil. But the White mausoleum is buried back in the trees, farther away. It's bigger, though. And it has Gothic columns. And a puzzling phrase carved over the doorway. You'll like it."

"I'm sure I will." River stumbled over a rock on the path, but caught himself before he fell. "Wouldn't I like it just as well in the morning? When it's warm, and we can see what we're tripping on?"

"No," I said.

Neely just laughed.

The moon was beginning to stick its face out into the night sky as we reached the cemetery, and the sea gusts were gentler now, having left the witching hour behind, I guess. The iron gate was open. The three of us squeezed through the gap.

I stood still and tried to absorb that calm, lonely, cemetery feeling. And then I led River and Neely to the White mausoleum.

Our family tomb was by itself at the back of the cemetery, along with some early suiciders' graves, and an abandoned caretaker's cottage that was spitting out old bricks and looking plump with atmosphere. Freddie was buried there, and my grandpa, and a mad uncle, and two poor little stillborn babies that Freddie had given birth to before my dad was born.

The Glenship tomb got mowed and trimmed now and again because it was near the graveyard's entrance. But not ours. Ivy poured off the stone roof as if it owned the place, and blackberry bushes crowded the walls like thorny leeches. Now that I was there, in front of our mausoleum, I was a bit shocked by the brutal neglect. It was tangible. Almost oppressive. I couldn't remember when I had last been to visit. When *anyone* had been to visit. Was it when Freddie died? Had it been that long?

I felt the bitter bite of guilt stirring up inside of me. Why hadn't I taken better care of Freddie's grave?

Maybe I had absorbed neglectfulness from my parents, along with art and snobbery.

Oh, it's okay, Violet, came Freddie's voice in my head. *I like my tomb this way. Forgotten and still.*

And it was true. Freddie had always liked abandoned, quiet things. Like ghost towns and rusted-out cars in junkyards and broken windmills standing where farmsteads used to be.

She'd had a collection of keys to buildings that had burned down in Echo. There were eleven of them, all looking pretty much the same, except for the great big key that had belonged to an old wooden church, reduced to ashes by some priest gone mad. She kept them in a pink handkerchief, and showed them to me one summer night when we both couldn't sleep. I remembered the fireflies, and Freddie's handkerchief smelling like rose petals, and the humid night air, and the ginger lemonade, and soft, wrinkled, familiar hands.

I reached up and tugged on a strand of ivy. It had been hiding the words carved into the stone over the door. They swooped and curled and glowed in the moonlight like something from Middle-earth.

"Is it in Elvish?" River asked, not two seconds after the thought of Tolkien danced through my brain.

"*Mea Culpa. By That Sin Fell the Angels. Exuro, Exuro, Exuro.*" I stood on tiptoe and traced the words with my fingers. "*Mea culpa* translates as *my fault*, which you probably know. The second line is from Shakespeare, *Henry VIII*. The end is *I burn, I burn, I burn*. Freddie had it carved up in there decades ago, and would never tell me what it meant. I finally had to do some research at the library. I translated the Latin, but as far as what Freddie meant by it . . ."

"She's sorry," Neely said, speaking for the first time since River had woken him up. He looked sweet and disheveled in wrinkled linen pants and his Windbreaker. "She's sorry for the sins she committed. And the burning is the fires of hell."

"I think not," I replied. Freddie wasn't burning in hell. I was sure of that, if nothing else.

I tapped the rusted-out lock on the door of the mausoleum, and it shook flakes of metal onto the ground. I supposed I could break it with a rock if I wanted to. Who the hell knew where the key was anyway.

But wait.

The names might be on the outside, buried under green leaves.

I moved to the other side of the tomb and pulled back the ivy.

The first name that came into view was True White. My aunt. The little girl that drowned. The ghost that River conjured up to scare Luke. The daughter that drove Freddie into the arms of God, and the Devil.

But the name we were all staring at wasn't True's.

ROSE REDDING
Beloved daughter, beloved sister
Murdered on her 16th birthday, June 8th, 1929

I pulled out the red card and the five letters I'd been keeping in my pocket. I gave the flashlight to River. He read everything. Silently. And then he gave the letters to Neely.

"Did you know?" I asked River, after a few more long moments of silence. "Did your grandpa talk to you about Freddie, and Echo, and is that why you came here? Did you know he had the glow too?"

River paused. His eyes held mine. Then he leaned back onto the blanket of ivy covering the mausoleum and nodded.

"My grandfather called it the *burn*. And yes. A few years before his death he started talking to me. That's when I first learned that this thing of mine, this glow, ran in the family. My father didn't have it, but my grandpa did. And I learned about a woman named Freddie, who was the only girl Will Redding ever loved. I learned about a town named Echo, where my grandpa lost control of his burn, and it got his sister killed. He tried to warn me, back before he died. But it was too late. Dad already had me working for him, and I'd gone too far with it. I was already addicted. I thought . . . I thought if I came here, to Echo, I might . . . I don't know. It might help me."

"It didn't," Neely said.

And I was thinking the same thing.

River looked at me, and his eyes were sort of pleading. "I got to Echo and found out Freddie had a granddaughter that looked just like her. And this granddaughter was looking for someone to rent the guesthouse. It seemed too good to be true. I thought it was fate. I thought . . . I thought you were going to save me, Vi."

"I'm *trying*," I said.

"I *know*," he said back. River reached for me . . . and then stopped. He put his hands back down. "It's not about that, Vi. It's not about Freddie, and my grandfather. It's not about the glow. It's about you sitting on those great big steps, reading in the sun. It's about the way you drink coffee on your tiptoes. It's about you being direct and shy at the same time, and caring and eccentric and kind of a snob. It's all of it." River stopped talking for a second, but his eyes didn't leave mine. "There's never been anyone before. Any girl. I don't know what I'm doing. Vi. Vi, look at me. Do you believe it? Do you believe what I'm telling you?"

He said the last part fast, really fast, like he was embarrassed, maybe.

"No. You're a liar." But it didn't come out as sharp as I wanted it to.

Neely laughed. "She's got you there, River. Told you there'd be consequences for all that ly—"

A shout. A kid's shout. Almost a scream. It came from the direction of the Glenship mausoleum.

We all looked around at each other, and then took off toward the sound. As we neared the old tomb, I saw two kids moving in the shadows. A tall, lean, black-haired boy. And a smaller boy, cowering on the ground by a headstone, his arms covering his face because the older boy was kicking the hell out of him. His wails filled the night air; they were ghostly, gossamer things, weak and pathetic and heartbreaking.

Neely shouted, *"No, River, let me do it, don't touch him,"* but it was too late. River threw his shoulder into the older boy, knocking him back against the mausoleum. He grabbed the bully by his shirt and dragged him into a standing position. Then he put a hand on the kid's throat and pushed him into the ivy-covered wall. Hard.

The boy's head jerked back and cracked against the stone.

"River, *stop*," I called out. It was the boy from a few days ago. The bully. *Casablanca* and the yo-yos. "He's just a kid. *Stop*."

River ignored me.

"Beating up a kid half your size?" River yelled. "You think that's *fair*? You think that's *okay*?"

The bully squirmed underneath River's hand. He raised

one arm and pointed it at the boy crumpled on the ground. "I came in here, looking for a place to smoke, and that kid had the balls to tell me to leave. Because of the Devil. The *Devil*. Those lying little brats told everyone they saw the fucking Devil, and made our town look stupid. And then I catch one of them, telling *me* to leave the cemetery. That little *shit*."

I knelt down by the boy on the ground. I recognized him. He was the blond kid who had hesitated by the gate when the other kids were leaving the cemetery. He was dirty, and his clothes were torn, and there was blood coming from his mouth and his nose. He swiped a hand across his eyes and glared at the black-haired boy.

"I'm not a liar. The Devil was here. We saw him. We all saw him."

The bully struggled in River's grasp. "*You lying little shit. I'm gonna kick you until your chest caves in and your lying little heart squeezes out between your ribs—*"

Neely shot forward and ripped River's hands away from the black-haired kid. The boy stood frozen for a moment, eyes staring stark white out of the shadows, and then he darted off into the trees like a deer.

Neely's hands were shaking. I could see them, moving in and out of the moonlight. His breath was coming fast. His shaking hands tightened into fists. "Did you? Did you, River? Did you use the glow on that kid?" Neely's voice had changed. It was low, and kind of eager, as if he *wanted* River to say yes.

River put his hands on his temples. "I . . . I don't know. I just— My hands were on his throat, and I was so mad, and I—"

Neely pulled his right fist back, the one with the scars that ended at his wrist, and hit River dead across the face.

River's head jerked to the side and he stumbled back. He brought his hand up to his cheek and looked at his brother. "Thanks" was all he said. He shook his brown hair away from his forehead, kind of cocky. Almost, *almost* like he was inviting Neely to do it again.

"Come on," Neely said, and his voice was tense and excited now. He circled River for a second. Then he threw his fist out again, smooth and fast and hard.

River glided out of the way like it was nothing to him. Neely put his head forward and ran his body hard into River's side. Both of them hit the ground and rolled. Neely came up on top, but River had him—his arm was wrapped around Neely's neck and wasn't going anywhere.

"Are you done?" River shouted. *"Are you done?"*

"Yes. Yes, damn it," Neely whispered back, because the

inside of River's elbow was pressing on his throat.

River let go. He got to his feet, and so did Neely. River looked at his brother, and then looked at me, and then he walked off down the hill.

I turned to the blond boy. "Are you hurt?" I asked, stupidly.

"A little," he replied, his right hand pressing into his ribs and his left hand swiping at the blood coming out his mouth. "But I'll be all right."

I moved his hand and felt around his little chest to see if anything was broken.

"Here, let me." Neely knelt down beside me. He was breathing fast, still, but he seemed . . . calmer, somehow, after the fight. "I've had first aid training. I did a summer as a volunteer EMT."

Neely searched the kid over. His knuckles were bloody, either from hitting River or from hitting the ground, but he didn't flinch as he moved his hands. He was gentle and efficient and not remotely bothered by the blond boy's dark, staring eyes, as I was.

"You're in luck," Neely said, after a few minutes. "No broken bones. Only bruises. You had better go home and let your mother put some ice on those."

The kid pressed his hands into the muddy earth and pushed himself to his feet.

Neely put a hand on his shoulder. "You shouldn't come back in here. There is no devil, and there never was, okay? Promise me you will stay out of the cemetery."

"I'll try," the boy answered, his dark eyes blinking at Neely, and his hand on his ribs. He turned and walked down the path.

I watched him until the stubborn black night swallowed him up.

And then I felt warm fingers intertwine with my own. Neely had grabbed my hand and now stood shoulder to shoulder with me, facing the woods. I could feel drying blood under my fingertips.

"I'll go look for the other boy later," he said. "I don't know what River glowed at him, but it . . . it couldn't have been good. I'll need to clean it up."

I nodded. And then we walked back to the Citizen, listening to the late-night creatures sing their late-night songs. Neely's fingers stayed tight around mine, until I let go.

≋

When we got back to the guesthouse, River was missing, still. Neely went looking for him around the grounds. It was late. A few hours from dawn. The grass was dewy and the air was moist and cool, almost cold. The moon was out, and everything was quiet, except the ocean. Even the crickets had gone silent.

I went home, dug around in the Citizen's freezer, and found some ice. I grabbed two washcloths, put four ice cubes in each, and went outside. I sat down on the front steps, in the spot where the light from the foyer spilled out the front windows.

Neely showed up a few minutes later. No River.

"Here," I said, handing him one of the cloths.

He grinned, and the bruise under his eye stood out stronger for a second. He put the ice on his swollen hand. "Thanks, sweetheart. A guy could get used to this—being taken care of after a fight."

"Everything's going to be all right with the bully, you know," I lied, because sometimes a girl needs to lie. "I'm sure River just made him see Cthulhu or something on the way home."

"Yeah. Maybe." Neely laughed. "I shouldn't have . . . My brother just really, *really* pisses me off. So . . ." He lifted his wounded hand and gestured to the bruise on his face. "Sorry you had to see that."

"It's all right. I've wanted to hit River myself, a few times."

"He'll do that to a person." Neely sighed, and I saw that sad smile, again, the one from before. "I know it seems like I'm not taking his problems seriously, but I am. I worry about him. Constantly. I just think you should know that."

"I do."

And Neely was grinning again. "Does anything get by you, Vi?"

I shrugged, thinking about Luke and Sunshine, and Freddie's hidden letters, and Daniel Leap's secret. "Yeah. Lots of things."

He laughed. "Well, I'm going for a walk. I don't want to be here when River comes crawling home because I'll probably just punch him again. I'll be back soon, okay?"

"Okay."

Neely left. The four ice cubes I'd kept for River melted in my hand and dripped onto the ground. I traced the edge of the red skirt I was wearing (Freddie's) and thought about the blood on the blond boy's mouth, and Rose Redding with her throat slit, and the letters, and River.

He showed up about twenty minutes later. He swaggered up the Citizen's front steps like always, and smiled at me like a damned angel.

"I think Neely's been wanting to do that for a long time." River laughed, putting his fingers on his cheek. It was swollen and evil-looking and starting to bruise. Brothers with matching smiles. And matching bruises.

I went inside, to the kitchen, and River followed. I fished some fresh ice cubes out of the freezer, put them in a dishtowel, and handed it to him without a word. A feeling had stirred in me, looking at River's bruised, smiling face, and it was hard and strong and bitter, like over-brewed black coffee without milk or sugar.

"Stop smiling, River," I said. "You don't even know if you used the glow on that boy. Do you understand how dangerous that makes you? Do you understand what that means?"

River pressed the ice to his face, and the cocky light dimmed in his eyes. "Do you think we can talk about this later? My face hurts. Tomorrow we can figure out what's to be done with me. I'll pack, and I'll leave, and I'll go home, screw everything up, and run off again." He paused. "The next town won't have you, though. Which kind of pisses me off, when I think about it."

And he sounded half sincere. Which was something.

I stared at him for a second. "The things you said in the cemetery, before we heard the kid's screams, about there never having been another girl before me. You were telling the truth, weren't you?"

River looked at the wall, and kind of, well, fidgeted, in a way that Neely would have laughed at had he seen. "Yes. Yes, I was."

"Are you lying?"

"Yes."

"Did you just lie, again?"

"Yes."

River let out a long sigh. And the last bit of his cockiness flickered, and went out. He looked younger, suddenly.

"Vi, would you please sleep next to me tonight? Please?"

"All right," I said. Because it would be the last time. Besides, I kind of believed him, about the things he said in the cemetery.

We went to River's bedroom in the guesthouse, opened his windows so a sea breeze could drift in, and slipped under the covers. River winced when his swollen cheek touched the pillow. I didn't kiss him, and he didn't kiss me, but I drifted to sleep with his arms around me and his face in my hair.

And I dreamed.

I dreamed about cemeteries. And a tunnel. And a man with furry teeth, and a slit in his neck. I dreamed about the Devil, who looked liked River except he had red hair and bloody red eyes. Only it wasn't the Devil. Or River. It was Neely, his blond hair red from the setting sun, his face red from fighting. Fighting with River, who was suddenly kissing me, and I was feeling so good, so good, because River was kissing my neck, and then my shoulders, and I slipped out of my clothes and he helped me and then I helped him do the same and we were naked, and I didn't care, and I just wanted the River kissing to go on and on forever and ever and ever amen and everything felt right and I knew it was time and I wanted him, oh how I wanted him . . .

A door slammed.

I jerked awake.

I took a deep breath. And opened my eyes.

It was almost dawn, the light an eerie bluish dark gray. I'd only been asleep a few hours. And I was in River's bed. I'd been dreaming. Just dreaming. Such a good dream.

Damn that door for slamming.

But wait. Something was different. I felt warm. Hot, even. My skin tingled. I moved.

And suddenly I realized what was different. I was naked.

And so was River.

Our bodies were pressed against each other, tight. My dream. *My dream had been real.* River's naked body was curled into mine, and it felt so right, like in the dream . . .

"Violet?" River whispered.

"Yeah," I said, really quiet. I took another deep breath, and my chest swelled into River's body. I let my breath back out. My eyes met his. He moved his hands and pressed them into my lower back.

"I think I was . . . I think I was using the glow in my sleep. I didn't even know I could do that. Aw, hell. We, we almost . . . God, I'm sorry, Vi. I don't know what's happening to me . . ."

I didn't move.

"Neely's right," River said, and his voice sounded unsure, and tense, and very un-River. "I'm out of control."

"Yes," I answered. And still, I didn't move.

"Violet, I'm not safe," River said, at last. *"You're not safe around me.* You should go. Get out. Vi, get *out. Now.*"

My heart shut down, shuddered, and started back up again. I slid out of River's arms, and out of the bed. My clothes were scattered on the floor, mixed in with his. I got dressed. Left.

Then I turned around, went back down the hall, and back into River's bedroom.

"River, you need to leave Echo," I whispered. I stood by his bed, with my hands on my heart, and waited. River shifted, and the blankets fell off his body, exposing his naked hip down to the thigh. "Tomorrow. And I don't want to see you before you go, all right?"

"Get out of here, Violet" was all River said.

And so I did. I left.

≈≈≈

Neely was in the guesthouse kitchen. He was drinking coffee from a small pink cup with a chip in it. His back was to the window, and the sunrise was starting up behind him.

"Neely, I don't know how you can drink so much coffee." My voice broke a bit when I said it. I took the cup from him and swallowed what was left in one go. I felt a little better, with the joe burning its way down my throat.

Neely looked at me. He was smiling, but his eyes were digging into mine.

"You all right, Vi?"

"Yep. Completely." But my hands were still shaking, and Neely knew I was River-lying.

"Okay," he replied. "I'll leave that for now. Want to know where I've been?"

I didn't.

"I tried to track down the kid that River glowed," Neely continued, when I didn't answer. "I went back to the cemetery and followed that trail through the trees for a while. But nothing. I'm worried about him."

I stared out the window and wouldn't meet Neely's eyes. "Me too," I said at last.

Neely looked at me. Really looked at me.

"So why are you awake?" he asked. "Why aren't you still sleeping in my brother's bed, buried in his arms, breaking your promise to not let him touch you?"

I shook my head and didn't answer.

"What happened?" Neely asked, his voice quiet. "Violet, what happened?"

I looked at Neely's right hand, the swollen one. The one that hit his brother across the face. "Will you promise not to start fighting again?"

"No." He paused, and ran his hand through his hair, and looked like River. "Yes. Yes, I promise. So help me God, Vi."

"River used the glow on me. In his sleep. He didn't mean to . . . but he did it anyway. And things were happening, and we were both letting them happen, but then I heard the front door open, and it woke me up. In time." I added that last bit of information, only because Neely's eyes were doing the antsy, eager thing they'd done before, a second before he punched River.

Neely took a deep breath and grabbed my hand. He squeezed it, hard, so hard, his fresh scabs split open and started bleeding again. And we just stood there, quiet, in the guesthouse kitchen, with the sun rising, and the sea breeze coming through the windows.

CHAPTER 25

SOMEONE WAS SAYING my name in a soft voice. I batted my eyes against the bright morning sun, and turned to see who had decided to wake me this morning. Sunshine? Luke? Neely? I stretched, and realized that there was no one next to me in bed.

River.

I sat up and rubbed my eyes. And then the memories from the night before flooded my brain and woke me up faster than a bucket of cold water. River leaving. He was in trouble, out of control. The glow. The letters—

"Violet?"

It was Jack. He was standing in a sunbeam at the end of the bed, looking serious as usual. "Jack. Hey. I was sleeping. Alone." *Concentrate, Violet.* "What's going on?"

"I went walking this morning," he said. "I wanted to find the perfect tree, and paint it. But I found . . . something else. In the ditch, by the tracks."

I looked at him, uncomprehending.

"I need you to come with me," Jack continued. "Now."

I nodded. "All right."

I brushed my hair, and my teeth, threw on a green skirt and a soft, long-sleeved button-down that my mom used to paint in. Jack waited for me outside. I didn't tell anyone I was leaving, not Luke, not Neely, not . . . River. I told River I didn't want to see him before he left. And I wasn't sure I still meant it.

Damn.

I followed Jack down the path to Echo, past the tunnel, past the cemetery. The sun was bright in the sky, and the dew on the grass was making my feet slick inside my flip-flops.

We heard a train whistle go off in the distance, and Jack's small shoulders stiffened in front of me. We had passed the town center and were walking by the empty field that led off from Glenship Street, and *still* Jack hadn't said a word. And it was making me nervous.

"For God's sake, what did you see, Jack?"

But Jack only shook his head. We walked another couple of minutes. I could hear the creek now, the one that circled the town and, some miles away, dropped into the sea. I swatted at a mosquito, and grimaced at the streak of blood it left on my arm.

When I looked up, Jack had stopped walking. He was pointing at the tracks.

Trains still went through Echo. The tracks near the Citizen had disappeared long ago, but there was still an active line that ran outside town, carrying cargo and, less often, passengers, all the way into Canada. Jack was pointing down a tree-lined stretch of those tracks.

He slipped his hand into mine, and together we stepped onto the rails. I listened for the sound of a train, but heard nothing but the mourning doves, coo coo-ing to each other in that husky, melancholy way they had. Jack pulled on my hand, and we half walked, half slid down the ditch on the other side of the tracks.

When we got to the bottom, I looked at Jack, puzzled. His red-brown hair was glinting in the sunlight. His face was pale.

And then I saw it.

Him.

Black hair, tangled, and clotted with dried blood. That's what I noticed first. The rest of the boy was hidden in the shadows cast by the trees. But his face was in the sun. I stumbled to the side, and almost stepped on the dead boy's hand. My mouth made a noise, a screaming, wailing noise, and the rest of me shivered at the sound of it.

"He was hit by a train, I guess," Jack said. "The conductor probably didn't even hear him. He bounced off, and . . . rolled."

I didn't answer. I was looking at the dead boy's eyes. His eyes, which had been so angry in the cemetery, with River's hand gripping his neck, were now wide and staring. And dead. Dead, dead, dead. This was different from seeing Daniel Leap, cutting his throat in the town square. The body in front of me had belonged to a kid. Just a kid. And his head was twisted at a horrid, unnatural angle, and his skin was purple and gray, and his black hair was dirty and full of leaves and blood and oh hell, I was looking at a dead boy, close enough to touch his poor dead boy body—

"Did River do it, Violet? Did he make him step in front of the train? I haven't told anyone else. I don't want River to get in trouble. I was going to tell the cops, but then I thought, what if it was River?"

I dropped Jack's hand, turned to the side, and threw up.

Jack patted me on the back, and I kept throwing up, again and again. And when there was nothing left I still threw up, the dry heaves racking my body and making me shake like the leaves on the trees that hid the dead boy's body from the light.

Finally, finally, I straightened. I walked over to the creek, put my bare knees on its muddy banks, and splashed cold creek water on my face. I rinsed out my mouth. And then went back to Jack, and the body.

"River is out of control, Jack. It was him, in the attic. I'm sure of it. He's dangerous. To me. To you. To everyone. So . . . so here's what is going to happen. You are going to go to the café, or the library, and stay there until I come for you. I don't want you to be involved in any of this. I'm going to Sunshine's. I'm going to use her phone, and call the police station in Portland." I ran the back of my hand over my forehead. My face was cold, but whether it was from the cold creek water or the clammy throwing up I'd done, I didn't know.

"Go back to town," I said, when Jack just stood there, watching me and not moving.

"Aren't you coming too?" he asked, and his voice was sweet and serious and concerned.

I shook my head. "I'm going to wait here for a few minutes. I don't want anyone to see us walking back into town together. I don't want anyone to know you're involved with . . . this."

Jack stared at me a second, nodded, and then he was gone.

The mourning doves cooed. A crow cawed from the

top of a tree. The shadows danced around as clouds passed in front of the sun. The boy's whole body was in dark now. I wanted to help him. I wanted to move him so he looked more comfortable, I wanted to—

"Hey there."

For a second, a wild, mad second, I thought it was the dead boy talking to me. I thought he'd come back to life. I thought I'd gone insane. I put my hand on my heart and leaned over and stared at the dead boy's mouth and eyes, waiting for them to move.

And then the back of my neck prickled.

I turned around.

A boy. A not-dead boy. Standing not ten feet away in the darkness underneath the closely packed trees. Fourteen, maybe, but still taller than me. Vaguely familiar. Did I know him? He was skinny, all bones and elbows and legs. And his hair. His hair was long, down to his shoulders, and red. Red like the sky in the morning, sailors take warning. Fire red. Blood red.

He was wearing black cowboy boots and fitted, expensive-looking black jeans, and a plain white T-shirt. His eyes were green, and wide open, and surprised.

He nodded at the body. "Yes, ma'am. It's quite a si . . . quite a sight," he said, his voice cracking halfway through. He had a southern accent, but not Deep South. McMurtry south.

Texas, maybe. "I stumbled upon it while watching the trains go by. That's how I got here." He nodded toward the tracks. "By train. I like to watch them. Ride them sometimes."

I stared at him. I tried not to shake. Tried not to panic. "How long have you been standing there?"

Please don't let him have heard that stuff about River, oh God, please, I thought. Even though I'd already planned to tell the cops, and it didn't matter anyway.

"Only for about five seconds, ma'am. I live in Echo. I started for town, to get help, but then I saw you and the other kid coming, so I just hid in the trees until I knew what you were about." He held out his hand. "The name's Brodie."

I shook his hand. It was skinny, but tough. His fingers gripped mine . . . and let go. "Brodie? I don't think I've . . . Have I seen you before? Did you just move here?"

He nodded, fast. His red hair parted at the movement and the tops of his ears broke through. They stuck out a bit and made him seem even younger. "I've only been in Echo a few days." He reached down and picked up something at his feet. It was a black cowboy hat. He slapped the hat on his head, and some of the red disappeared in a flash, like a lightbulb going out. "I'm from Texas."

I'd seen that hat before. The kid, sitting on the swings, when Daniel Leap killed himself—he'd been wearing a hat like that.

The clouds shifted, and the sun broke through again. The dead boy's face was back in the light. And I realized I'd just been having a get-to-know-you conversation with a kid from Texas with my toes twelve inches from a corpse.

"Texas, right . . ." I said, barely noticing. All I was thinking about again was River, and turning him in, and what they would do to him, and what it would do to me. "I've got to go make a phone call, so I . . . I can't talk right now. I've got to go home and . . ."

"Would you mind if I came with, ma'am?" Brodie took his hat back off and held it at his side. "You're going to call the cops, is that right? Well, I can wait with you and then tell them what I saw. I'd like to help you out. You look a bit pale, to be honest. I've seen a dead boy before. There are lots of dead bodies in Texas. So I don't mind so much."

But my mind was a million miles away and I didn't answer. And when I started walking back to town, Brodie just followed me. The part of me that could still notice things noticed this. But what difference did it make? What difference did it make if he came with and told his side of the story to the cops too?

We took the back roads when we reached town, so we could skirt the main square. I didn't want to explain to anyone why my legs were covered in mud, why my hair was dripping with creek water, why I looked sick, why I was walking next to some kid named Brodie. I was certain that if one person stopped and asked me what was wrong, I would open my mouth and confess everything. The glow. River. The Devil. The dead boy. Everything.

If Brodie talked on the way home, I already couldn't remember.

Everything was silent at the Citizen. I went to the shed, but Luke wasn't painting. The guesthouse was quiet. When I put my ear to the door and listened for sounds of breakfast being made, coffee sizzling in the moka pot, eggs frying in the pan, Neely and River fighting, there was nothing.

I stood in my backyard and shivered. There was a bad feeling in the air, like a storm brewing. Except the sky was clear. The sun was bright, and the air was warm. Something was making my skin crawl, though. *Something* was giving me the feeling that I was being watched.

I looked around. No one. No one was anywhere.

"I don't know where anyone is," I said. "It's . . . strange."

Brodie just smiled and shrugged.

I started to waver. I walked toward the Citizen's front steps and considered crawling back into bed. Forgetting what I saw. Forgetting the dead boy, his hair clotted with blood. Forgetting Daniel Leap slicing the razor across his throat. Forgetting it all.

But then I looked at Brodie, with his red hair and his hat and his ma'ams.

He'd seen the body too.

There was no forgetting. No covering it up.

"Just stay here," I said, not being all that polite and not caring. "I'm going to go to the neighbor's and use the phone. It's easier if you stay here. Okay?"

Brodie tipped his black hat at me and then pointed at the ground by his feet, as if to say *I'm glued to this spot*.

I took a deep breath. And started walking down the road. To Sunshine's house.

Sunshine wasn't outside, sitting on her swing. *She must be sleeping too*, I thought. I wondered what the hell time it was in the morning. Sunshine was an early riser, like Luke, and I didn't really know what early morning people did, when they got up and when they ate breakfast or how they spent their early morning time. I had never been one of them, except for the times serious boys woke me up at the crack of seven a.m. to show me dead bodies by the railroad tracks.

The front door of Sunshine's house was open. I knocked on the screen, but didn't wait for a reply. I stepped inside.

I saw Sunshine's parents. Sam and Cassie stood beside each other in the living room—Sam was lost-looking and corduroy as usual and Cassie was black hair and glasses. They were staring at something on the floor.

The thing on the floor was Sunshine. She was lying on her stomach, and she was bleeding. Blood oozed from a slick dent near her temple, dripped across her face, and pooled on the floor beside her.

Sunshine saw me. She opened her mouth. She was trying to say something, but the only thing that came out was spit, and more blood. She coughed, and blood sprayed between her teeth.

"Maybe you need to hit it again," Cassie said. "Look, it's trying to move."

Sam had a bat in one hand. I hadn't noticed. *Why hadn't I noticed that bat? When did Sunshine's bookish parents get a baseball bat?* Sunshine's fingers reached out and touched my bare toes, and I wanted to help her, I wanted to help her, but I couldn't move. I was stock-still and frozen, trying to scream but making no sound and Sunshine wasn't moving at all anymore and Sam's bat had blood and matted hair on it, and why hadn't I seen it when I first came in, Sunshine, blood, bat, I was shaking and screaming a silent scream—

And Cassie finally saw me.

She smiled. Her eyes had a funny, staring, dead-boy-by-the-tracks look in them. "Hello, Violet. Do you want some tea? We've had quite a morning. A rat got into the house. But Sam has killed it with his bat. Look at it there, by your feet. Isn't it disgusting? It's probably carrying rabies. Sam is going to take it out back and burn it. Violet, you look upset. Is something wrong?"

Sam looked up then. He took one look at me and raised the bat in the air. "I told you there'd be more than one, Cassie. Rats come in hordes. Get out of the way. I've got to kill this one too—"

He swung the bat, and I ducked. The hard wood bounced off my temple and I stumbled backward. I didn't fall, but there he was swinging again, and God, I didn't want to leave Sunshine, but I could hear the bat cutting through the air and—

I ran. I ran out the door, stumbled, ran down the steps, stumbled again, ran past the woods, past the ocean, down the driveway, and straight toward Citizen Kane.

Brodie was waiting for me. He was standing by the fountain. He saw me running and didn't seem surprised, didn't seem surprised at all. He was stroking the dirty nude fountain girls with one hand and smiling.

"How is Sunshine?" he asked, nice and slow, as I came to a stop in front of him, sweating and sick because my whole damn world was shaking and falling apart. "Is the little slut dead yet?"

And then he looked at me, *right* at me, and he winked.

CHAPTER 26

I TRIED TO RUN. My feet slipped in the gravel and I fell. My palms skidded across the small rocks and maybe it hurt but I couldn't tell, because I was already up and running again, running toward the Citizen, to safety.

He caught me on the steps. Grabbed me, hard.

"Maybe we should introduce ourselves again. The name's Brodie." His skinny fingers gripped my left elbow. He jerked me back to the ground. "And you must be Violet."

He let go of me, as if he knew I wouldn't run. And I didn't.

"What do you want?" I asked. Though I didn't want to know. "Who are you?"

Brodie opened his mouth, and shut it again. He tilted his head to the side, and his expression went slack.

His eyes looked younger for a second, younger and—

He straightened his head, and the look went away.

"Who am I?" He flipped his cowboy hat off with one hand. His boots tapped on the driveway, tap, tap, tap on the old, cracking pavement. "Well . . . I could be the Devil, I suppose. Or I could be River and Neely's younger brother. Which would you like? Take your pick." His voice had changed. It wasn't fast and kind of eager and enthusiastic. It was low. And he spoke in a slow, languid drawl now, dragging out the words as if reluctant to let them go, like a miser with his gold.

Brother. *Brother.*

He stepped toward me. His eyes had changed too. They were narrow, as if from squinting in the sun. And cocky. Those cocky, narrow eyes. They were familiar.

I moved back. He laughed. It was a hoarse sound. A hoarse, *familiar* sound.

I'd heard that laughter before.

In the Glenship attic.

I smelled smoke, and gas, like I was still back there, with Gianni and Jack.

"Not going to let me come near you, then. Right. Because River told you about the glow. Both of my brothers have big mouths, but of the two I think River's is the biggest. You?"

I didn't answer. I pressed my hands to my heart, pushed my palms in deep, tried to make the beat slow down.

Brodie laughed again, took a step closer. "Hey, you don't need to worry. I don't glow like River. Not by touching. I spark. And I need blood to do it." Brodie paused. His narrow eyes went strange again, like before—they looked very green, and a little bit . . . lost. Then his face softened and became almost dreamy. "If I wasn't such a violent youngster, I probably wouldn't have figured it out, not for years. And wouldn't that have been a shame? Look at this."

Brodie slipped his hand into his boot and pulled something from it, a thin, four-inch piece of silver with a pearl handle. A knife.

I'd seen that knife before, cutting up an apple to give to a little kid at *Brief Encounter* in the town square.

"I got this thing made special," he said, waving it in front of my eyes. "For my girlfriend. She was a sweet thing, sweet as sugar with sugar on top, and innocent as a day-old colt. I liked to cut her. I liked to watch her cry."

He slid the knife back into his boot.

"I'll be damned if we didn't just meet and yet I'm talking away as if we've known each other for years. I think it's because you look like Sophie. My little Sophie. Blond hair, pale skin, drippy fear in your drippy blue eyes.

Hmmm . . . I would like to cut you sometime. Watch you cry. I think you'd like it. I *know* I would."

He hesitated, and the fingers of his right hand tapped the ends of his red hair. "Let's see, where was I? Oh, yes. So I live in Texas. Or I used to. I'm only River and Neely's half brother, to be frank. Different mothers. Pa, he didn't have much use for me. He paid the bills, and came to town once in a while, on account of some Redding oil interests in Abilene, and to get himself a bit of Texas honey. Until Ma up and went deranged, that is. Now she's rotting in some asylum and I haven't seen her since." Brodie's body went still. No boots rapping, no fingers tapping. The only thing that moved was his red, red hair, lifting in a breeze coming off the sea. "She used to call me the Mongrel. Did you know that?"

I shook my head.

Brodie's eyes shifted to the side for a second, not looking at me. "Well, she's locked up with the screamers and the droolers and she got hers, didn't she. But back to the point. The last time Papa Redding came for a visit, we had a strange talk. William Redding II, he's as cold as ice in hell, so when he tells me about a glow, and starts asking me questions, questions about my thoughts coming true, and making people do things just by thinking them . . . well. I paid attention."

I snapped my head around, trying to spot River, or Neely, or Luke. *Someone*. Where were they? Had Brodie already gotten to them? Had he already—

"Pay attention, Violet." Brodie's voice was harsh, suddenly, his words fast. "I don't like to be ignored. Eyes on mine. *Eyes on mine*."

I put my eyes on his. Brodie's eyes were green and narrow and mad-mad-mad and I felt that I would go mad too if I stared into his eyes for much longer. But I clenched my fists and didn't look away.

"There, that's better," Brodie said, his voice slow and languid again. "So, a few months ago, I was using my little knife on Sophie, and, well, I tried making her do something. With my mind. It had never worked before. I'd been trying it, off and on, since Pa and I had our chat. But it worked then. Oh, hell, did it work then. So much for saving yourself, darling Sophie. I took it from you, and you were happy to give it, oh yes you were."

He opened his mouth and licked his bottom lip.

"Sunshine," I whispered. "What did you do to Sunshine?"

He shrugged, his narrow shoulders disappearing into his red hair. "Nothing. She flashed those bosoms at me, white and fine as a bucket of fresh cream, peeking out of the top of that whore-red dress. So I asked her where you were, and she said you were walking toward town with the orphan brat. I followed her back home, and met her parents. And they met my little knife. I'm pretty quick with the thing. You'll be surprised. I knifed both their skinny palms as easy as shaking their hands. And then I found you ten minutes later, and Jack brought us both to the body. I'm pretty quiet, when I need to be. You didn't hear a thing."

Tears were running down my face now. They were slipping out the corners of my eyes and leaving a wet trail down my neck. River wasn't the Devil. He had never been the Devil. The red boy standing before me with his knife was the true Devil. In the flesh. I knew it like I knew the smell of paint drying on a canvas. I knew it like I knew the feel of my own heartbeat in my chest.

"But . . . but Sunshine's dad hit her in the head with a bat. A *bat*." There was a high, pleading sort of sound in my voice. I hated it. "She's hurt—"

"Way to go, Papa Sam." Brodie stuck his thumbs inside the pockets of his jeans and then let his gaze slide down my body. "Want to know a secret, Violet?"

I shook my head.

"Oh, yes, you do. I, Brodie Redding, have been in this nowhere shit town for three days. I can tell by your face that you're surprised, Violet. As was I—I track down one brother and the other shows up too. Of course, both are too stupid to notice I'm here. If there is anyone more tedious than you and River, with your glow talk and your kissing, it's Neely. Always fighting, like a damn savage. This whole trip has been dull from one end to the other. I had to burn a witch on the way here, just to stop me from blowing my brains out with boredom."

Brodie smiled, as if he liked thinking on that. "But back to the point, Vi. I've been watching you. You and River and Jack and Luke and the rat girl. Eating pizza. Painting. Sleeping. Oh, yes, ma'am. All the windows in the guest-house are wide open and three feet off the ground, and I've been in and out of Citizen Kane more times than I can count. I've seen it all. Heard it all. Has it never occurred to you to lock the Citizen's doors once in a while? I've been coming and going as I please these last few days, watching all of you paint together and kiss each other and adopt random redheaded orphans who don't even— Who can't even—" He paused.

"Anyway, it was too damn easy. And easy things bore me. I'm bored. Bored, Violet."

"It was you," I whispered. "The laughing in the attic. The bully. River didn't forget. He didn't do it, just like he said." I felt dirty and exposed and weak with fear and I just wanted to go back to bed and wake up, *except that it wasn't a nightmare. Sunshine was really hurt and the boy was really dead and everything was going to get a whole lot worse than it already was.*

"Now, Violet. Give River his fair share. I sparked up your Italian pizza boy, it's true. Once I found that rotting mansion, I knew I had to use it as a setting for some mischief. What a fine place to set someone on fire. And it was all going so well until Neely stuck his nose in, that fist-slinging halfwit. But that dead brat by the tracks was all River's. Yes, ma'am. Neely was out prowling for the boy, trying to save him, the sentimental simpleton. But now we know that the brat was already lying in the ditch, bloody, swollen, and dead as a widow from the waist down."

Brodie whistled, low and long.

He'd been here, the whole time. It was true. He'd been right in front of us, laughing and spying and plotting evil.

My head was tingling and my throat stung, like I was swallowing smoke.

He was going to kill me. He was going to kill us. All of us.

"Why?" was all I said. And then I said it again. *"Why?"*

Brodie just kept whistling the first few bars of something sad and folksy. "Well, should we go see what my brothers are up to?" he said finally. "Hmmm? Don't shake your head at me, darling. Come on now."

I lunged forward. I was going to run. Run to Echo, get help, *just go, go*—

And my head jerked. Pain rippled over my scalp. The red boy had grabbed my hair in his fist. He yanked me back to his side.

Brodie's green eyes stared down at me, through me, like they were trying to dig their way into my soul. "You're going to play a part in this thing I'm planning, whether you like it or not. So you might as well save time and do as you're told."

A scream. Coming from the woods. Jack. He was running and screaming *Let her go let her go* and he came right at us—

I saw a flash of silver.

And Jack was down.

Down in the dirt, blue eyes shut, and a line of blood breaking out across the freckles on his cheek.

Brodie crouched over Jack's still-as-stone body. He grabbed a bit of his hair, and twisted it between two fingers. "It's not even pure red," he said. "Just this shit muddy auburn color. Frankly, I don't see the appeal."

Brodie stood up, took the toe of his boot, and slid it under Jack's body. One quick kick and he'd flipped Jack over on his belly so his face was in the dirt. Brodie shoved me out of the way, reached down, and yanked the back of

Jack's shirt up. Jack's pale skin gleamed in the bright sun.

"You'll want to watch this," Brodie said. "I'm going to cut him. Slower this time." His tongue ran over his lower lip. "You're thinking about running for help, aren't you, Vi. I can always tell when my victims are about to bolt. But do it and I'll kill Jack instead of cut him. No"—he glanced up at me— "you aren't going anywhere, Violet White. I have great plans for you. I'm going to make you bleed. I'm going to cut you and cut you and make you bleed and bleed."

I thought when Sunshine fainted, I was scared. I thought when I saw the Devil over River's shoulders, I was scared. I thought when I saw Jack tied up in the attic, and the dead boy by the tracks, and Sunshine bleeding from the head, and Sam with the bat, I thought I couldn't get more scared. But that was only the beginning. The beginning. And the middle. All leading up to the red boy in front of me.

This was the end.

CHAPTER 27

HE DRAGGED ME to the guesthouse, one hand pulling me by my shirt, the other clawing through my hair, his thin, hard fingers twitching and jerking until his nails drew blood.

I tried to turn, tried to call out to Jack—he was still on the ground, not moving, his skin crisscrossed with red—but the nails went in harder.

Brodie opened the door and shoved me through it. The first thing I saw was River, kneeling on the floor of the kitchen. Neely was standing behind him, holding a kitchen knife to his throat. River's head was back, the edge of the blade pressed into the soft skin near his Adam's apple, so deep that River's heartbeat was making the knife quiver slightly.

The room began to spin. I saw dark spots in the corners of my eyes. I was going to throw up again. And I didn't want to be sick in front of the red boy. *Don't be sick, Vi . . .*

"Neely," I whispered. "Neely, *stop*. Brodie's tricking you. It's just a trick. *Put the knife down.*"

Neely was bleeding. A thin line of red ran down his left cheek, just like Jack.

Neely looked at me when I said his name, but his eyes were odd and empty, like Cassie's, and Sam's. And Gianni's. "Violet," he said, "I caught this boy trying to sneak into the Citizen. He was going to kidnap you, take you back to his men, and rape you. He and his posse have been causing hell in these parts for years. But I got him good now. Run to the prison and get the sheriff, would you? I can't seem to move my arms. I've got to keep the knife at his throat, you see, otherwise it hurts . . ."

I reached out my hand. "Neely, put the knife down. It's River, your brother, *you have to put the knife down*—"

Brodie grabbed me. Thin fingers wrapped around my wrist, and he jerked my hand back. "Don't want to do that, darling," he said, the words crawling out of his mouth as slow as molasses. "The people I spark tend to respond pretty violent if you interrupt them in the act."

I screamed, but Brodie didn't drop my arm. River's eyes were watching me over the knife. They weren't empty, like Neely's. They were alive, and sparkling, as always.

"Don't do anything stupid, Vi," he said. His words made the blade cut deeper into the skin of his neck. Blood began to drip from the wound down onto the collar of his shirt, where it bloomed like a flower.

I fell. My knees, still muddy from the creek bank, hit the kitchen floor with a loud crack. I moved my head back so I could look up. The ends of my blond hair swished across the black-and-white tiles, and I met Brodie's eyes.

"Just undo it," I said.

Brodie stared at me. Seconds passed. He breathed in and out. Then he grinned. "Your degradation amuses me," he said at last. And shrugged.

I heard the knife crash to the floor behind me. I got up and turned around. Neely was rubbing his eyes. River got to his feet. Slowly. He put one hand to his neck, where the knife had been, and swiped away the blood. Then he reached out and pulled me up. But he didn't look at me. He didn't even look at Neely. His eyes were fixed on Brodie.

"How did you do that?" River asked, and his voice shook. Just a little, but it was enough. River had never lost his cool, not since I'd known him. That was the thing about River. He was calm. Calm as a summer's day. Calm as a gentle nap in the sun. Even when girls were fainting and men were slitting their throats in front of you. He'd been upset, about thunderstorms and his dead mother, and not knowing he was using the glow on me in his sleep, but he'd never been *scared*. Not like this.

And if River—*River*—was scared . . .

"Tell me how you did it." River reached out his arm as if to grab Brodie by the collar, but Brodie stepped back out of the way, lightly, on his toes, with his knees bent like a skinny, leering marionette.

"What, take my spark back?" Brodie put a hand on his sharp chin and stroked it. "Well, eventually my victims shake off the spark on their own, but it can take hours. Otherwise, I rip the spark out of someone's head manually, so to speak. Easy as pulling apples off trees, old boy. I'm pretty good at it." He was watching River's face, closely, so closely. "I could show you how, if you wanted."

River just stood there, staring.

Brodie took his cowboy hat off and set it on the table. He ran a hand through his red hair, and it reminded me so much of River and Neely that my stomach twisted, tight. A bad taste filled my mouth, rotten and evil.

They really were brothers.

"I suppose it's time for introductions," Brodie continued when he realized River wasn't going to talk. "I guess I was being rude. I came in here, cut up Neely, and never once said, *Hello. I'm your brother Brodie. Our pa knocked up my mad mother and then went back to his real sons, which happen to be you. And here we are. Nice to meet you.* I got distracted by that full-figured strumpet who sauntered into the yard. I took off without a word. And then I followed Violet and some little brat to a dead body. I meant to come back sooner. As I said. Rude. Here, let's meet proper like." Brodie held out his hand.

River's eyes went sly. He reached out. My heart jumped and I thought, *Here we go,* but Brodie swept his arm back to his side and laughed. "Ha. Not a chance, River. I know how you work. How your glow works. Our papa filled me in, long before I got here and had to listen to the three of you yak and yak about it. You look surprised. Yes, I've been prowling around here this whole time, eavesdropping and being bored dead as a doornail. What, still surprised? Didn't you know you had a brother, River? Didn't anyone tell you about me?"

"You were supposed to be younger," Neely said, his voice off and weak and strange. "Dad probably has dozens of half-Redding brats, but they're only kids. You're supposed to be a little kid."

Brodie laughed, his low hoarse laugh. "That's right. *Half*-Redding. Kids grow up, Neely. Yes, old Papa Redding couldn't keep it in his pants. He knocked up my poor mother when she was just seventeen. He met her at one of those rich-ass garden parties the worthless and wealthy like to hold to bore the shit out of themselves. Of course, he didn't find out until later that my mother's family has their own curse."

Brodie paused, one hand on his hip, the other in the air, spinning around on one heel of his boot. "We tend to go insane. Down in the dirt, rootin' tootin', tear-your-hair-out insane. Oh, how I love thinking on Ma, barefoot, red hair down to her waist, howling in the asylum, fingernails scratching at the stone walls. I hope the rats are chewing on her toes. Mongrel. Mongrel. Ha. Ha. Hahahahahaha. My grandparents tried to raise me right after she got locked up, but hey, they're old and I've got a lot of energy. It didn't work out so well."

River put his hands on me while Brodie was talking and pushed me behind him.

"Next thing I know I'm reading a story in the newspaper that was so floor-stompin' crazy, it spread all the way from the East Coast. A story about some kids seeing the Devil in a cemetery. And I thought . . . hey, that sounds like me. Like my spark. *Shoot*. I jumped a train and here I am. What do you think, River? Are you impressed? You like what you see so far?"

"It was you, wasn't it." Neely was standing still now.

Frozen, not breathing, not moving. "The kids in the park. Texas. The witch burning. The attic. And now you're here. You've found us. So what do you want?"

Brodie smirked. "You noticed. Austin. That city's full of pigs and whores. I walked by this group of rat-faced youngsters who were running around like they owned the place. I challenged them to a Neely-fight, fist to fist, but they just laughed. *Laughed.* So I thought, you know, what the hell. I'd make them burn."

Neely stopped rubbing his eyes. His hands snapped into fists and he hit him. Left cheek. Dead center. So fast that even Brodie couldn't slide out of the way.

Brodie did nothing. He just took it, and kind of smiled.

"Fight back," Neely said, his face brick red, his eyes bright. "Right here. No glow."

"Spark," Brodie interrupted, touching his bruising cheek and still smiling. "I call it the spark."

Neely ignored him. "You set people on fire, you make me shove a knife in my brother's throat. I blamed River for that stuff at Glenship Manor. He tried to deny it but I wouldn't listen, I didn't believe him—"

Neely's fist flew. But Brodie dodged out of the way this time, quick and light, like it was way too easy and he was only half trying.

Neely's face was red as blood. Red as Brodie's hair.

River put his hand on Neely's arm. "It's all right."

Neely pushed him off.

"I should have known." Neely was almost yelling now. "I thought you were just some little rancher kid Dad was trying to do right by. But of course you've got the glow. Why else would he be supporting some skinny Texas spawn?"

Brodie grinned. "I bet he told you all the other half-Redding bastards are just kids too. Not nearly old enough to have the spark. And you believed him?"

Neely was circling and pacing, trying to get closer to Brodie. River reached out and grabbed his arm. "Don't, Neely," he said quietly. "He'll just cut you."

"Boooooored," Brodie's voice drawled. He sat down on the kitchen table and wrapped an arm around his knee. His other leg swung free, boot heel rapping against the table leg. "This is *so* boring. Neely, *shut up*. River, you too. You are both boring the shit out of me. Look, I came all the way here to see what my legit, non-mongrel, sparking brother was like. I wanted to bond, brother-style. Maybe see if he'd want to team up and have some real fun. I even allowed myself to fantasize about it on the way here—the two of us, taking on the world, destroying our enemies, celebrating our victories, cutting up women . . . But so far you aren't impressing, River. I think it's because do-gooder Neely is a bad influence." Brodie turned and stared at Neely. And as he stared his eyes narrowed. Slowly. Then he faced River again, and grinned. "Thoughts?"

I heard a noise, but didn't take my eyes off Brodie. None of us did.

I hoped it wasn't Jack. I prayed it wasn't Jack. I didn't know what Brodie had done to him with the knife. Maybe put him to sleep so he'd be out of the way.

Please just be unconscious, Jack.

Brodie tilted his head and looked toward the doorway. "Well, well, well. This must be the twin brother. Sunshine mentioned you, before her father killed her with a bat, that is."

I followed Brodie's gaze. Luke was standing by the door, a worried expression on his face. He looked at me. "What the hell happened to Jack? He's knocked out cold on the ground outside and bleeding. We need to call an ambulance. *Now*." And then he saw Brodie. "Vi, who is this cowboy on our table?"

Luke nodded at Brodie. He didn't walk over to him, though, or try to shake his hand. Some deep, instinctual part of my brother told him that Brodie was wrong.

Off.

Bad.

"Run," I said to Luke. But my mouth was dry and made no sound. I coughed, swallowed. "*Run*," I whispered.

And that time Luke heard me. He backed out of the door, turned—

But Brodie was faster. He flew off the table and landed on his feet, softly, his boots making small clinks on the floor. In the corner of my eye, I saw something glint in the light coming through the windows. And then my brother was bleeding. Wet round beads of blood formed a line down his left cheek. Luke's eyes went from surprise, to shock, to anger.

To nothing.

I stepped forward, my arms outstretched, wanting to help him, take him in my arms, shake the nothingness out of his eyes, but River held me back. I remembered why, and froze.

Luke walked into the kitchen. He bent over and picked up the kitchen knife from where it had fallen on the floor. He spun around and threw his body into Neely. Neely went flying against the kitchen wall. And then the knife was at his throat. Neely's neck was stretched taut; my brother had one hand on the black knife handle, and one hand on Neely's chin, forcing his head up.

Brodie clapped his hands. "Let's see. The first order of business, I think, is to get rid of Neely on a more permanent basis. He can't spark, and even if he could, I wouldn't want him around. He doesn't have your . . . morally ambiguous nature, River. You and me, we're the same, brother. You just don't know it yet."

River ignored him. "Luke. Drop the knife. Drop that knife."

"Can't," Luke said, his voice strained, his eyes never leaving Neely's neck. "This bastard was going to set my sister on fire. I have to keep this knife here so he doesn't get away."

"Luke," I said, over and over, my hands gripping my skirt and squeezing, squeezing the material between my fingers and my palms. *"Luke, Luke, Luke, Luke."*

River tried again. "No, you don't, Luke. It's a trick. Put your arm down."

Luke shook his head. "Can't. It hurts."

I wanted to shout at Luke like I had shouted at Neely. I wanted to fall to my knees and beg Brodie to let Neely go, as I had for River, but I knew it wouldn't work again. *"Stop it, Brodie, stop it, just stop it,"* I screamed anyway.

"I'm going to kill you," Neely whispered. "I'm going to beat your face in with my fists. Try to laugh while choking on your own teeth, you mad fucker." The knife cut into Neely's neck when he spoke, just as it had River's. A red smudge formed underneath the silver edge. River saw it and let out a loud, angry, chest-rattling moan.

He clamped his hands around my brother's arm and

began to pull. "Drop the knife, Luke," he yelled. *"Drop it."*

Luke's arm began to lower, and then he began to scream. He screamed and screamed. He screamed like the time he fell out one of the Citizen's windows when he was ten and landed with his leg twisted and broken beneath him, scream, scream, scream.

River let go and stepped away. Luke's arm flew up, the knife went back to Neely's throat, and my brother's screams stopped.

"I told you," Brodie said. "Don't interrupt my victims. They don't like it."

River turned his gaze away from Luke and from the blood that was beginning to drip down Neely's neck, saturating his shirt. He looked at Brodie, and his eyes were deep, dark hurt and horror and rage.

River put his hand on his heart. "You know, Brodie, that I can see colors. People's colors. I'm not sure if our dad told you that."

Brodie nodded. "He did. But I didn't give a shit, because I can't do it, and it's not worth doing anyway." Brodie shrugged and looked away.

"Well, most people are made of bright colors," River continued, as if he hadn't heard him. "Pink, yellow, blue, green. But not you. You're black. Black as coffee poured across a night sky. I've . . . I've never seen that before . . ."

River's eyes were scared.

Brodie smiled. It was a crooked smile. River's smile. Neely's smile. "I'm pretty special, ain't I? I've always said it, but now everyone else will be saying it too. River, would you please look at me when I'm talking to you? I can see that you're trying to use your glow. I can sense it, like an electric current running from your body to Luke's there. But you don't exercise your madness. You're much, much, much too sane. Dried up and weak. You can only stand around, ignoring me and staring at Luke, wishing you could make something happen with your glow. But you can't. You can't, River. My sparks dance circles around yours. Doesn't that bother you? You're the true blue Redding and yet I've got you beat before I even start trying. This isn't how it should be. Let me help you, brother. Let me show you how it's done."

Brodie waved his arm above his head in a circle and then tapped the heels of his boots together, like Dorothy and *There's no place like home*.

"Heck, *this* is only the beginning." Brodie's eyes were jumping and crazy and green as sea glass. "Wait until you see what I can do. Count on it, this is going to be one hell of a ride. And by the end, you're going be my biggest fan. Believe it, brother. Our time has come."

We didn't move. We didn't say a word.

Brodie stared at River. He closed his eyes a second. Opened them. "After all, River, I'm the only one that knows what it's like to have a spark. A glow. Halfwit Neely there, he doesn't know. He'll never know. But I do. It's us against them, brother."

River still didn't move, still said nothing.

Brodie's body slunk back into a slouch. "Shoot, I'm bored," he said, slow and easy and soft. And his voice was convincing enough, but his shoulders slumped forward.

And that's when I saw it.

A glimmer.

Underneath the tall, the skinny, the knife, the red, the bored, the mad.

A Jack-like glimmer of a lonely, unwanted kid.

And, underneath the glimmer . . .

Rage.

Black as the night sky, empty as Montana, bitter-as-burnt-joe, howling, shrieking, screaming rage.

Seeing this, knowing what it meant . . . it disturbed me. Deep. Down to my bones.

Maybe Brodie wasn't insane.

Maybe he was angry. Just really, really, really angry.

And this . . . this was so, so much worse.

A second passed, and then Brodie sat up straight, suddenly, like he'd just thought of something.

He looked at me.

I started to see the dark spots again.

"Violet," Brodie said. "Come here."

I closed my eyes and shook my head.

"Violet, come here. You are going to help me convince River. Come here. Now."

Something flashed in the light. River threw himself in front of me, but Brodie spun out of the way, and I felt a sharp sting on my cheek. I put my hand to my face.

And then it began.

CHAPTER 28

RIVER HAD USED the glow on me. Many times, probably. He used the glow to make me see Jack's devil. And my mother. He used it to calm me down, after seeing the dead body of Daniel Leap. But River's glow was a soft thing, a seductive thing; it crept up on me like twilight, and became such a part of me that I missed it when it was gone, like the sun at the end of the day. River's magic might have been bad, but it felt . . . *good*.

Brodie's did not.

I felt a hand, a hand as hard as steel, grab my brain in its fist. I could feel its steel fingers clamping in, as it began to press, harder, and harder.

It hurt. God, it hurt.

I fought it. And the grip got worse. It squeezed so

hard, my mind turned to mush, thick, oily, oozing mush.

I stopped fighting.

I tilted my head and looked down at my shirt. It seemed far away. As if it belonged to someone else. My hands went to the buttons of my mother's soft painting shirt. The shirt suddenly felt itchy. And hot. Like it was burning me. Like all of its tiny threads were scratching and sparking at my skin, trying to burn me up. I clawed at the buttons. I had to get the thing off of me. My teeth gritted with the pain of it. Long red welts puckered up over my body, and now I was ripping at the cloth and I could hear River yelling my name but it was far away and I spun and ripped and *at last* it was off and down on the floor where it belonged.

I gasped with relief as my shirt fell to the floor. The itching eased. The grip relaxed. My brain stopped dripping through the steel hand's fingers, and I could think again. As long as I did what the hand wanted, I was okay. As long as I *believed* what the hand wanted, the hurting would stop.

My upper body was naked now except for a thin black chemise I'd found in Freddie's closet last summer. I had slept in it the night before, and hadn't bothered to change before I followed Jack out to the dead boy. I was wearing nothing but a sheer nightgown and my green skirt and the mud on my knees. I wanted to wrap my arms around my body and crawl into the corner.

But the hand wouldn't let me. So I did nothing.

I could hear Brodie's hoarse voice. It sounded hollow and deep and miles away. It said, "Boys, you haven't seen anything yet. Getting them naked is only the beginning. I'm going to cut her. Slowly. Gently. Like a knife sliding through butter. Watch this, River. You'll love it."

"Brodie, let her go," River said, and his words drifted toward me, as Brodie's had done, and they sounded tired and pleading and sad, like the fight had been taken out of them. "Take the spark back and I'll hear you out. I'll . . . follow you, do whatever you want. I won't put up a fight. You won't even have to use your glow. I'll be as peaceful as a newborn lamb."

Brodie laughed. "All right. That's more like it, brother."

The steel hand disappeared, just like that. My brain shuddered, swelled. My palms went to my eyes, and I rubbed them, hard. I rubbed the steel hand out of my mind, rubbed and rubbed, and took deep breaths. Then I opened my eyes—

And River jumped forward. He grabbed Brodie and yanked him sideways into the table. A bottle of olive oil fell to the floor and shattered. Brodie and River twisted and pulled and struggled and fell to the ground, right over the green shards of glass. Brodie was laughing and laughing. He was kicking his boots on the floor and laughing and laughing and laughing. River had Brodie's hand, the knifing hand, pinned behind his back, and I thought, *This is it, River's going to win, River's going to save us . . .*

But none of it mattered. Brodie turned his head to the side and sunk his sharp white teeth into River's forearm.

His teeth came back with blood.

River's arms dropped to the floor. His eyes went dead.

Brodie jumped to his feet, quiet and quick as a cat.

Why is he so damn nimble, I thought, somewhere far back in my mind. *How did he get to be so damn nimble? Is that how the Devil moves?*

Brodie stepped over River's still body, went to the sink, and spat out blood. "See, Violet," he said, after wiping his mouth on the little lamb towel, *"that's* why I use my knife. So much neater. I do like being tidy. I suppose some might call it vanity, but there you go. I don't like biting people. It just ain't civilized."

I wasn't looking at Brodie as he talked, even though I knew that made him angry. I was looking at the blood that was trickling down River's forearm. I couldn't even see Brodie's teeth marks, from the blood. And River's eyes were empty now. And the emptiness was uglier in his eyes than it had been in Neely's and Luke's.

River went to the stove, grabbed the teakettle, and filled it with water. He lit the burner and set the kettle on it.

And then he put his arms to his sides and just stood there, facing the stove. Waiting.

"What's he doing?" The benign nature of River's movements had me more worried than if he was holding a knife. The room was spinning. I rubbed my eyes again, to make the spinning stop. "What the hell is he doing?"

Brodie lifted his arms into the air and stretched, as if he was getting up from a long nap. "River is going to boil that water, and then pour it over Neely's head. It's childish, but I was pressed for time. And it'll kill two birds with one stone, so to speak—River will learn what I'm made of and show some respect for me, and for what I want to do. He'll join his glow to my spark. He'll begin to understand that Neely is just a no-sparking halfwit who can't stop people from boiling up his face. I may be a bastard mutt from Texas with a mad ma, but River won't care, not after this." Brodie paused, and I saw that look again, the one that made his green eyes seem big, and deep, and young. But it only lasted a second. He shook his head, and grinned. "Then there's the added benefit being that either way, it will allow me to finish playing with you."

He came to me. Brodie reached a finger forward and ran it down my body, over my chemise, from my neck, between my breasts, to my belly button. Then he reached down, put his hand into his boot, and pulled out his little knife.

"You've got until the water boils, Violet." Brodie's voice was low and old. Old like time. Old like mountains. Old like the seasons. And the oceans. And good. And evil. "You do what I want, and you do it well. Then maybe, *maybe*, I'll release River before he melts our brother's pretty face off."

I went quiet and still. *Okay, Violet. You just do it. You just do whatever he wants and you save River from hurting Neely. That is your job here and you are just going to do it. No, you can't start seeing the spots again. You can't faint, because then you can't save them. Don't think about it, just nod your head, NOD YOUR HEAD, VI.*

I nodded.

Brodie held the knife out. He put it against my belly. I could feel the sharp edge through the thin black silk. I sucked in my breath.

"Relax," he ordered.

I let my breath back out.

"You sleeping with him? You sleeping with River? Is that what you're doing?" Brodie's voice was singsong, gentle, like he was talking to a baby.

I shook my head, my eyes glued to the silver knife pressed against me.

"Sophie killed herself, you know. My girlfriend, Sophie. She slit her wrists, right before I left Texas. She was . . . troubled." Brodie paused. "Sometimes I regret that I had to use the spark on her before she would let us be together. Carnally speaking. Sophie, she was raised a good Catholic and she believed in God and hell and virgins and whores. Nothing worked on her, not even my cutting her, until the spark. Did River have to use the glow on you too? Or did you hop into his bed of your own free will?"

Don't you dare try to run, Violet. Don't you do anything but stand there and take it; don't you run, don't you even move, or he will hurt River, and Neely, and Luke, and Jack, as easy as breathing . . .

Brodie sliced the knife across my belly. It cut through the chemise, and through my skin. It was a shallow cut. It barely even bled at first. Still, I closed my eyes. I couldn't let myself faint. The blood was pounding in my head, making it hard to hear the water in the kettle. I strained my ears. Nothing. Nothing yet. How long did it take water to boil? What could he do to me before it did?

"*Yes. Oh, yes.*"

I opened my eyes again.

Brodie's mouth was slightly open, and he was taking short inhales through his teeth. His gaze was on my stomach, on the wound spitting out plump circles of red . . .

Hang on, Vi. The water has to boil soon, and then Brodie will make it all stop. He's just having fun. He'll get bored soon,

*just hang on, don't faint, it will make him mad, madder than
he already is, just hang on. No, that's not the kettle whistling,
it's just the blood in your ears, hang on, hang on . . .*

"Tell me you love me, Sophie," Brodie whispered. His
eyes were on mine now, and they were bright green and
shiny with tears and *mad mad mad mad mad*. "Tell me you
love me."

"I love you," I said. But I was crying and the tears slipped
between my lips as I spoke the words, making them sound
fake and forced.

Brodie grabbed my left arm and lifted it away from my
body, halfway up in the air. Then he pressed his torso into
mine, hard and harder and hardest, hardest, hardest. So
hard, I could barely breathe. So hard that the blood on
my stomach squeezed out between us and began to trickle
down my sides.

"I'm going to cut you again, Sophie. I'm going to cut
you like I mean it. River, you hear that? I'm going to hurt
her. And there's nothing you can do about it. Yet. But I'll
teach you. I'll teach you how to be mad. I'll teach you how
to cut. You'll learn to love it. I promise."

River didn't turn around. He just kept staring at the
kettle, like it was the only thing in the whole world.

Brodie's knife flashed, and this time it went deep. He
cut my left wrist, dropped it, and cut my right.

Blood flowed.

It was hot and thick and wet and God, it was coming so fast. How could it come so fast? I saw my spots and the room spun and my brain began to drift away from me . . .

Double, double, boil and bubble. Fire burn and cauldron bubble. I was going mad, straining to hear the kettle and trying not to faint *even though the blood was gush and mush and it was turning my skirt a soggy black and how could there be so much blood in me?*

My eyes rolled around in my head and finally landed on River, who was still standing, facing the stove. The water was making that hot, hollow sound. *Soon, soon . . .*

"Kiss me, Sophie."

Brodie leaned down and put his mouth on mine. I tried to fight back. I pushed him away, but I was feeling so weak all of a sudden, so, so weak . . .

Brodie put his hands on my shoulders and shook me. "Kiss me like you *mean* it, Sophie. Or I'm going to kill your brother and then go find that little red-haired brat and make him drink his own blood."

I did. So help me God, I did. I put my bleeding arms around him and slid my mouth onto his. My insides recoiled. Bile rose up my throat. But none of it, *none of it* reached my lips. I kissed Brodie like I was a desert and he the cooling spring rain. Like I was seven years at sea and he the first sight of land.

I kissed him like he was River.

Brodie's eyes closed.

Then I bent over, reached down to the floor, and grabbed a thin, oily sliver of green glass.

I screamed as my fingers closed over the shard, from pain, and from joy. The glass sliced into my palm, deep.

I reached my arm back, swung it forward, and stabbed Brodie in the chest.

Blood bubbled out of the wound, started dripping down his shirt. Brodie opened his eyes, looked down at the blood, and laughed. His shirt was going red, a sopping red, like Daniel Leap's, and he laughed and laughed. He wrapped his fingers around the glass shard and yanked it out. It made a sharp ping as it hit the floor. And then the blood really poured. Brodie screamed. He screamed as the kettle screamed.

And then I saw dark.

CHAPTER 29

I WAS SUPPOSED to die.

I was left to die.

But, instead, I woke up in the hospital with bandages around my wrists and an IV tucked into my arm. Luke was next to me. He put his hand over mine as soon as my eyes opened.

"Vi, how are you doing?" he asked, all worried and trying to hide it.

The doctors thought I tried to kill myself. I was given concerned looks and numbers to call and pamphlets to read, but then they left me alone. For a while. For which I was grateful.

I lost a lot of blood. A *lot* of blood. I was almost dead. I was supposed to be dead. But River, he woke up from Brodie's spark, and then Luke too, and they put me in River's car and I got blood all over the vintage seats, but I didn't die. Neely knew what to do and he kept me alive during those last minutes that really mattered.

Brodie was long gone by then. Long, long gone. To the ends of hell, for all we knew where.

Sunshine was in a coma for four days.

Cassie and Sam woke up, rubbed their eyes, and found their daughter unconscious on the living room floor, bleeding from the head. The police figured it was one of the homeless people that jump off the train and cause the only crimes that ever happen in our town. A man broke in to steal something, Sunshine surprised him, and he hit her with a bat he found lying nearby. Then he climbed on the next train out of town and disappeared. That's what they figured. And everyone was content to believe it.

I was there when Sunshine woke up in the hospital. I asked her, in a gentle way, what she remembered about the bat that hit her. And the man that held it.

She turned away from me and curled into a ball.

"Shut up" was all she said. And then: "The police already asked me all those questions and I told them I don't remember. So now I'm telling you. *I don't remember, Vi.* Now, can you go get me some iced tea?"

Maybe that was part of Brodie's spark, the forgetting.

Like River's glow, sometimes. I don't know. I damn well remembered what Brodie did to me. And maybe Sunshine remembered too. But she never talked to me about what happened to her.

We passed some boys, a few days after Sunshine got out of the hospital, on our way into town. They wore Little League outfits, and one of them, a skinny kid with red hair, was tossing a bat back and forth between his hands. Sunshine flinched each time the bat smacked his palm, and I saw tears come into her eyes. But I didn't say anything. And she didn't say anything. And then we went into the café and soon she was smiling and flirting with Gianni behind the counter, and life moved on, as it does.

Gianni had stopped talking to me, after the fire. He wouldn't even look me in the eye when he handed me my coffee. I supposed he was afraid. I supposed I reminded him of the night he went mad . . . the night Neely paid him to keep his mouth shut.

I wondered if he would come around, eventually. I wondered if Neely and River left, if he'd start looking at me again. I wondered how much I wanted him to.

The police found the dead boy, when they were searching the railroad tracks for signs of the man who attacked Sunshine. An accident. Boy on tracks, doesn't hear the train, gets hit, falls down the ditch. What else could it be?

I kind of thought, in the back of my head, that some-thing would happen. That town meetings would be called and people would gather in basements and swear to seek out answers and track down culprits and attempt to under-stand Echo's strange summer of kids with stakes and kid-napping devils and girls beaten with bats and boys dead by the railroad tracks.

But there was nothing. People moved on, just as Sun-shine did.

I thought, sometimes, that Sunshine seemed . . . differ-ent, after Brodie. There was something in her eyes that hadn't been there before. She stopped sitting out on her porch as much, just drinking tea and doing nothing. She started reading books on the environment, and wilderness survival. She said she wanted to start going camping, just me and her, and I said all right. Once I went down to the beach, to that hidden spot to read, and found her swimming. She was out there in the waves, alone, just her and that tight white swimsuit, and I couldn't tell if she was swimming toward something, or away from something. Maybe both.

I liked the new Sunshine. And so did Luke. But I think we both kind of missed the old one too.

≋

I was watching River pack his vintage leather suitcases. It was a few weeks after Brodie. I had just taken the last bandages off my wrists, and my scars were red and mean-looking, and I hated them. I rubbed the red welts as River threw the last of his clothes into the second case, slammed the lid down, and snapped the four clasps into place. I flinched each time metal hit metal and locked. It was such a definite sound. Such an *ending* sort of sound.

River stood up, a suitcase in each hand. He looked just the same as he had the first time I'd seen him. Except for the still-healing bite mark on his forearm. Except for the look in his eyes.

His eyes weren't just cocky, and confident, and indifferent, and noticing, like that first day. There was something new there now. Something . . . *more*. And I wondered if it had anything to do with me.

I hoped so.

People said time was relative, and I guess that explained why my life before River felt like a handful of seconds—brief flashes of small events that added up to very little. But my life after River was a three-volume saga. Epic. With quests and villains and murders and unsatisfactory resolutions and people being torn apart.

"Want some coffee?" River asked.

Though what he meant was: *Want some coffee before I take my bags and get in my car and leave and never come back?*

"Yeah," I said.

So he brewed one last batch of espresso in the moka pot, and we sipped it, searing hot, by the kitchen sink.

And I looked at him, at his long, lean side, while he was sipping and narrowing his eyes. He didn't look mysterious anymore, or exotic, or full of secrets. He just looked like River.

And it was enough.

"You just look like River," I said.

And River looked back at me sideways, his cup halfway to his lips. "That's good," he said, kind of half laughing, half serious, "because I *am* River."

And then River West William Redding III picked his suitcases back up and I followed him outside. Neely was there, waiting, and Jack, and Luke. The four of us stood in a semicircle around River's new-old car, its seats still stained with blood.

River looked at Neely. "You know why I have to do this, right?"

Neely laughed. "Yeah, I do. Go get a grip on your glow, so we can go after Brodie, and beat the shit out of him. If he's still alive."

"He is," River said.

I shook my head. "I stabbed him. In the chest. I saw the blood. I *heard* him screaming." I'd said this before. I'd said it so many times, I was starting to chant it like a prayer.

River didn't say anything.

Jack caught my eye. "He ran. While I was still on the ground, after he cut me. I couldn't move my arms or legs, but I could still see. He left the guesthouse and he was running."

Jack was right. We'd talked and talked about this, and it always ended with Jack, seeing Brodie run, and us knowing what that meant. Brodie lived. He was gone and he didn't leave a trace. And we'd looked. Hard.

Luke gave River a cool, manly half hug. Then River squatted down and pulled Jack into him. Their hug wasn't cool and manly. It was just strong, and genuine.

"I'm going to get this kid some coffee," Luke said, finally. "Jack, should we see what's going on in town? Maybe some kids in the square saw a pack of zombies. That sounds about right on schedule."

Jack grinned. He detached himself from River, and, without a backward glance, followed Luke down the path into Echo.

It was just River and Neely and me.

River ran his hand through his hair and leaned against his car. "Grandpa told me something once. Do you remember when I visited him in the French Alps, Neely? We were sitting together and watching the sun go down behind the peaks. Grandpa was not as sharp as he used to be, and his mind would drift sometimes. Mostly he would talk about Freddie, and things that happened to them when they were young. But this time, he looked straight at me. *You've got to abstain,* he said. *You've got to abstain if it starts getting out of control. It's the only way."*

There was silence for a little while, as we all thought about that. I listened to the leaves shake in the trees, and the waves hit the rocks below. I listened to my heart cracking, re-forming, growing, because it was no longer small, and shriveled, and starving.

"If I'm going to go after Brodie," River continued after a minute or so, "I'll need to abstain. I'll need to be alone. Completely alone. Otherwise . . . otherwise I don't trust myself to do it."

"Brodie said you had to go mad, to make the glow obey you." I slid my hand into River's and squeezed. "What if your grandpa was wrong? What if stopping does nothing, and Brodie just gets stronger and stronger?"

River shrugged. "I've got to try, Violet. I either stop, or I keep going until I'm as mad as him. Which would you choose?"

Neely shook his blond hair at that and laughed. "I'd be willing to go mad if it meant I got to kill that little cowboy. I'd kill him so hard—"

River put his arms around his brother and hugged

him. Then he released Neely and grabbed me. We held on tight, as tight as we could, and River put his lips to my ear.

"I'm going to disappear," he whispered. "If I screw up, and use the glow, Neely will find me. But if he doesn't find me, then I'm doing something right. Let me stay hidden. And when I come back, I will be stronger. Better."

River's fingers went into my hair, and he held me even closer. "Brodie thought you would die. What is he going to do when he finds out you didn't? Maybe he won't care. But I'm not taking any more risks. Neely is going to stay in the guesthouse. He'll stay until I get back."

I nodded, my cheek moving against his shirt. I didn't mention that Neely hadn't been able to stop Brodie from trying to kill me before.

River kissed my cheek, and my forehead, and my earlobe. Neely was watching, grinning, but River didn't care and neither did I.

"How am I going to sleep without you?" River murmured into my neck. "Vi, I've never been scared of anyone in my life, but my red-haired cowboy brother scares the hell out of me. But I don't care. I don't care if I have to sell my soul to the Devil. I don't care if Brodie *is* the Devil. I'm going to kill him. Like he tried to kill you. And I'm going to make it stick, so help me God."

And then he kissed me. On the lips. *Deep.* I closed my eyes and sunk into it, trying to feel that melting feeling I felt before, at the cemetery, that first time.

But the scars on my wrists started hurting. And I saw a flash of red hair. And then *just like that* I was feeling Brodie's lips on mine as my blood soaked through our clothes.

I pulled away. And I could tell by the look in River's eyes that I didn't have to say anything, not one damn word, because he understood.

River reached into his pocket and pulled out another bookmark. It was a hundred-dollar bill, folded into the shape of a star. He put it in my hand.

And then he got in his car.

And drove away.

CHAPTER 30

RIVER LEFT. AND Neely stayed.

Jack was living with us now too. He'd been through devils, suicides, attics, witches, fires, knives . . . but he was all right somehow.

Neely built a fire pit in the backyard by the guesthouse, and the five of us—Luke, Sunshine, Neely, me, and Jack— liked to roast sweet Italian sausages and corn on the cob after dark. We did it all summer long.

Sometimes I slept in River's bed, out in the guesthouse. Neely didn't mind. Besides, I liked his laugh. I liked that he looked like his brother. We didn't talk about River. And we both stopped reading the papers. We didn't want to know. Not about him, and not about Brodie—what they were doing, and who they might be hurting. Not yet.

The last night in August, a week before I started my senior year, I was sleeping in River's bed again. I rolled over onto my side and sunshine hit me full in the face.

But it wasn't the light that had woken me up. It was voices. Outside. I pulled my clothes over my head, my heart racing.

It couldn't be.

But it was.

I stepped outside, and there were my parents, pulling suitcase after suitcase out of a taxi. My mom caught sight of me, dropped her bag. I walked into her arms and we hugged like hugging was breathing and we'd been holding our breath for a long, long time. My nose was buried in her long hair and she smelled of strong European coffee and delicate French perfume and fresh Parisian rain. But underneath all that was the tang of turpentine, like always.

I was mad that she left, and then came back, like it was nothing. Like she had no explaining to do, like she had no responsibility to be around. But my parents were going to do what they were going to do, regardless of what I thought about it. I had to take them as they were, and hope they did the same for me.

My mom talked fast. She talked like how my thoughts ran on in my head, fast, fast, fast. And she started talking fast now. She talked and talked about Europe and museums and an art show in Paris and I only half listened because I was hugging my dad and just taking it all in.

"Violet, did you hear me?" My mom put her hand on my arm. "Your dad sold out a show in Paris and what do you think that means it means we have some money to spare finally that's what it means. Oh, here's *Luke*."

Luke was outside by that time and he came running down the steps. He started crying a little bit, which was strange because I'd never seen Luke cry. Our dad had that far-off look in his eyes as he hugged him, a look I suddenly realized I had missed like crazy. Then Neely and Jack came out and we had introductions. Introductions led to talking about art, which took us to the shed, and then the guesthouse, and we talked about everything that had happened since they left, which was almost nothing, because we didn't tell them about River and Brodie and Freddie's letters and Jack's blood being thicker than water and Sunshine and the bat and the boy by the tracks and my shaking hands with death and stabbing the Devil in the chest and what I was hiding under the long sleeves I was wearing in August.

Later that evening, I was sitting on the steps all by myself, wondering again what forgotten corner of nowhere River was holed up in. Night was falling on one of the last days of summer, and my River blues hit, as they tended to do near sunset. I could hear Neely and Luke laughing as they gathered twigs and branches. We were going to spend the night camping in the backyard. My dad was putting up a dusty green tent he found in the Citizen's cellar, and Mom was painting in the shed with the door wide open so she could watch everyone. Jack was churning ice cream in an old hand-crank machine, and Sunshine was sitting beside him, squinting in the dying light, trying to read some old Boy Scout handbook from the library about how to build a fire.

I was wondering if River was getting his glow under control. And if he was lonely. If he missed me, like I missed him. But then Neely was in front of me, holding out a stick with a marshmallow on it and demanding I join in the fun. So I did. I roasted things and ate homemade ice cream and painted by moonlight and slept in a sleeping bag on the ground. And the night blurred into one big blaze of nothing and everything. I was safe. And content, even with my River blues.

I glanced over at Neely, lying on his side by the fire. I thought he was asleep, but he opened his eyes and looked at me, as if he knew I was thinking about things. He grinned. And that grin cut me deep.

Freddie often told me that you've got to be happy when you can, because life won't wait for you to take the time. And she was right. She'd learned that the hard way. Freddie was human, and she'd made mistakes. But she learned how to hold on to her happiness somewhere along the line. She prayed to God, and held on.

I ran my fingers over the scars on my wrists. Life was safer, without River. And less. Less breathtaking. Less terrifying. Less stirring. Less . . . everything.

Damn. I really miss you, River.

Maybe it was just the leftover glow talking. Maybe it was the glow giving me my River blues . . . but it felt real. And my feelings, pure or not, were the only thing I had to go on. River had manipulated people. And murdered people. He was wicked. Not as wicked as Brodie, but . . . still wicked. It was better that he was gone, better that he was out of my life. I knew that, logically. What I *felt*, though, deep, deep down in the darkest dark of my heart, was that I didn't give a damn if River was evil. I still liked him. Maybe I even kind of loved him.

And maybe that made me wicked too.

A Q&A with
April Genevieve Tucholke

About the book

1) Where did you get the idea for the story of *Between the Devil and the Deep Blue Sea*?

I happened to read a bizarre, stranger-than-fiction article when I was living in Edinburgh, Scotland, about how hundreds of children in 1954 gathered for three days in Glasgow's Southern Necropolis to hunt a "seven-foot-tall vampire with iron teeth." The kids were armed with sharpened sticks and knives and claimed the vampire had already kidnapped and eaten two boys.

What I find so inspiring about this story is that one kid probably started it all. One charming, magnetic little liar of a kid told all the other kids there was a vampire in the cemetery and made them all believe him. Why did he do it? Where is he now? What kind of person did he grow up to be? Eventually these thoughts formed themselves into a kids-with-stakes, devil-hunting cemetery scene in my book. And the lying kid? That became River.

2) Why did you choose to name the book *Between the Devil and the Deep Blue Sea*?

I originally titled the book *Devil River*, because I thought it sounded Southern Gothic. When I was almost finished with the first draft I happened to hear Cab Calloway singing "Between the Devil and the Deep Blue Sea." And I just knew. The song itself is far too cheerful, but the lyrics are dead perfect.

3) Can you tell us a little about the glow? It's a really creepy ability. Would you say that the ability is supernatural, or that it comes from your genetic code—like *X-men*?

It's genetic. River and Brodie inherited the glow through their father, just as they inherited his amorality.

4) Do you think it's possible that there really are people out there with abilities like the spark and glow?

I think there are people who have certain unexplainable abilities, like clairvoyance and telepathy. My grandfather claimed he could do water witching—I watched him do it when I was young. He held out a thin, forked stick and found an underground water source. There is still magic left in the world. There are still delicate, mysterious things we don't entirely understand.

5) Honest question: Would you date River West?

If I was still a teenager in my small rural town, attending my small rural school? Yes. I would have been truly, madly, deeply in love with him. I had a big, hungry imagination and nothing to feed it, except the books I read. And read. And read. River is mysterious and troubled and worldly. He cooks. He cares about his brother. He lies, but then, so did every boy I dated as a teenager, except one. River believes in justice and vengeance. He does questionable things. He takes the law into his own hands. He has no regrets. He wants life to be interesting. River is not the tender, sweet, flawless boy next door. But then, I didn't know any of those kinds of boys growing up.

As an adult, though? I'd take Neely. Hands down.

6) Is the town of Echo based in part on somewhere you've lived or visited?

Echo is based on pieces of all the places I've lived. I chose a coastal

Maine setting because I've read a lot of Stephen King ... and when I think of horrific things going down in small towns, I think of King. And Maine. But I've lived on both coasts and spent a great deal of time in the Scottish countryside. I've seen my share of eerie things, of crashing waves and abandoned manors and paths that lead into deep, dark woods. All this went into Echo.

7) Are any events in *Between the Devil and the Deep Blue Sea* based on experiences that you've had personally? Which ones?

My husband and I used to go for long hikes in the bucolic country-side south of Edinburgh. I've never been able to resist the road less traveled. I once walked down a neglected woodland path that dead-ended at an old train tunnel set into a tree-covered hill. Now, because it was Scotland, there were no fences or KEEP AWAY signs, nothing to stop you from just waltzing right into the pitch-black tunnel and disappearing into the thick gloom. Forever. God knows where that tunnel went. I only ever got three feet in and it was enough to haunt me for days. This inspired the Blue Hoffman tunnel scene in the beginning of the book.

8) Anything special we can watch out for in the sequel, *Between the Spark and the Burn*?

Between the Spark and the Burn has snow, madness, and pig's blood. River is missing. There are Bright Young Things. Someone goes mad. Someone goes sane. There are islands. Forests. Creepy small towns. More cemeteries. A girl named Pine. A boy named Finch. Wild horses. A frozen lake. Red hair. Violet finds her grandmother's diary, and it's full of scandal and sex and secrets. River's apple doesn't fall far from the Redding tree.

9) What were you like as a teenager?

I was independent and wary. I read all the time. I dreamed all the time. I was a straight-A student. I liked to take risks. I was excruciatingly soft-hearted, but I tried to hide it.

10) What do you think your teenage self would think of you right now?

She would be too afraid to talk to me.

11) If *you* had the glow, what would you do with it?

Use it for good, hopefully. I'd try to bring mischief and wonder into people's lives—I think a lot of adults are chronically deprived of mischief and wonder.

12) What do you do in your spare time?

Walk in the deep, dark woods with my dogs. Cook. Daydream. Read.

13) What five things can't you live without?

> Books.
> Coffee.
> Dogs.
> Nature.
> Travel.

14) If you could choose any place on Earth, where would you visit?

Northern Italy. And I'd like to see the fairy pools and the fairy bridge on the Isle of Skye again someday.

15) What is your favorite movie of all time?

It changes, depending on my mood. *Amélie*, *The Illusionist*, *The Fellowship of the Ring*, *Jane Eyre* with Toby Stephens, Joe Wright's *Pride and Prejudice*, *The Eagle*, *Brief Encounter* ...

ABOUT WRITING

16) What made you want to become a writer? What do you love best about it? What is most difficult?

What made me want to be a writer: being a long-term reader.

The best part of writing: the readers who like my crazy stories.

The worst part of writing: sitting still, in the quiet, cranking out the cunning little words. Sometimes it makes me want to scream. And not in a good way.

17) What books and authors inspire or influence your work?

Authors that inspire me: Susanna Clarke, Margo Lanagan, the Brontës, Dickens, Poe, Larry McMurtry, Daphne du Maurier, Stephen King, George R. R. Martin, Scott Lynch, L. A. Meyer, P. G. Wodehouse, Agatha Christie.

18) Why are you interested in horror as a genre?

I liked being scared as a child, and now I like scaring children.

19) What was the writing and revision process like for *Between the Devil and the Deep Blue Sea*? Do you have a writing routine?

Learning to draft and edit is an acquired skill like anything else. I'm better at it now. I've got the melody down. It's still hard. Brutally hard. Especially drafting. I spend days and days thinking about the plot. Then I read things and watch things and go places to get inspired. Then I write a two- or three-page outline . . . and begin. And after drafting comes the year-long revision.

20) Can you describe what it was like when you were first informed that *Between the Devil and the Deep Blue Sea* was going to be published? What was the process like from writing the manuscript to finally seeing the book in your hand?

I was, coincidentally, at a place up in the mountains called Devil's Lake when I called my editor for the first time and thanked her for buying my devil book.

How did I feel? Relieved, nervous, blissful.

What was the process like? Shocking, harsh, merciless, brilliant, thrilling.

21) *Between the Devil and the Deep Blue Sea* is at times very dark and disturbing. What would you say to someone who argues that it should be censored for a YA audience?

First of all, teenagers can handle dark things. They understand the difference between reality and fiction.

Secondly, I put in nice, comforting scenes of the characters hanging out in sunny kitchens, drinking coffee, or sitting by a bonfire at the edge of the ocean, or spending an afternoon digging through old trunks in the attic. All the lazy, dreamy things that make teenage summers so magical. It takes the edge off the horror, I think.

22) What advice do you have for an aspiring author?

Read everything. Every genre. Westerns, mysteries, romance, science fiction, literary fiction. Read it all.

READ ON FOR A PREVIEW
OF THE CHILLING CONCLUSION...

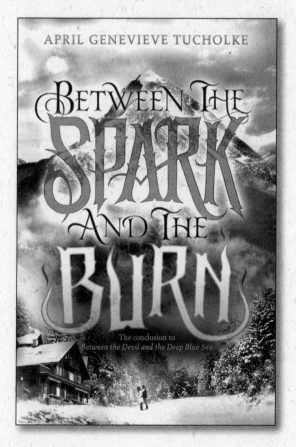

APRIL GENEVIEVE TUCHOLKE

BETWEEN THE
SPARK
AND THE
BURN

The conclusion to
Between the Devil and the Deep Blue Sea

CHAPTER 1

MY DEAD GRANDMOTHER Freddie once told me that the Devil created all the fear in the world.

But then, the Devil once told me that it's easier to forgive someone for scaring you than for making you cry.

The problem with River West Redding was that he'd done both to me.

Since then I'd spent months just waiting. Waiting on my rotting mansion's wide front porch, on its secret little beach at the bottom of the cliffs, in its nefarious guesthouse. And I was getting antsy. I'd tasted love and terror last summer, and it left a sweetness in my mouth. I wanted to go somewhere. Anywhere. I wanted to make something happen. I wanted to get bone-shaking scared and face my fear. I wanted to get scratched. Bruised. Bloody.

River and his brother Brodie were gone. Long gone. Doing God knows what. Alone. Or together. Who knew.

Was River the Devil?

Was Brodie?

Mostly I tried not to think of them. Either of them. Of what they were up to or the trouble they were causing or the lies they were lying.

And mostly that didn't work. At all.

Where are you, River?

Silence and not a word. Not for months. Neely had gone looking, but nothing. Maybe this was a good thing. Maybe it meant River was keeping his promise. But then why hadn't he come back? He'd glowed up my damn heart last summer and then left without a trace. He'd been gone so long now that I could barely remember the smell of his skin. Or the way his eyes lit up when he lied. And lied. And lied.

River, what would you say if you could see me now, lonely little book-reading Violet, talking about getting in trouble and making something happen? Would you crooked-smile at me with that glint in your eyes and say, "I like you, Vi"? Or would you look worried and run your hands through your hair, and wonder what the hell had changed inside me since last summer?

A gust of cold wind blew in off the sea and smacked me

in the face. Instead of wincing, I smiled. I had a blanket around my shoulders, coffee in a nearby thermos, and a pair of binoculars in my hand. The sea stretched on forever before me, and my thoughts went with it.

I'd read stories of widows who never recovered from the Death at Sea of their captain husbands. Widows who spent their days wandering the seashore, waiting.

But that wasn't what I was doing down here, under the moody sky by the capering waves in the hidden little cove by my cliff-hugging tumbledown mansion that my grandmother Freddie had named Citizen Kane.

My Freddie-blue eyes squinted under the cold, glaring sun. I'd starting watching the ships again, out there on the Big Blue. I'd started wishing I was on them.

I sighed as a freezing winter breeze blew across my neck. A wave crashed into the sand and stretched its long fingers toward me. It drenched my feet and the hem of Freddie's red dress—which I had stupidly worn down to the beach when I knew better. The seawater made the dress look redder, like it was blushing.

My hands pressed into cold ground. I leaned back. Closed my eyes. The sand rubbed against the Brodie-scars on my wrists, and they started hurting. But it was a good hurt, like cold snow melting on warm skin. Or like kissing River's lips after he lied.

Maybe it was River's magic that made me think of him still. Made me talk to him like I used to talk to Freddie. Maybe it was that bit of glow still lingering in me like the last tingle of opium in an addict's blood.

River, I found something.

Heard something.

Freddie once caught me climbing a tree in the Citizen's backyard. I was twenty feet off the ground and still going up when I heard her voice. *GET DOWN RIGHT NOW, VIOLET WHITE.* The second my feet hit earth she wrapped her arms around me and hugged me for five whole minutes, maybe more.

"Your life is not your own, Vi," she said. "Don't you know that? It belongs to the people who love you. So you need to take better care of it."

Freddie was right, I supposed.

I wasn't taking very good care of my life. Not since River came into it.

And yet . . .

I walked back up the steep trail toward home, my wet dress hitting my boots with a smack, each step. And I sang a little song to myself, something that I made up as I went along, something that was melancholic and nursery rhyme, something that sounded a little bit like *A-hunting I will go, a-hunting I will go.*

CHAPTER 2

I FOUND MY parents painting out in the shed—it got great afternoon sun, even in winter, which it was. It sat there, squat and chipping paint, in its little shaft of sunshine, wedged in between the skeletal winter woods and the overgrown maze and the now empty guesthouse and the beautiful, buffeted, browbeaten, salt-stained Citizen Kane.

I loved the ocean. Its sounds were like lullabies and mothers' voices—I'd grown up on them, a soundtrack of lapping waves and seagulls and storms.

Yet the rollicking sea sea sea was a bully. I reached up to the low roof of the shed and knocked off a couple of icicles. A rotted piece of wood fell with them. I left it on the ground and went inside.

My brother was in there too, painting away, and the redheaded orphan boy, Jack. My next-door neighbor Sunshine was sitting on the floor, watching. I sat down next to her and enjoyed the cluttering bodies and the burnt smell of the space heater in the corner.

It was Christmas Eve and pretty much everyone I knew was packed into a painting shed. There wouldn't be any baking, or decorating, or caroling. Not with the Whites, not at the Citizen. But that was all right with me.

"So I've decided to go after River."

I said it quick, just like that, before I had a chance to think better of it.

"Who is River?" my mother asked, head snapping up, looking straight at me. *Really* looking, for once. Most of the time her eyes were distracted and dreamy when she talked to me, as if her mind were clicking through colors, figuring out the exact peachy shade of my skin, the perfect wheat-yellow combination of my blond hair. My parents painted and the rest of us moved around them in a blur.

"Neely's older brother," Luke said when I didn't answer. They searched my face, Luke and Jack and Sunshine, trying to puzzle out why I'd brought up River after all this time, why I'd dipped my toes into that mess of lying, glowing, out of control, brown-eyed, brown-haired rich boy.

The hell if I knew why I did it. The words just fell out of my head, out of my mouth, like leaves off trees. Like snow out of the sky.

Maybe there was something in the air.

I sighed.

I wondered if Neely would be back for Christmas.

I missed him.

I missed the way he reminded me of River—the way he drank espresso with narrowed eyes and ran his hands through his hair.

Though Neely's hair was blond, like mine, not brown, like River's.

And Brodie, the other brother, the half brother, his was red. Red, red, red.

I missed the way Neely laughed at everything. Red-headed cowboys with knives. River's lying. Everything.

I missed the way he loved his older brother so damn much and at the same time really liked putting his fists in River's face.

Neely had run off three times already, trying to find his older brother, trying not to think about his younger one.

But nothing.

I wanted Neely to come back.

Acknowledgments

Nate.

Joanna Volpe. Agent, Stephen King lover, fellow night owl. You watched *Diabolique* for me. I owe you.

Jessica Garrison. You knew exactly how to squeeze the goodness out of my little devil book. If you ever want to run from some coyotes, I know a place.

Everyone else at Dial and Penguin, especially Kristin Smith for that drop-dead cover.

Simon Ålander, for his brilliant hand-lettering.

Sandra, for letting me stay up reading as late as I wanted. Jason, for your active imagination—I always really liked that about you. Erin and Todd, for playing the Egypt Game with me that one summer night. Loren, for the tree house.

Joelie Hicks, for your love of books.

Erin Bowman, for always being there.

The Lucky 13s.

The Friday the Thirteeners, for that thread about unicorns.

And the red-haired boy, for the skull.